A SURPRISE PREGNANCY ROMANTIC COMEDY

# LOVE IS *Ale* YOU NEED

BREWS & FLINGS SERIES

# GIA STEVENS

Love Is Ale You Need: A Surprise Pregnancy Romantic Comedy by Gia Stevens

www.authorgiastevens.com

Published by: Gia Stevens

Copyright: Love Is Ale You Need: A Surprise Pregnancy Romantic Comedy by Gia Stevens © 2024 Gia Stevens

Print ISBN: 978-1-958286-17-3

Editor: My Notes in the Margins

Publisher: Wild Clover Publishing, LLC

v033024

All rights reserved. No portion of this book may be reproduced in any form without permission from the publisher, except as permitted by U.S. copyright law.

This is a work of fiction. Names, characters, places, and incidents either are the products of the author's imagination or are used fictitiously. Any resemblance to actual persons, living or dead, business, companies, events, or locales is entirely coincidental.

*Find someone who's kind, patient, loving, makes you laugh, and enjoys a good clam joust.*

While this story is a romantic comedy there may be situations that are triggering to some. For a list of those content warnings please visit my website and scroll to the bottom of the page.

## SINGLE BROS. LIFE

*Trey*

Humans are not swans. Outside the obvious regarding appearance and being able to fly, though it would be pretty sweet to fly, we're not meant to mate for life. Not me anyway. I can't even call myself a wolf because guess what? They also mate for life. Suckers. One by one all my friends have been pairing off because they've found the love of their life. Their soulmate. Their better half. Don't get me wrong, I'm happy for them, but again, it's not for me. There's only one person I can depend on. Myself. And it's better that way. Less feelings. Less complications. Relationships are a hard pass and Single Bros. Life nights are for exactly that.

"Can I have your attention?" With a heavy hand, I

smack the gavel against the table, sending vibrations through the wood. "Attention, everyone."

Bang! Bang! Bang!

I hit it again but this time in rapid succession until everyone turns their head toward me, including all the customers in the main room of Porter's as everyone goes whisper silent for a second. Well, shit, maybe that was a little harder than needed. Soon enough the chatter and clinking of glasses resume in the main bar area while a hush settles over the small crowd in front of me. By small, I mean three people. Placing the gavel on the table, I roll up the sleeves of my white dress shirt. When I glance up, I'm met with a menacing glare from a six foot four, broad shouldered Jake stalking toward me.

Since he always sports a resting glower face, I offer him a wide grin in return. "Are you joining us for our meeting tonight? These guys could learn a thing or two about being single from you." I hold out the gavel and wave it over the table, where three guys are seated. "I'm sure we can find another chair for you."

Jake comes to a halt inches away from me. His face is stoic, like a marble statue, but with much harsher lines and a distinct tick to his stone jaw. With every flare of his nostrils, I have the urge to boop him on his nose, but with the storm clouds rolling in his eyes I'm sure it would lead to him booping me on my nose with his fist, so I think better of it.

"Oh. Um. I stand up here. Everyone else sits down there." I point my gavel over the table again.

Without saying a word, he rips the gavel from my hand so fast I'm surprised I'm not left with splinters, or at least wood rash.

"If you use this," he holds up the gavel, "in my bar

again, I'm going to be forced to use it on you." He's so close his hot breath rolls over my face. "I said you could host whatever meeting you're doing, but you're not disrupting my bar with this shit. Got it?"

My lips press together, and I nod. "Duly noted." Don't poke the bear. Don't poke the bear. If my face wasn't so pretty, I'd totally poke the bear. "Can I have my gavel back?" I stretch out my arm to grab it, but Jake pulls it away.

"No." He twists around and storms off.

"So, we don't need to find you a chair?" I ask as he departs. "I guess that's a no," I mumble to myself.

I shift my attention to the table in front of me. "Sorry about the interruption. Thanks for coming to Porter's for our Single Bros. Life meeting."

Shortly after graduating from college, I created SBL. That's what happens when your heart is ripped out of your body and tossed to the ground. From then on, I realized relationships weren't worth the hassle. Everything is tremendously less complicated when all you offer is a few hours of companionship. And by companionship, I mean fucking. Nothing more.

A hard and fast rule of mine is to always go to her place, it's a lot easier to run away than it is to convince her to leave. I've heard all the excuses: I'm too tired, I don't have my car, I don't want to wake my roommate. My response is always: here's a cup of coffee, I'll call you an Uber, and I don't care about your roommate. I don't actually say the last one, even though I really should. Maybe it will drive my point home. Most importantly, no sleepovers. My plan works because nine times out of ten my phone is ringing asking for a repeat. That brings me to my next rule. No more than twice. A third time screams this could lead to more and I don't want to send mixed signals.

"While the man cave is under construction, we'll be meeting here over the next few weeks, since no one else has a place we can go." My gaze narrows at every single guy sitting before me.

"Sorry. My apartment is too small. Two of us could sit in the living room, one in the kitchen, and someone in the bathroom." Owen shrugs with a sheepish smile.

"With how much you don't clean, I don't think anyone wants to do that," Miles says.

"What about your place?" Owen counters.

"My place is spotless right now. Mostly because my parents are visiting me for the next month and Mom cleans when she's bored and I'm not going to say no." Miles adjusts his black-framed glasses.

"So, your house is the cleanest, why don't we go there?" Darren asks.

"Because my dad's idea of relaxing is sitting in front of the TV in his underwear," Miles adds.

Everyone's faces scrunch like they got a whiff of rotten cheese.

"Remind me to never sit on your couch," Owen says.

"I just got a cat, Mittens, who hates everyone, including me." Darren rolls up the sleeve of his button down dress shirt. Giant red scratches stretch from his wrist to his elbow. "I'd hate to subject anyone else to this type of violence. Who knew a cat named Mittens would be so angry?"

"Cat therapy." Owen points a finger in the air, turning toward Darren. "It's a thing. My co-worker goes with his cat."

Darren digs his phone out of the front pocket of his khakis. "That's an idea. Do you know who does that?"

"Guys. Guys! Let's rein it in. Anyway, we can all thank Jake for allowing us use of Porter's backroom. Also, we can't bring our own snacks, which might be for the best since Owen got sick from the cheese dip Darren provided at the last meeting."

"Sorry. I had no idea the cheese went bad." Darren's tone is somber as he drops his head.

"With the cheese in the past, Porter's has apps and beer. But everyone is responsible for their own tabs." I glance around the room. "Where's Tim?"

Owen raises his hand.

"You don't need to raise your hand," I say.

His hand slinks to his lap. "He texted me and said he can't make it today. Something about needing to pick up the kids from school because their mother is too busy"—he reaches into the breast pocket of his red polo and pulls out his phone. He glances down at the screen and then at me—"and I quote, 'fucking her piece of shit boss.'"

"Fucking Tim," I mutter under my breath.

The other two guys gasp, while Owen nods his head in confirmation. I'm not sure if it's because how Tim worded it or because his ex is still sleeping with her boss who is also Owen's boss. They've bonded over their mutual dislike of the guy.

After Tim caught his now ex-wife cheating last year, he eventually filed for divorce. Granted, she wasn't doing much to conceal it, but for the longest time Tim put on blinders for the sake of the kids. When Owen invited him to come to SBL, we all welcomed him with open arms.

"We can use this as a learning experience. First," I hold up one finger, "avoid having kids at all costs. Things will always turn to shit, then you're left with nothing but a pile of shit. Tim's already a lost cause, but we're slowly guiding him back toward the light. And second," I hold up another finger, "if your wife, girlfriend, or partner says they have to work late and come home smelling like cheap perfume. Run. Run like Forrest Gump. Right the hell out of there." I hold up a third finger. "Most importantly, paternity tests are your friend. And always confirm she's actually pregnant. Ask to see a test. Go with her to an appointment."

Miles pulls out his phone and types notes on the screen, absorbing everything like a sponge.

"Learn from mine and Tim's experiences. Now that we got that out of the way, let's continue with the rest of the meeting."

Over the next hour, we discuss everything I'm doing with the man cave remodel, including installing a state-of-the-art bar. Miles tells us about the new drone he purchased and the three-camera system it has. Owen animatedly discusses the ins and outs of a new virtual reality video game console he bought. Darren rounds out the conversation by debating if perhaps the reason his cat is acting out is because he's lonely and maybe he should get another cat so he can have a friend.

As they continue to discuss the pros and cons of Darren acquiring a second cat, I excuse myself. I stroll through the crowd, meandering in and out of tables filled with customers. Along the way, I duck and weave away from previous hookups, vying for my attention, but get stopped by a few acquaintances to talk business. At the end of the long bar, I claim an empty seat. I drum my fingers on the smooth, worn wood bar top as I wait. My gaze drifts to the opposite end of the bar where Rylee, a bartender squares her shoulders at a guy across from her. By the way she's clenching her jaw, I'm sure she's ready to rip his jugular out Mortal Combat style.

He reaches across the bar, and she pulls away. My

molars grind together. That's all I need to see. I shove off the wood edge, the screeching of the metal on the linoleum tile draws the attention of a few customers around me. The stool nearly topples over, but someone behind me catches it and I stalk to the other end.

## BANTER STRANGLEHOLD

# Rylee

In one smooth motion, I slide the knife through the lime. The two pieces fall to the sides. I toss them into the condiment tray and set another lime on my cutting board and repeat the process.

"What are The Boy Scouts of America doing back there?" Nora, the newly hired bartender, asks from next to me as she fishes olives from a jar. She's been on the job for two weeks and luckily, I haven't had to do too much handholding, so I know she'll fit right in.

"It's some bachelors forever meeting. I don't know. Jake said they could use the backroom for the next few Thursday nights." Clamping the lid tight with a snap, I tuck away the container into the bottle cooler and grab the lemons.

"Do they call themselves bachelors because they can't score any dates? Especially the guy on the end with the plaid collared shirt, khakis, and black rimmed glasses. I bet he sells car insurance and still lives in his mom's basement." She pulls her long, beach wave blonde hair back and secures it with a hair tie. "All of them except that dark haired Greek god. White button down flexing all his forearm deliciousness. What's his story?"

Bang! Bang! Bang!

Without glancing up, I know exactly who she's referring to. Every time he's here, he's the topic of conversation. "That's Trey. I don't know his deal. Women flock to him like he has a golden dick. But also, it's a different woman every time, so it can't really be that special." I slice through a lemon.

With a loud stomp, Jake passes by us, the liquor bottles shaking on the shelves as he beelines it to the backroom where Trey and the others are hanging out. We exchange glances and shrug simultaneously.

"I won't lie. I'd be willing to take one for the team and test it out." She rises to her tippy toes, peering over the heads of the bar patrons for a better view of Trey.

I roll my eyes and continue slicing the lemons. "Have at it, but double protection might be necessary. Anyway, Jake said we don't need to wait on them. If they need anything, they have to come to the bar."

Nora turns toward me, resting her elbow on the edge of the cooler. "Have you ever hooked up with him?"

"Hell no." I shake my head. "He's not my type. In fact, my type and him are in completely different area codes. Not even in the same state. More like opposite ends of the country."

"Okay. Okay. Got it." She raises her hands up, palms

out in defense. "You seem a little riled up over someone who's not your type."

"Guys like him are all the same. Hell, I was married to a guy exactly like him. They're not worth your time." Amongst many other things, like knocking you up and promising he'll take care of you while also sticking his dick in other women, but I keep that to myself.

Our gazes anchor to Jake as he storms past us and down the hallway toward his office. This time sporting a wooden gavel in his hand.

I stab the knife into a lemon. "Anyway, the more money they have, the bigger assholes they are. Based on the designer suits he wears, he's plenty of both."

She twirls her blonde ponytail around her finger. "I don't know. I think you're judging him too harshly. What if he fosters puppies and kittens because he has so much love to give." With a hand on her waist, she pops her hip. "Wouldn't you feel like an ass for judging him so harshly?"

I bark out a laugh. "No. Plus, I highly doubt it." Images of Trey with a gaggle of puppies and kittens pouncing all over him as he lays on the floor, shirtless, flash before me. Ugh! Of course, he's shirtless. All my daydreams of him are shirtless. Trey and his friends have been coming into the bar since before I started working here. My first impression of him was he's hot. But it didn't take long to see him for who he really is. A playboy. Night after night he would have a different girl on his arm. That's when I slammed the door on anything happening outside my daydreams. A customer takes a seat at the other side of the bar, and I abandon my thoughts and the conversation with Nora.

Over the next hour, we busy ourselves with customers serving drinks and taking food orders. After everything settles down, I pour myself an ice water as a guy sits on the abandoned stool across from me. His dark hair matches the scruff along his strong jaw. His lips tip up in a sexy half-smile I wouldn't mind waking up next to. But the most attractive thing is, he's sporting a t-shirt and not a three-piece suit.

"What can I get you?" I ask.

His gaze drifts from my face and lingers on my chest before sliding up. "Are you an option?"

Scratch that. He just went from semi-cute to jackass in two-point-two seconds. "No."

"Are you sure? You look a little tense. I could ease that for you." He rests a hand on the smooth wood surface and the silver band on this left hand glints from the overhead lights.

If Jake wouldn't fire me, I'd punch him in his smug face. According to him, it's his bar so he does the punching. Not only is the guy in front of me a jackass, but also a cheating bastard. I rest my hand on the bar top and lean in. He does the same. I jerk my chin toward his hand before squaring my gaze with his. He snaps his hand back and hides it behind the bar.

Too slow, asshole. "So, drink or no drink?"

He clears his throat. "How about a Vodka Collins and your phone number." He flashes me another half-smile. That must be his signature move and the only thing he can offer.

"Oh, you want my phone number?" He unlocks his phone and waits as if he believes he's charming enough that I'll give it to him. "Five. Five. Five. Go to hell."

His head jolts up from his phone. "That's too many numbers."

"Fucking hell," I mutter, pushing off the bar. Twisting around, I grab a bottle of vodka and a glass. When I'm finished with his drink, I slide it in front of him. Before I can pull my hand away, his fingers wrap around my wrist.

Red-hot rage courses through my veins as I glower at his hand on mine. Slowly, I lift my head, my glare as sharp as broken glass. "Touch me again and I'll shove this vodka bottle down your throat... sideways." I hold up the half-full bottle. Immediately, he releases his grip but keeps his hand on the bar.

"Is that some new, kinky foreplay?"

"I wouldn't test her. I've seen her throw bigger guys out on their ass." Out of nowhere, Trey wedges himself between the asshole and an empty stool.

He sizes Trey up and huffs out a laugh. "And what are you? Her enforcer?"

Trey shrugs. "More like a cheerleader. By the daggers she's throwing your way, she doesn't need my help."

The asshole's glare cuts to me. "You're not worth it," he sneers and grabs his drink before shouldering past Trey.

A cocky smile covers Trey's face. His gaze is glued to the asshole as he disappears into the crowd. Once he's out of sight Trey turns his attention to me. "That guy's a dick."

I hold up the bottle again, done with the bullshit. "The same offer extends to you."

"Got it." His smile never falters as he holds up his hands in defense.

I blow out a small breath. Trey's not the enemy. I lower my arm, setting the bottle on the bar. "Thanks, but I had it covered." Reaching over, I grab the empty coaster and toss it into the trash. There's only been one time where a guy got too handsy and I needed Jake and Lach to help escort him out. Other than that, I've always held my own.

He rests his elbows on the bar and leans in. "But I can be your enforcer if you need."

"I'll pass. I know how to handle guys like him," I snap.

"Well, if you ever—"

"Don't. I can take care of myself. I don't need guys like you trying to come and save the day like a knight in Armani armor."

He tilts is head. "What's that supposed to mean? Guys like me?" he asks, not in indignation but curiosity.

"You save a girl," I use air quotes around the first four words, "and expect her to be wooed by your manliness and fawn all over you. Which I'm sure leads to a night between the sheets. Then, once it's over you throw her out like discarded trash."

"So, my manliness does nothing for you?"

"Not. A. Single. Thing."

When my gaze shifts to his, dark steely gray eyes meet mine as a slow smile spreads across his face. I've seen him flash that same smile at countless women here, but this is the first time it's aimed at me. I understand how it could entrance them, but I have more willpower. I think.

Needing his attention off me, I nod at a table where several women gather around. "Don't you have some girls to flirt with? There's a bunch here, or have you already been with them all?"

Without taking his eyes off me, he shrugs his shoulders. "Nah. The only girl I want to talk to is standing in front of me."

I shake my head, fighting hard to hold back a smile of my own. He must have an entire book full of one-liners. "Too bad I'm immune to whatever charm you think you have."

"I'll have you know I have more charm than one of those overpriced charm bracelets with all the dangling hearts, butterflies, and chat bubbles."

"Chat bubbles?"

He nods viciously. "Oh, it's a thing."

"It sounds like you've been scorned by a charm bracelet."

"Nah. Just the women who wear them."

"I'll be sure to wear my charm bracelet next time."

He flinches. "That's harsh."

"How about a beer to cheer you up?" Mostly, I need away from him. He has me in a stranglehold with his playful banter. Never would I think I'd be bantering with Trey. He's only good at getting women to take their clothes off. Not this.

"Deal. IPA." He nods to the row of taps.

I reach for a pint glass. Once the golden liquid kisses the rim, I slide it across the bar top. From across the room, one of his friends yells for him, motioning him over with a wave. As he reaches for the glass, our fingers brush against each other's. My gaze flits to his as a burst of electricity flows between us. It's like the slow motion moment before a bolt of static electricity zaps you, catching you off guard. I yank my hand away, grab a rag, and wipe down the already clean bar. What in the fresh hell was that?

The corners of his lips twitch, telling me he felt it too. Before walking away, he turns toward me. "Just so you know, I wouldn't throw you out."

Before I can respond he pivots on his feet. Halfway to the backroom, a woman at a nearby table halts his progress. She runs her hand down his arm and shoves her chest in his face. My jaw clenches with each graze of her finger over his buttons of his dress shirt. When he flashes his dimpled smile at her, I roll my eyes and return to serving the next customer. It was nothing. Absolutely nothing.

## CUDDLE FOR ONE

# Trey

I'll admit, Rylee was never on my radar until four days ago. She's not a damsel in distress, but a damsel who will karate chop you in the jugular if you cross her and, damn, it's hot. Our verbal sparring is some of the best foreplay I've ever had. It's something I haven't had in a long time. After I walked away, a former hook up rubbed herself against me, vying for my attention. Oddly enough, I wasn't interested. Instead, my mind was still on the feisty brunette behind the bar.

The leather executive office chair is cool against my back. I kick my legs up on the mahogany desk, crossing one ankle over the other. After graduation, I got a junior agent position at Harbor Highlands' largest and fastest growing real estate and development firm. Throughout the years, I've been able to climb the ladder to managing director at The Blue Stone Group.

I pull my phone from my pocket, unlock the screen, and click on my messages.

**TREY**

Hey, what are you doing tonight? Catch up with beers at Porter's?

**BENNETT**

I can't. I have a table I need to finish sanding and staining before the weekend.

**TREY**

That sounds boring.

**BENNETT**

The thrilling life of running a business.

**TREY**

Again, sounds boring. I'll ask Seth.

**BENNETT**

Good luck with that.

**TREY**

Hey, what are you doing? Beers at Porter's?

**SETH**

Currently, I'm cleaning puke off my shirt.

**TREY**

Have you already started drinking?

**SETH**

No. The baby isn't feeling well. Parisa's sick too. I think the flu's going around.

**TREY**

Fuck that. Stay home and away from me.

**TREY**

I mean, hope everyone gets well soon.

SETH

Thanks asshole.

TREY

Anytime.

My feet drop to the floor with a thud. Sitting up, I rest my elbows on the desktop. Well, shit. My number one and number two are out. I guess this is a solo mission. Wingmen only slow me down, anyway. Decision made. For the rest of the afternoon, I busy myself with checking and answering emails, along with making a few phone calls. Anything to keep my thoughts off Rylee for the last few hours of the workday.

At 4:45 p.m. I'm pulling into the parking lot of Porter's. I throw my SUV in park and jump out. The moment I open the door, a wave of laughter and conversation greets me, filling the room with lively energy. Immediately, I'm hit with the scent of grilled onions and beer, making my stomach growl.

Every corner is bustling with customers. Some sit at tables and others are shooting darts or playing pool. Luckily, I find an empty stool at the far end of the bar and take a seat. My foot bounces on the foot ring. The new bartender, Nora, is at the opposite end of the bar serving a group of college kids. Glancing over my right shoulder, I scan the bar for anyone else who's working. Most importantly, Rylee.

Jake pushes through a swinging door from behind the bar and my heart and something else shrivels up. While he'll be perfect for someone, I am not that someone. He jerks his chin in acknowledgment, and I return the gesture. A few minutes later, he stops in front of me, resting his hands on the smooth wood.

"What can I get you?"

I glance at the lineup of beers on tap. "I'll take an IPA."

Jake grabs a pint glass and pours me a beer while I work up the courage to ask if Rylee's working. Honestly, I've never had a girl consume my thoughts like this before. It's a little unnerving, actually.

When Jake passes me the full glass, I immediately grab it and take a gulp. The icy liquid hits my throat and for a brief second, it gives me something else to think about. Too bad it doesn't last long. Jake twists around and it's now or never.

"Is Rylee working tonight?" I spit out as casually as I can.

"It's her night off." Jake's gaze lifts to mine, eyebrow raised. "Why?"

*Shit. Abort. Abort.*

"No reason." I swallow another big gulp of my beer to buy myself a few seconds to recover and to think of a change of subject. "Can I use the backroom again next week? For another SBL meeting."

He eyes me warily, jaw clenching before answering, "Fine. But if you use another gavel in my bar…"

"Heard loud and clear. Speaking of which, can I have that back?"

"No," Jake says matter-of-factly. Then he's shuffling down the bar to serve drinks for other waiting patrons.

Alright. Thursday. Only three more days. I can wait. I pull out my phone and send a group text to the other SBL members.

> **TREY**
> Meeting is at Porter's again. Same time.
> Tim, you better show up this time.

**DARREN**

Cool. I really want to try those mini beer-battered corn dogs. At the last meeting on our way out, I saw a table with those. They smelled delicious.

**OWEN**

Yes! I heard they make their own honey mustard dipping sauce.

**DARREN**

Only ketchup for me.

**TREY**

Guys...

**MILES**

What's really good is dipping them in just a little bit of honey. No Mustard. Just honey.

**TIM**

Were those the things on a stick? I've seen them there. Those looked good.

**TREY**

Enough about the corn dogs.

**DARREN**

I think those were the Tot Kabobs. No stick is required for the corn dogs.

**TIM**

You know what I really want to try, the Italian nachos. Instead of salsa, you dip them in marinara. Whoever thought of that... Genius.

Shit. This went sideways, fast. I swear herding cats would be easier than keeping these guys on track.

**TREY**

Thursday. Porter's. See everyone then.

I mute the group text to let them finish playing Betty Crocker and tuck my phone into my pocket. Since my original mission was a failure, let's try Plan B. I swivel my stool around and take in the crowd. There is a plethora of women here and I'm sure I could have my pick of any of them. No reason to waste my effort in coming here tonight. I make a sweeping glance over one face and then another. Soon enough, I've scanned the entire bar, twice over, and nothing. They're all just faceless women. None of them are the feisty brunette that seems to have embedded herself into my thoughts. I huff out a deep breath. Spinning around, I guzzle the rest of my beer, throw some cash under my glass, and push it toward the rail. I guess I'll be cuddling with myself tonight.

## EIGHTY-FIVE-FIFTEEN

# Rylee

"Son of a bitch!" Jake's booming voice sounds from his office, almost rattling the liquor bottles off the shelves.

Nora and I glance at each other. Her eyes are wide, but this isn't anything new from Jake, especially since he passed on some of his responsibilities to Chad.

"Don't worry about him. He may seem big and scary, but he's more like a giant teddy bear... mostly." An alive, feral teddy bear. I keep that to myself though, so I don't scare off the new hire. I pull two beer bottles from a cardboard case and set them in a cooler. "Finish stocking these. I'll see what the problem is." I dry my hands on a towel before spinning around and strolling down the length of the bar until I reach the hallway. Low grumbles and the slamming of a fist into a file cabinet flows through the open doorway. I peek my head through the opening to ensure the coast is clear before fully committing myself. Jake's sitting behind his desk. Stacks of papers are scattered in front of him as he rubs his temples.

Moving a step inside, I lean against the doorframe. "I would ask if everything was alright, but the raging Hulk sounds coming out of your office tells me otherwise. So, what's up?"

Jake's hardened eyes meet mine as deep frown lines etch into his forehead. "How hard is it to count? One. Two. Three. Four. Write it on a piece of fucking paper."

I slink through the doorway now that it's evident the anger isn't directed toward me and take a seat in the pleather armchair across from him. "Let me guess, Chad messed up the ordering again."

"For the third week in a row. I can't explain it. He was a model employee, then after I gave him a promotion, that he asked for, everything goes to shit. I can't keep double checking his work because I might as well just do it myself." He scrubs his hand down his face. "Wait. Didn't you say you went to college for business?"

"Yeah. But I didn't graduate." I was in my third year and then life threw me into a tailspin, and I've never been able to fully recover. Before he can ask any more questions, I hold out my hand. "Here, let me see."

He passes me the paperwork of what was ordered and what was delivered. From a quick glance everything between the two papers appears correct, so that's not the issue. Then I see it. I don't even need to go look. "He's over ordering all the bar garnishes. We don't go through two cases of limes in a week. Over half of this is getting thrown out." With the papers in hand, I storm out of his office and into the storage room. By the brief inspection, I can tell he's not even paying attention to anything he's ordering.

Jake steps up next to me and I pass him the papers. "There are already eight bottles of this brand of vodka. Why is he ordering more? Rail vodka, sure, but not the top shelf stuff."

"More importantly, where is he putting it?"

Both of us dig through the entire shelf to count all the bottles until we find the extra sitting on the whiskey shelf, which threw off the count for the entire second shelf. After some rearranging, Jake and I were able to gather the accurate tally of everything.

"Thanks Rylee. I was five seconds away from losing my shit."

"Lose it? Based on the yelling earlier, it's long gone." I flash him a smile. He gives me a half nod, half shrug, which is practically a smile in Jake's book. "I'm surprised Nora didn't hightail it out the front door. I'm going to see if they're finished stocking up front."

I exit the storage room and as soon as I'm behind the bar, a familiar face is staring back at me. His smile is somewhat charming. Okay, a lot charming. Half devilish. Half boyish. It's devoyish. I stride toward him. His piercing gaze locks onto mine. The way he's looking at me right now sends a bolt of lightning straight between my thighs. I can't control it. And I can't deny it. But he can't know it either.

I come to a stop in front of him and rest my palms on the bar top. "Another boy scout meeting today?"

A hearty laugh escapes him, but then he leans in and whispers, "I assure you, there's nothing boy about me."

"So, man scouts?" I tuck a strand of hair behind my ear.

He lets out another boisterous laugh. "Actually, it's our

weekly Single Bros. Life meeting." He leans back, resting an elbow on the backrest.

"Oh. Well then. Does the bro need a beer?"

"Yes, please."

"At least you have manners."

He flashes me a dimpled grin and there goes the lightning bolt to the lady bits again. I shake the thought away and reach next to me to grab a glass. While pouring his beer, I glance at him from the corner of my eye and our gazes connect. Quickly, I look away, warmth spreading over my cheeks as I pray he didn't catch me. When the beer reaches the rim, I set it down. Reaching over, I snatch a straw, drop it in the pint glass, and push it toward him. "I'm fresh out of sippy cups."

My snark doesn't even phase him. Instead of giving me some snappy come back, he leans over, wraps his lips around the straw, and sucks. I'm fixated at the way his Adam's apple bobs up and down as he swallows. When he's finished he rests an elbow on the bar leaning in so only I can hear. "Are you flirting with me?"

I swallow down the rock in my throat. An Adam's apple should not turn me on right now. "How do you get flirting from that?"

"The tucking the hair behind your ear, ogling from the corner of your eye like I'm a fresh cut ribeye ready to be served up for your enjoyment."

I roll my eyes and bite the inside of my cheek to hide my smile. "I wasn't ogling you."

"I'm pretty sure you drooled a little."

I whirl around and as nonchalantly as I can, I brush the corner of my lips with my finger.

"You know, it would work better if there wasn't a mirror right there."

I glance up and sure enough, Trey's smug smirk is

peering back at me. A rush of heat floods my face. Spinning around, I inhale a deep breath and slowly blow it out. "Fine. You caught me. I was staring. But mostly I wanted to see if your head could get any bigger." I lean in, his leather and spice scent tantalizing my senses, almost distracting me from my thoughts. "Just so you know, it did."

"Have dinner with me." Confidence oozes from his tone.

Hypnotized by his full lips, I nearly forget he asked me a question. "Excuse me? Do you randomly ask women who you've had a five-minute conversation with to dinner?'

"Sometimes." He shrugs.

"And it works?"

"I'm batting about ninety-ten. But also, between us it's been more like *two* five-minute conversations. So, I'd consider it one ten-minute conversation and you can get to know a lot about a person in ten minutes. What do you say?"

I'm flabbergasted. So much so, I'm surprised my jaw doesn't hit the bar top. He's so cocky and sure of himself. Plus, he reminds me too much of someone else, which dampens my entire mood. "I don't think so."

"So now it's eighty-five-fifteen," he mumbles. "I get it. You want to get to know each other more—"

"No. Not really," I say but he ignores me.

"I'll go first. My full name is Trey Alexander Wilson. My favorite beer is IPA. I like spooning and baseball. Not always together but sometimes. And I really want to take you to dinner. Now it's your turn."

I stare at him, mostly curious if he's being serious but his bright steely gray eyes and raised eyebrows indicates he is. "Okay, my name is Rylee. That's all you're going to get because I don't date guys in suits so that's a no on dinner."

"Come on. Give me a full name, at least. If you don't tell me, I have ways I can find out." He leans back on his stool.

I lift a shoulder and let it drop. "Oddly enough, I don't doubt that so I guess you'll have to work for it."

"Dessa. What's Rylee's last name?"

She steps up next to me, brushing her raven locks over her shoulder. "I'm team Rylee." She extends her arm, fist in the air. My bestie always has my side.

Dessa has worked at Porter's for as long as I have. She's our resident mixologist and is always creating new weekly drink specials for Lach to add to the chalkboard with his phenomenal artistic skills.

"Nora?" he asks.

"Seeing I'm new here. It's best I take their side." She raises her fist in solidarity.

"Lach, twenty bucks." He pulls a black leather wallet from the inside pocket of his suit and holds out a crisp twenty-dollar bill.

He yanks it out of his grasp. "Hart."

Out of all of us, Lach has worked here the longest. He's also Jake's best friend and clearly doesn't have my back. I guess that's one less Christmas card I need to send this year. Who am I kidding? I don't have time to send cards.

"Hey, you never offered me twenty bucks." Dessa clasps her waist.

"You wouldn't have given it up for twenty bucks." Lach tucks the bill into his pocket.

"No. You're right. I would have asked for fifty." She smirks.

"Thanks guys. Glad to know you can all be bought." My attention jumps back to Trey. "You got your info. Can I get you anything else?"

"Yes. Dinner?"

Before I can respond, a woman with long, perfectly styled, blonde hair and runway ready, airbrushed makeup strolls up to the bar. "Hey, Trey." His name rolls off her tongue as she brushes her hand over his bicep. "A few friends and I have a spot in the corner with an extra seat if you want to join us."

He glances over his shoulder at the table before shifting his concentration back to the woman on his left. "Maybe next time."

"The invitation is always open," she purrs, dragging her flame red fingernail down his arm.

I choke down the bile that rises in my throat. "Desperate isn't a good look on anyone," I mutter under my breath. The woman doesn't pay attention to me, but Trey's gaze lifts to meet mine. I offer him a snarky smile and shrug. His throat resonates with a low laugh as he shakes his head and he sends the woman on her way.

Trey swings his focus to me and rests his elbows on the bar, a full-fledged smirk on his face. "Jealous?"

I scoff. "Of what? Her? If anything, I'm embarrassed for her."

"If you say so."

The way his gaze bores into me sends a rush of heat coursing through my entire body. It's like he's trying to read every dirty thought floating through my mind right now and that would be terrible. I need him out of my space before I grab his tie and haul him over the bar to slam my lips to his. "You better not keep your fan club waiting."

"Which one?"

"All of them."

His lips tip up into a half-smile. "I'll talk to you later,

Rylee." He taps the bar before sauntering away and into the backroom.

My gaze never wavers from his retreating frame. When he's in a room, he commands attention and people give it to him. How could you not? He's tall, broad shouldered with a tapered waist, and an ass that fills out a pair of slacks perfectly. Mentally, I slap myself across the cheek. No dirty thoughts about Trey.

"Did I hear you correctly?" Nora's voice startles me, causing my heart to jump to my throat. "You turned down dinner with that Greek God. Do you think I can take your place?"

"Go right ahead. I've been with guys just like him. It's nothing but a rollercoaster and by the end you're left sad, empty, and disappointed." I walk away, mostly because I need to clear my head and Nora going on and on about Trey isn't helping.

"But the ride is at least fun, right?" she yells.

It's always fun until you end up pregnant and dropping out of college, only to wind up as a single mom. Been there, done that, and I have the daughter to prove it.

## THE UNEXPECTED TINGLES

# Rylee

When I arrive home from work, I shove the key into the lock and twist. The TV is blaring the latest episode of whatever bachelor farmer seeking love with a rose dating reality show Marcie, my sixty-five-year-old neighbor, likes to binge watch.

Fifteen years ago, she lost her husband, Marcus, in a car accident and never wanted to find love again because he was her swan. From the stories she's told me, his shoes would be hard to fill. Their love is one every couple aspires to and a far cry from my last. So instead of finding love again, she watches others do it on TV. I've warned her it's all scripted, but she threatened to stop babysitting if I told her any more lies. Since she lives in the apartment next to mine, doesn't charge me, and adores Abby, I keep my mouth shut and nod and smile.

I lean over the couch and gently shake her shoulder.

She startles awake, mumbling, "DJ better not have given a rose to that bitch Tonya."

"Hi Marcie. I'm not sure, but why are you hating on Tonya?"

She ambles to her feet and neatly folds the blanket that was covering her. "I don't trust her. She's too... nice." Her lip curls on the last word.

"Well, you've always been extremely perceptive of people. Like when George was stealing packages. You knew right away it was him."

"His eyes were always too shifty."

I nod because everything about him was shifty. "Thanks again for watching Abby."

"Anytime. You know that."

I give her a tight-lipped smile as I walk her to the door. She's been my saving grace since my divorce from Kyle. My life would be a hot mess—hotter mess—without her. After she leaves, I close and lock the door. With a flick of the switch, the kitchen goes dark. Then I swiftly move to power down the TV in the living room. On my way to my bedroom, I peek my head through the doorway of Abby's room. Her soft snores fill the room as she sleeps sideways on her bed. I'll never understand how that could be comfortable. Once I'm through the doorway of my bedroom, I kick the door shut and the latch clicks into place. I tear off my clothes and toss them into the laundry basket next to the closet. Next, I yank out a pair of sleep shorts from the dresser and grab a t-shirt from the closet. After I'm dressed, I flop on to the bed.

Over the next hour, instead of sleeping, images of Trey flit through my mind. He's good looking. Okay, he's fucking gorgeous, and he knows it. Nora was five seconds away from throwing herself at him. But it's the cockiness disguised as confidence that always tricks me. My ex was the same way. Apparently, it's my type, even though I don't want it to be. After what feels like hours, I eventually close my eyes and fall into a restless sleep.

The buzzing of my alarm clock stirs me awake. My heavy lids drift open. I'm convinced I only got an hour, two tops, of sleep. That's how my body feels, anyway. Reaching over, I smack the top of the clock to stop the noise. I roll onto my back and stare at the ceiling. Shit. Even after a night's sleep, my situation isn't any better. In fact, it might be worse. Not only am I angry at myself for thinking of Trey, but I'm also sexually frustrated because I'm thinking of Trey. It's a wicked combination, which in turn makes me hate myself even more.

After dropping Abby off at school, I came home and did the one thing that I needed to do... work out some of this frustration. Everything was going perfectly until it wasn't. While in the middle of executing some self-love with images of badass Jax Teller playing on repeat, out of nowhere, he morphs into Trey. Dirty blond hair turns dark, and the leather cut transforms into a three-piece suit. The most infuriating part was I had the most explosive self-served orgasm I've had in years. While I'm not sexually frustrated anymore, the self-loathing is very prominent.

All day at work, I was on edge. Between terrible customers, Chad screwing up the inventory again, and Trey, I was over everything including the *Rylee say yes to Trey* written on the blackboard behind the bar. Based on the scripty font and heart doodles, I suspect it was either Dessa or Nora, but neither would admit it. As I shot daggers at both of them, I wiped away all traces of the words.

Luckily, it was time for me to leave for the night. As I'm

standing in front of my locker in the staff room, my phone vibrates against my butt. When I pull it out, Kyle flashes on the screen and my shit night just got worse.

"Hi Kyle."

"Hey Rylee. So, I know this weekend I'm supposed to take Abby, but something came up."

"What are you talking about? You can't bail on her again." I press my phone between my ear and shoulder as I yank my wallet from the small metal cage, slamming the door shut.

"I'm sorry. I have this work thing I can't miss. But I promise to make it up to her."

My heart thunders in my ears, causing an instant headache. Same excuse, different day. I hate that he always does this to her, and I hate that I always have to be the one to tell her. As much as I regret ever meeting Kyle and the three years I spent with him, it gave me Abby. And that's the only good thing that happened.

"I'm sick of your excuses and I'm sick of your bullshit. You better keep your word."

"Rylee—"

I end the call and shove my phone into my back pocket. Adrenaline races through my body. My fists clench. Everything he does irritates me. I exhale a deep breath and stomp out to the main bar area. All heads turn toward me as a hush rolls down the bar.

"Why does it look like you're about to go on a murderous rampage?" Dessa asks.

"It's never good news when I speak to Kyle." I stop at the corner of the bar and rest my elbows on top. "Would you guys still visit me if I were in prison?"

"Depends on where you end up." Lach shrugs a shoulder. Dessa snaps the end of a towel on his chest, but he grabs it, snatching it away from her.

A few stools down, Trey raises his hand. "I'll come visit, especially if you need conjugal visits. I'm pretty good with those."

"And how many of those do you do a week?" Dessa asks.

"Okay. I'm good at practicing them. Rylee would be my first." He leans over the bar, his gaze instantly connects with mine like the opposite ends of a magnet, and winks.

Ugh! It shouldn't be so sexy, but my vagina really wants to wink back. With a shake of my head, my hair drapes over my face, concealing my expression from the outside world. Yet, a subtle smile creeps onto my lips. What the hell? I don't get shy or giddy, but right now I'm doing both and it's all Trey's fault. Somehow, he's implanted a tiny piece of himself in my head and oddly enough, I don't hate it. Especially right now, it keeps the focus off my piece of shit ex. I exhale a deep breath and regain control of my thoughts. "I'm going to go home, eat a pint of ice cream, and forget that Kyle even exists. I'll talk to everyone later." With my wallet in hand, I stroll toward the exit.

When I'm halfway across the room, Trey jumps off his stool and meets me in front of the door. "I'll walk you out. It's dark out there."

"Thanks. But I got it."

"I insist. Plus, I'm now closer to the door than I am to my seat, so it would take more effort to go back than to leave."

"Not really because now you have to go across the parking lot—never mind. Do what you want." I shove the door open, and Trey follows closely on my heels. Immediately, the cool spring air does nothing for my heated skin. My stride increases with each heavy footfall. I hate that Kyle always does this. There's always an excuse for why he can't spend time with Abby. Mostly, I hate that because of this I'm always thinking about him.

"Slow down. Is this a race?" Trey jogs up from behind me until he's meeting me stride for stride.

"Sorry. I'm just a little... irritated. Annoyed. Angry. I can't believe Kyle would do this to me again. He's the most unreliable human ever."

"Is Kyle a boyfriend?"

Bile shoots up my throat hearing the words Kyle and boyfriend strung together. I meet Trey's gaze. "Ex-husband."

He releases a slow whistle. "So, a little more baggage with that one."

I exhale, my shoulders dropping. "You could say that. He shouldn't gnaw on my last nerve, but he does. I don't want to think about him. Just the thought of him drives me crazy. I can't believe I wasted so many years of my life on him." When I reach my SUV in the far corner of the dimly lit parking lot, I whirl around to face Trey. "I don't want him occupying any more of my thoughts."

Trey's large but gentle palms cover both of my cheeks. Car horns blare in the distance and slowly meld into a dull hum the moment his lips touch mine. It's soft at first, as if he's testing the waters. Alarm bells should be blaring in my head right now, telling me I shouldn't be kissing him, but they're not. In fact, a rush of euphoria flows from the tips of my toes to where my lips are touching his. It's the highest of highs and something I haven't experienced in a really long time. His tongue sweeps over the seam of my lips. He tastes like spice and hops. A moan rumbles in the back of my throat and he deepens the kiss.

I break away, but his palms are still on my cheeks. I need a moment to gather my thoughts. Because whatever just happened should not have happened. My body shouldn't be tingling as much as it is from that kiss. "What was that for?" I press my fingertips to my lips, the residual heat radiates to my fingers.

He rubs the pad of this thumb against my cheek. "I wanted your thoughts to be occupied with something else. Did it work?"

Dumb question. Of course it worked. My nipples are still hard because of it. But it's Trey. I can't be kissing Trey. Then why can't I stop thinking about his lips on mine? And why do I want them there again?

"Fuck it," I mumble, more to myself than him. I'm taking this one for me. With a hand around the back of his neck, I haul his mouth to mine, crashing our lips together in a bruising kiss.

## Chapter 6

### STRIPPER CONDOM

# Rylee

I melt into him. He takes that as a sign to deepen the kiss and I let him. With our lips still fused together, he spins us around, slamming my back against my SUV. A moan rumbles from my throat as he grinds his growing erection into my stomach. I'm going to regret this later, but I don't care. I need to feel something, anything else besides the utter disappointment that is my life. All I need is a few seconds, so I don't rage call Kyle to yell at him about how much he sucks. Also, it better last longer than a few seconds or I'll be hulking out for a completely different reason.

Like a mental rolodex, I run through everything in my backseat. Car seat. Toys. Good chance there's a lot of fruit snack wrappers scattered between the seats. That plan is out. I've got to go with something else. With my palm on his hard, muscular chest, I shove him away, causing him to stumble backward. His gaze flits to mine with a mixture of shock and surprise. "Where's your car?"

His eyebrows pinch together. "Behind us." He nods to a black SUV parked next to mine.

"Get in the backseat."

"Wait. What?"

"Get in the backseat. I want to work out some frustration."

"Are you sure?"

"Are you trying to talk me out of sex right now?" My irritation grows exponentially with every passing second. After the last shitty fifteen minutes of my day, I need my thoughts consumed by something else, even if it's Trey. At this point, I won't even be picky. I'll take his tongue, fingers, or cock. Or maybe one of each. I don't care. I just need it.

"Fuck no." He shoves his hand into his front pocket, pulls out his keys, and fumbles to hit the unlock button on the key fob. After a second, the lights flash and he yanks the backdoor open.

I crawl inside over one of the bucket seats, tossing my wallet to the floor, and Trey follows close behind. As soon as the door slams closed, I pounce. Leaping over the gap between the seats, I straddle his lap as I palm his cheeks and slam my lips to his. His firm hands roam over my ribcage as his thumbs graze the underside of my breasts until he's holding me in place as if he's afraid I'll leave. Right now, that's not happening. In fact, I moan and rock my hips into him. Needing to feel him. Everywhere. His rock hard erection rubs against my pussy and I half moan, half mewl. The sensation sends a million tiny pin pricks over my entire body.

I break our kiss and frantically pull apart the buttons on his shirt. I'm surprised I don't rip any of the threads. Once they're all undone, the side of his dress shirt falls open and I'm met with chiseled and toned muscles. All I want to do is spend several hours running my hands up and down his chest and over every ridge and valley of his six-pack abs. But I don't have hours. If I did, I'd talk myself out of it. Less thinking. More doing.

"A couple of housekeeping guidelines." His hands skate up my sides, taking the hem of my shirt with them. I raise my arms and he removes my shirt, tossing it on the seat next to us. "One. This is only happening once."

"It's like you're speaking my language." He cups the outside of my black lace bra and places open mouth kisses on the swell of each breast.

My back arches and I moan from his touch. "Two. Tell no one."

"Done." He bites down on the soft flesh, and I grind myself against his now fully hard cock.

"Three. When was the last time you got tested?"

"Like a month ago. Everything's negative." He pulls down the cup on one side and sucks a nipple into his mouth. His tongue swirls around the stiff peak, and I'm on the verge of seeing stars.

"Same." I pant. "And you haven't gone bare with anyone since?"

"Nope. I always suit up." He repeats the action with the other breast but this time his fingers knead the tender flesh of the other. "Fuck this." He mumbles against my skin. His hand slides to my back. In one swoop, the clasp of my bra releases, and the straps slide down my shoulders. He finishes removing it and tosses it to the floor somewhere next to us. "Much better." With both hands he cups my breasts, pressing them to the center. His thumbs brush over my pebbled nipples as he places open mouth kisses on one and then the other.

I whimper and arch into him. "Last one. I don't have a condom unless you do, but I'm on birth control."

He freezes, and a blank expression takes over his face for a brief second. I'm slightly terrified he's going to tell me he doesn't and back out. Which would probably be for the best since all my moral judgement has taken a vacation.

"Oh! Wait!" He grips my waist and moves me to the other seat. He bends over, lifts the center console, and rifles around inside. I count the seconds by the thumping of my heart. The longer he takes makes me question my decision to go through with this, but my vagina is leading the charge, keeping me rooted to the seat. He slams the lid down and holds up a square plastic wrapper.

I snag it from his hands. From the dim street lamp shining in through the tinted windows, a shimmer of text catches my eye. Glancing down, I read the words, mostly to myself, "Sugar Daddy's." My gaze shoots up. "The strip club?"

"Uh. Yeah." He rubs the back of his neck. "I got it from a bachelor party."

I stare down at the white plastic square with gold imprint as I contemplate having sex in the back of an SUV in the parking lot of my work with a strip club condom as if I was in my twenties. Granted, I wasn't actually doing this when I was twenties, but I'm pretty sure Kyle was. Fuck it. Fuck all of it. I'm thinking with my vagina tonight.

With the wrapped condom in hand, I climb on Trey's lap and crash my lips to his. His fingers wrap around the nape of my neck, and he deepens the kiss, causing me to see stars. And not just one star, but a meteor shower of stars raining down on us.

Without breaking our kiss, my hands fumble to

unbutton his pants while he does the same to mine. Once both our pants are haphazardly pushed down our hips, I rise to my feet. With my back hunched, I shimmy my jeans down one leg, then shift my weight to do the same to the other side. He lifts his hips and pulls his pants the rest of the way down until they hit the floorboard. Despite the lack of light, the outline of his impressively hard, thick cock casts a distinct shadow on the floor. A rush of heat lands directly between my legs and I freeze. That's going to be inside me. I have the urge to wrap my hand around the girth and lick the head, but that's not why we're here.

I finish yanking off my jeans, and they drop to the floorboard with the plop. I rise to my knees. With my finger hooked on the fabric of my panties between my legs, I begin to pull them to the side, but Trey stops me with his hand on my waist.

"These can go too." He lowers his head. The stubble on his chin scrapes over my sensitive skin as his heated breath skates across my pelvic bone sending a rush of goosebumps over my entire body, peaking at my nipples. The tip of his tongue carves a path following the line of the elastic waistband from my hip to right below my belly button. His teeth dig under the fabric, and he does his best to pull them down with his teeth until he loses his grip and they snap back into place.

I inhale a sharp breath from the slight sting.

"This works better when I have more room." He hooks both thumbs under the fabric and shimmies them down as far has he can until I have to stand up. After they drop to the floor, I rest a knee on the seat to get back to penis insertion position. Before I can slide down on his monster cock, he stops me, his fingers dimpling my waist.

"I'm not done yet." With his other hand, he slides two fingers down my slit until he reaches my entrance and then back up to rub a circle around my clit. "Fucking drenched." The deep timbre of his voice sends a shiver up my spine. He continues to slide his fingers up and down, smearing my wetness all over my pussy and his fingers. He leans forward and places a kiss in the center of my chest. My heart flutters until I tamp down those feelings. That's the last thing I need right now, especially with him. This is a no feelings operation.

With one hand gripping the dark leather of the backseat, I splay my other hand against the roof. I rock my hips against his fingers, needing more of him. "That feels so good."

"But my dick will feel way better." He pulls his hand away. Long, slender fingers wrap around his girth. One. Two. Three pumps.

With my teeth, I tear open the condom. Remembering where he got it, I cringe and spit out the top half and then pass it to him. He pulls it out and rolls the latex down his length. With a steady hand around his cock, he holds it still. I take that as my cue, lowering myself onto the crown. A jolt of electricity courses through me as the tip grazes my entrance. Inch by inch I slide down. My mouth gapes open, unable to form words, as he stretches me wider and wider.

"Ah. Fucking hell. Your pussy feels amazing gripping my dick." His fingers curl around my waist.

I continue to slide down, surprised I haven't bottomed out yet. In one swoop, Trey thrusts upward until he's fully inside me. My yelp morphs into a moan as I adjust to his size.

"Oh. God." My head falls back as I collect my breath.

"Fuuuck." His hands grip me tighter.

Slowly, I rise and savor the stretch as I slide up and down on his cock. My pace grows faster with each pass.

My moans and whimpers mix with his grunts and groans, each thrust increasing in intensity from the previous one. I roll my hips, the new angle driving his cock even deeper. His lips wrap around my nipple, sending a lightning bolt directly to my clit.

"Harder. Don't stop," I pant. His teeth clamp down, shooting my pleasure to the stars. "Oh! Yes!"

He reaches up and wraps his fingers around the grab handle and uses it for leverage to push deeper into me. Each and every time, he hits my g-spot, and I can't help but moan out his name. I rest one hand on his shoulder, my nails digging into his skin as my orgasm draws nearer.

"Trey. I'm close. So close." I continue rolling my hips, keeping a steady pace.

"I'm right there with you." He sucks a nipple into his mouth and softly bites down. He pounds into me from below. "Oh, shit!"

"What?" I freeze. "Are you coming already?"

"No! Ah! Ah! Charlie horse!" His arm goes slack.

"Shake it off!"

He drops his hand from the handle and stretches his leg as far as he can in the small space.

"Shit. That sucked." He blows out a breath. "Okay. Go." His fingers grip my waist as he guides me up and down on his cock again.

I rock my hips. The sensation on my clit draws me closer and closer to climaxing. He continues the assault on my pussy from below. My orgasm detonates, sending a rush of white, sultry heat through my entire body. I cry out Trey's name, my nails digging into his skin as wave after wave of pleasure rolls through my body. Every second is more magnificent than the last.

"Fuck. Rye. Your pussy is so tight. I can't."

A deep groan rumbles from Trey's chest as he thrusts

his hips up, his hot cum filling the condom. He continues thrusting, riding out his own orgasm, until he slows to a stop. His hand hits the seat with a thud and my forehead drops to his shoulder. The steady rise and fall of his chest is hypnotizing. He glides his palm up my thigh, stirring me to meet his gaze. My breath hitches as his finger caresses my cheek before tucking a lock of hair behind my ear. Without saying anything, he presses his lips to mine. It's sweet and tender and everything I don't need right now. This isn't a fairy tale. I stopped believing in those a long time ago.

Instantly I crash down to earth. What did I just do? And I can't even use alcohol as an excuse because I'm stone cold sober.

"Oh god. Oh god." I scurry off Trey's lap and flop down in the seat next to him. A million different emotions smack me in the face. Anger. Annoyance. Confusion. Lust. Circling back to anger. My frantic gaze darts from left to right, searching for my clothes.

"I'm used to women using those words while they're riding me, not searching for their clothes."

I stop and glare at him before I desperately go hunting for my underwear again. Once I find them, I yank them up. Then I swipe my pants off the floor and do my best to tug them up in the small space, but my foot collides with Trey's solid knee in the process.

"Sorry," I mumble.

"Hey, where's the fire?" He reaches over and rests a hand on my thigh.

Currently, the fire is raging through my entire body and heading straight to my heart, and I need to pull the pin on the fire extinguisher. Stat. "I have to go." Reaching behind me, I clasp my bra and then I grab my shirt. Without putting it on, I pull the lever of the door and push it open. A shiver runs up my spine as soon as the cool air hits me. I shove the shirt over my head and slam the door. My fingers fumble pushing the button through the hole of my jeans. As I pass the gap between our two vehicles, the pavement illuminates red from the taillights and the back driver's side window slides down. Trey's deep voice sends me ten feet into the air.

"Forgetting something?" He holds out my yellow wallet.

I clutch my chest. "Yes. Thank you." In two long strides, I'm standing in front of him while avoiding eye contact. I grip my wallet and tug, but he doesn't let it go. My gaze lifts to his.

"Are you sure you don't want to stick around? I might be able to find another stripper condom." The corner of his mouth tips up into a smile.

It's a panty dropping smile that makes it hard to not drop my panties for him... again. Because he set the bar high with round one so I'm sure round two would be equally as good, if not better than the first. But I can't.

"I don't think so." This time when I pull my wallet, he lets go. With a quick spin, I sprint to the driver's side of my SUV, my heart pounding in time with my footsteps. I fire up the engine, press the pedal, and reverse out of the parking spot. I spare a quick glance in the rearview mirror, Trey's SUV receding into the distance. Unfortunately, the enormous knot in my stomach doesn't dissipate with the added distance. What was I thinking? A sigh escapes my lips and I lower my eyes, fixating on the windshield in front of me. Biggest mistake ever. Okay. Maybe only the second biggest mistake. The first one started with a phone call that got me here in the first place.

# Chapter 7

## THE BESTEST FRIEND

# Rylee

"Be good and I'll see you in the morning, okay?" I drop to a knee in front of Abby.

"Okay." Her voice is soft.

"I love you always." I hold up my hand, curling my pointer finger and thumb in the shape of a half heart.

"I love you forever." She holds her hand up, mirroring mine. A warm smile covers my face as her bright hazel eyes sparkle. She's my entire world and I hate that I can't always spend my nights with her. I'm so thankful Marcie babysits her for me while refusing to let me pay her. Especially during school closures, like today. She's familiar with the single mom life and knows how hard it can be. Plus, she adores Abby like a second granddaughter.

Once I'm in my SUV, I turn over the ignition and shift

into drive. Houses and street signs pass by me in a blur. At the end of the road, I pass the neighborhood park as kids race around the playground and climb all over the equipment. A black SUV eerily similar to Trey's draws my attention. Immediately, thoughts of the other night in the parking lot of Porter's with Trey in his SUV flash in my head.

It was as if I was having an out-of-body experience. Like it wasn't really me in the back seat, yet I can still feel every kiss on my lips, every caress of his hands, but most importantly, the stroke of his cock inside me. A chill runs up my spine and my nipples pebble. But it's Trey. The same guy who's declared his eternal bachelorhood with his weekly meetings at Porter's. But what niggles me the most… he's just like my ex. Work first, everything else after. I've already lived that life. I don't need a repeat. But with the snap of his fingers, or his fingers inside me, he ignited a spark unlike anything I've ever experienced. It was a euphoric high that I want again. Damn.

After arriving at Porter's, I busy myself with rearranging perfectly organized shelves in order to keep all thoughts of Trey at bay. That only lasts a whole ten seconds until the flashbacks of us in his backseat start playing. It was only sex, so why can't I stop replaying it in my mind? Maybe because it was some of the best sex I've had in… ever. Dessa strolls behind me with a jug of pineapple juice in her hand, mentioning something about a dream, but I'm barely paying attention. He's short circuited everything in my body. There's only one thing I can do.

"Then a T-Rex burst into the room and used his little arms to ravish my naked body." With her arms close to her body, she wiggles her hands. After a second, she drops them to her sides. "Are you even listening to me?"

I lift my chin, abandoning the box of beer bottles. "Uh. Yes?"

She rests a hand on her waist and pops her hip. "Then what did I say?"

"T-Rex with little arms." I hold my arms close to my body and wiggle my hands.

She giggles and goes back to pouring the pineapple juice into a shaker. "What's with you today?"

My gaze shifts left and then right before I lean in. "I made a mistake."

She freezes mid-pour and stares at me. "You really killed him, didn't you? I left my shovel at home, but after work, I got you. There's an old gravel pit—"

"No. Not that." Even though I'd rather deal with the aftermath of that versus what I'm about to tell her. I peer over my shoulder before I cup a hand over my mouth, shielding my words from anyone else. "I slept with Trey."

"You had sex with Trey?!" The bottle in her hand nearly drops to the floor, but she recovers.

I slap a hand over her mouth. "Shhh. I don't need everyone in the bar knowing."

Her eyes widen and she mumbles incoherently under my palm.

"Ugh! I know. The last person I should ever want to have sex with. But something came over me and it happened, and it was earth shattering." I sigh and lean my hip against the beer cooler.

"Did you tell him about Abby?"

"No. What was I supposed to say while his dick was jabbing my uterus? 'Oh, by the way, I have a daughter.'"

"Is it really that big?" she whispers.

"Not the point."

"Okay we'll circle back to that." She swirls her pointer finger in the air. "So, what does that mean? Are you two dating?" She presses the cap onto the shaker and turns it sideways, giving it a firm shake.

"No," I spit out entirely too fast to be casual. "Definitely not." I pause. "Friends?" I tilt my head as I test out the word to see if it fits. Since it doesn't give me hives, I go with it. "We're friends." Mostly I need to shove him into the friend box for me. He's everything I don't need in my life. Been there. Done that. Built the brick wall, surrounded by concrete with barbed wire strung around the top and I don't want to take it down now.

"Like naked friends?" She wiggles her eyebrows. "I bet he'd make a good naked friend."

"Just friends. I don't sleep with friends."

She raises a perfectly sculpted eyebrow.

"We're friends," I point between us, "and we haven't slept together."

She pours the chilled liquid into a low ball and pushes it my way. "I am missing a key male anatomy that you seem quite fond of, so that theory is out. Also, try this."

I take a sip of her newly created concoction. "Yum. It's sweet but not overly sweet. What's it called?"

She taps her chin. "I think I'll call it… Friends with Benefits."

My lips flatten into a thin line. Lach walks past and I grip his bicep, spinning him around. I link my arms around his waist because I can't reach around his shoulders. "Lach and I are friends, and we haven't slept together."

"Wait. Was sex an option between us?" He peers down at me, his sapphire colored eyes sparkle with intrigue.

"No. Because we're friends and I don't sleep with my friends."

"Friends can have benefits." Lach wraps his arms around my shoulder in a bear hug.

"No naked friends." I glare at Dessa. "And no benefits." I flash Lach the same look I just gave Dessa.

"What about Jake?" She nods in his direction as he strolls along the opposite side of the bar.

"Whatever you guys are talking about, leave me out of it," Jake grumbles without sparing a glance our way.

"We're just talking about how friends can have benefits," Dessa says as she pours another drink and passes it to Lach. "Try this."

Jake rounds the corner of the bar and stops at the computerized cash register. "Yeah. Definitely leave me out of it."

"Oh, come on." Dessa strolls past me and Lach.

My shoulders drop, thankful I'm no longer the center of her questioning.

She stops next to Jake and leans her butt against the edge of the counter. "You're telling me you've never had a friend with benefits?"

Without taking his eyes off the register, he answers, "No. I'm saying whatever you three are discussing, I want no part of it."

"You must have a friend with bennies because we certainly haven't seen you with a girlfriend. So, who's the lucky lady? Is it Katy? She seems to always be here while you're working. I bet it's Katy. She's cute! Definitely worth the benefits." She nudges Jake with her elbow.

"For one. No. Second. No." He slams the register shut and stuffs the money into a bank bag.

Dessa rolls her eyes. "You're no fun."

"I never claimed to be." Jake holds up the bag. "I'm going to the bank. Then I might throw myself into the lake just so I can avoid the rest of this conversation."

"Don't worry. Like I told Rylee, we'll circle back to this." She smirks, swirling her pointer finger in the air.

"Looking forward to it." The slamming of the door echoes throughout the bar.

Dessa twists to face me, a knowing grin spreads across her lips. "Now, back to Trey—"

"There's nothing to go back to. It was a mistake. A lapse in judgment. I shouldn't have even said anything since it meant nothing." I absentmindedly straighten straws and napkins that are already organized.

"This is really good." Lach holds up the now empty low ball. "We should make it a special. What's it called?"

"This one is a nod to Rylee. It's called Friends with Benefits," Dessa sing songs.

I hate my friends right now. All of them. Except Jake. He's the only innocent one. "It was nothing."

"If you ask me, if it meant nothing," she flashes air quotes around the last two words, "we wouldn't still be talking about it."

"What are we talking about?" Lach asks.

Dessa leans toward him and whispers, "I'll tell you later."

"Exactly. You're right. Conversation done." I finish counting bottles and slam the cooler door. "I'm going to grab another box." Before anyone can say anything, I stride down the length of the bar and around the corner to the walk-in cooler. As soon as I pull the handle, a blast of chilly air slams into me, instantly cooling my heated skin. This is the right decision. Anything more with Trey would only take me down a path I've already walked down. Plus, I've heard his comments, he doesn't want kids and I have Abby.

I shove my hands into the handles of a box of beer bottles and carry them out. Behind the bar, Dessa is busy making drinks for a couple of customers and Lach's off to the side, prepping the garnish trays. Good. Now we can move on.

I rest the box on the edge of the cooler, slide open the door, and fill it three bottles at a time. When the box is empty, I glance up and freeze. I'm met with a pair of familiar steely gray eyes. I suck in a sharp breath that doesn't go unnoticed based on the lazy smile that creeps over Trey's face. Heat floods up my neck and over my cheeks because I won't lie, his smile alone can cause a girl's thighs to clench. I'm going to need another trip to the cooler.

"Fancy seeing you here." His hypnotic, dimpled smile makes an appearance.

I close the flaps of the box. "I do work here."

"That you do. And I think I need a beverage."

"I'm sure that's not the only thing you need."

"What are you offering?" He smiles again.

It's the same smile he gave me right before I kissed him. And it's beyond tempting to do it again. *Look away, Rylee. Look away.*

"Not that." My gaze drops to the cardboard box as I fight the urge to become distracted by this man.

"But last week—"

I huff out a breath and rest my forearms on the closed box. "Are we doing this? The awkward 'we had sex talk.'"

"We don't have to do the talk, but we could always do the sex again." A slow smirk graces his lips. It's equally sexy and cocky, and a trap I can't fall into.

"That's not going to happen."

"So, you're just going to resist my charm."

I want to say no, crawl over this bar, grip his tie, and kiss the smirk off his face. Instead, I say, "Yes. But we can be friends." I need to cram him into the friend box. Like yesterday.

"Like friends with benefits?" He quirks an eyebrow at me.

What is with everyone needing benefits? Can't two grown adults of a different sex be friends? "Only friends."

"Then I'm going to be the bestest friend you've ever had." He flashes me a wink before rising to his feet, taking his beer with him as he strolls to the backroom.

My heart hammers in my chest. His words seem more like a promise than a threat, and that's what I'm afraid of.

# Chapter 8

## DATING ADVICE

*Trey*

My fingers curl around the edges of the round pub table and I roll it on its edge of the base from the corner of the backroom, so it stands at the head of the small rectangular table. While I wait for the rest of the guys to arrive, I pull out my phone. With a mind of their own, my fingers type out Kyle Hart on social media. It doesn't take long to find him as he's the only one in Harbor Highlands. He works as a financial advisor at a mediocre firm. His side part comb-over screams douche. While one social media page is set to private another one isn't, and he has no qualms about posting pictures of himself cuddled up with a variety of different women. While I've been with my fair share of women over the years, I'm not posting pictures of them like a trophy collection. First impression, this guy is a piece of shit.

"Hey, Trey. What are you doing?" Darren says as he sets a beer down next to me.

His voice startles me, and I fumble to exit out of the app. I was so distracted I didn't even realize he was here. "Uh. Nothing. Checking my stocks." Or stalking someone's ex-husband. Quickly, I tuck my phone into my pocket. "Thanks for the beer." I lift the glass and take a giant gulp. I pull out gavel two point oh and smack it on the wood.

Squeak. Squeak. Squeak.

The plastic toy hammer draws everyone's attention as I smack it against the wood. Everyone takes their seat with Tim and Darren on one side and Owen and Miles on the other.

"Tim, it's so good you could join us."

"Yeah. It was a hectic week." He rubs the back of his neck.

"What happened?" Miles asks.

"Julie got a flat tire, so she wasn't able to pick up Mallory and James from school, so I had to do it. Then school was canceled because of a water break and since I already had the kids, Julie told me to keep her for the night and that turned into the weekend." He blows out an exasperated breath and his shoulders deflate.

"I admire that you can stay friends with your ex," Owen says. "It never works out that way with mine."

"I wouldn't say friends. She's still sleeping with her boss, but we stay cordial for the kids," Tim adds.

"It always ends badly with my exes." Darren swallows a gulp of his beer.

"Exes are exes for a reason," Miles says.

"Good, now that we got all that out of the way." I grip the edge of the table.

Miles' eyes light up. "You guys will never guess what happened. I met a girl."

"No way. Where did you meet her?" Owen asks.

"At the library. She was sorting books while I was searching for something new to read. I've seen her around a few times, but never worked up the courage to say anything to her. Then, out of the blue, she asked me if I needed any help. I panicked and pulled a random book off the shelf. I tell her I got it. Then she asked if I had a son. I glanced down at the book I was holding, and it's titled *So Your Son is a Centaur*."

The entire table bursts out laughing, and I can't help but join in because that's pretty funny. This is the first time I've heard Miles talk so much. Usually, he's the quiet guy who keeps to himself. Maybe he just needed to find himself a girl. I slam the plastic hammer down on the table and it squeaks. "Okay. Let's move on. Darren last week you were telling us—"

"What happened after that?" Tim asks.

"I told her I don't have a son or a centaur. Then she released the sweetest laugh," Miles says.

"I dated a girl who had the best laugh. It was infectious," Owen's eyes gloss over as he reminisces.

I roll my eyes. We're not here to talk about girls and how they sweetly laugh. That's not the point of SBL. This is the opposite of SBL.

Miles continues, "So I shoved the book back on the shelf and then asked her if she wanted to go to dinner sometime, fully expecting her to tell me no or she has a boyfriend, but she said yes. Now, I don't know what to do. Where do I take her? What should I wear?"

Darren rubs his chin. "That could be hard. You don't want to go too extravagant and appear pretentious, but you also don't want to seem cheap."

Miles points at Darren. "Exactly. What do I do? I have to let her know by tomorrow."

"You can take her to Le Uve," Owen says.

"Isn't that too elegant, though? I was thinking maybe The Lake Café." Miles presses his lips into a firm line.

"But their menu selection is limited. Do you know if she has any dietary restrictions?" Owen asks.

This is not how guys' night is supposed to go. I need to step away. "I'll get drinks." As I drop the toy hammer, it emits a high-pitched squeak. I'm not even sure if anyone heard me and I don't care. Somehow our single guys' meeting has turned into gossip and relationship hour. It's pretty much the opposite of everything being a single guy entails. Once I'm at the bar, I throw myself onto a stool.

Nora sees me first and nods in my direction as she elbows Rylee. As soon as she lifts her head, our eyes connect. As much as I want to flash her my signature dazzling smile, continue our verbal sparring, and flirt with her until a blush covers her cheeks, I don't have it in me.

She saunters my way and stops once she's in front of me. "Why do you look like someone kicked your puppy?"

"They went rogue."

She grabs a pint glass and pours me an IPA. Once it's full, she slides it my way. "The Boy Scouts went rogue?"

I swallow a gulp as the hoppy liquid flows down my throat. "I don't know what happened. One minute I was starting the meeting so we could talk about our run of the mill topics like sports and cars, but then it turned into a Dear Abby column with terrible dating advice."

"Why does all this guy talk have to be centered around sports and other masculine topics?"

"It's called Single Bros Life. Emphasis on single. We're not here for relationships."

"Is that because the longest relationship you've had is with that beer?" She points at the pint glass in front of me.

I bark out a laugh and then lift the glass to my lips for a gulp. "Maybe so, but I'll also treat this beer like it's the best damn beer I've ever tasted." I toss her a flirty wink.

She shakes her head, but the corners of her lips tip up into a smile. Quickly, she leans down, so her dark brown hair flows over the side of her face and digs in a cooler so I don't notice, but I noticed. And hell, I wish I could read her mind right now because if it has anything to do with me and how I'd treat her, I'd gladly show her. In the meantime, I'll mess with her a little more. I lower my voice so it's deep and seductive. "Sometimes you need to roll it around on your tongue, so you experience all the different tastes. Depending on the beer, one taste is never enough. Instead, I want to spend alllll night enjoying the taste."

Her head shoots up, cheeks stained pink, with a can of whip cream in her hand. Her finger slips and presses against the tip, sending a spiraling spray of the fluffy cream hissing into the air.

"Shit," she mutters as a deeper shade of pink covers her cheeks. "Chad must have forgotten to replace the cap again."

I bite back a laugh, my mood slightly lighter, as she scrambles to clean up the mess. If I had to guess, my words played a part in the volcanic eruption out of the whip cream can, much like my dick from the night in the parking lot.

After the couple minutes it took for her to wipe off the sticky mess from behind the bar, her gaze connects with mine as she diverts her attention back to me. "So, everyone's expected to just stay single?"

I shrug. "That's the plan."

She leans in, her nose wrinkling in curiosity. "There

wasn't a weird oath like blood brother's type of thing, was there?"

I huff out a laugh. "It's not a cult."

She holds her hands up in defense. "Just checking, because it was kinda teetering on the edge." She leans against the bar. My gaze lifts to hers. "Look, these guys seem to be your friends, I'm not fully sure why," the corner of her lips tip up into a playful smile, "but be a friend to them. If they're seeking advice, give it to them. And the advice can't be don't date."

"That defeats the entire purpose of the group."

"Sometimes things change." She shrugs her shoulders.

"I was hoping it wouldn't be today," I mumble and rise to my feet. "Can I order a round of beers?" Change sucks. I hate change. Things were going just fine. Everyone was happy and single, or so I thought. Wordlessly, Rylee pours the beers and sets them on a tray for me. Maybe she's right. These guys have been with me for years. Every Christmas I get a card from Miles' parents and how do I know it's from them? Because it's signed Miles' Mom and Dad.

When I return to the backroom, I set the tray of beers on the table and pass them out. "Take her to The Boat House. Be sure to call to make reservations. They'll probably tell you they're all booked, but tell them you want the Trey Wilson special. They'll hook you up."

Miles beams up at me. "Really? Thanks. I really appreciate it." He pulls out his phone and types out a note to himself.

I give him a curt nod. Clearly, a date with this woman would make him happy, so I'll be happy for him. Once I'm behind the makeshift podium again, I take a swig of my beer, working up the courage to ask the next question. After swallowing, I set my glass down. "Anyone else have dating problems they need solved?" My gaze flits to each and every guy, they all shake their heads, and we continue with the rest of the meeting.

A squeak fills the room as I hit the hammer on the table. "Thanks for another great meeting. Next week, same time, same place." Everyone stands, but Owen stops and turns toward me.

"Are they still remodeling? That's like three weeks now. I thought you were just putting in some new flooring and a bar?"

"Uh. Yeah." I shove my hands into my pockets. "They ran into a few snags, so it's taking longer than usual."

"That sucks. Well, I can't wait to see it." Owen throws his hand up in a wave as he strolls toward the exit. Tim and Darren are close behind him.

Miles lingers off to the side until everyone is out of sight. In a few steps, he's joining me at the pub table, hands shoved in the pockets of his khakis. "I know tonight got a little off topic, but I really appreciate The Boat House recommendation. She'll really like that place."

"Don't worry about it. I hope the date goes well." I nod and give him a tight smile.

"Thanks again." He turns around and strolls away.

Fuck. I'm going to regret this. Before he's out of earshot, I yell, "You'll have to tell us how it goes." He'll be bursting to talk about it along with everyone else.

*Embrace change.*

He glances over his shoulder, a small smile covers his mouth and he nods, before meandering through the crowd until he reaches the exit.

Since the night's still young and Rylee's still here, I finish moving the tables to their original spots and make my way to the bar. Luckily, as I approach, a man and woman vacate their stools, and I score a spot at the end of the bar. Within seconds our gazes connect and a small smile graces her lips. Even though the evening started out like shit, her smile shoves all that away.

I'm out of my element with her. She's constantly on my mind and all I want to do is be around her. Truth be told, I want another round of our night in the parking lot, but she clearly said it was only one time. Call me an asshole, but women don't turn me down so this is uncharted territory, and they never gave me a map. But if life has taught me anything it's that sometimes you need to make your own map.

Rylee stops in front of me. "Beer?"

I wave my hand. "Nah. Two beer limit during the week."

"That's commendable."

"I try."

A smile flirts on her lips as she fills a glass full of water, tosses a slice of lemon in it, and slides it my way. "You seem like a lemon kind of guy."

"I do appreciate the refreshing taste." She flashes me another one of her dazzling smiles. So, I shoot my shot again. "Have dinner with me."

"I thought you don't date."

"Relationships. I don't do relationships. It's totally different from a date. Plus, it's only dinner."

"I don't think so." She pulls the lever down, filling a pint glass.

"So, you don't eat?"

A laugh springs out of her as she passes the glass to a customer two seats down from me. "I eat." Her hand rests on her hip. "But dinner sounds too… datish and I don't date friends."

"It would be a friendly meal shared between friends."

Nora saunters behind her and fake coughs into her fist. "Just do it."

I point to Nora. "Yeah. Listen to her."

"It sounds like terrible advice, if you ask me," Rylee quips.

Since this isn't working, I try another tactic. "Word on the street is you like to listen to people's problems and tell them what to do? You did it with Bennett and Van. Maybe I need some of your wonderful advice."

She narrows her gaze at me, knowing exactly where I'm going with this. "Do you need someone to listen to your problems?"

"I do actually. Thanks for asking." I sit up in my seat. "I just don't know what to do."

Rylee dramatically wipes a rag along the top of the bar, encouraging me to continue.

"There's this girl I know—"

She stops and the rag that was once in her hand hits me in the chest.

"Hey, that's not what a good bartender does. I don't recall Bennett and Van getting towels thrown at them."

She crosses her arms over her chest. "I like them more."

I bark out a laugh. "Where was I before I was rudely interrupted? Oh yes. There's this girl and no matter what I do, she keeps turning me down. It's like she's immune to my charm."

"You want my advice?" She leans in.

I inch closer to her until we are face to face, fourteen inches of wood between us. "Yes."

"If I were you, I'd give up." A slow tight-lipped smile spreads over her lips. "It seems like a lost cause."

I rub my chin, pretending to consider her words, then square my gaze with hers. "Nah. I don't give up that easy. Plus, she hasn't told me no. I'm wearing her down."

She presses her lips together and nonchalantly shrugs a shoulder.

"Same time next week. Have a good night, Rylee." I rise to my feet. Her gaze never leaves mine. I'm unsure why she's keeping me at arm's length, but I'm determined to tear down her walls, even if I have to do it one brick at a time.

# Chapter 9

## THE TREY WILSON SPECIAL

*Trey*

With one eye closed, I line up my shot. I pull my arm back and sling shot it forward. The dart soars through the air and pierces the small red dot in the center. Bullseye. I throw the next dart. Bullseye. Then I throw the last one. Triple one. What the fuck? The dart must be defective. I stroll up to the dartboard and yank them out.

On the center of the wall are two dart boards, flanked by two pub tables. Then on the opposite side of the room is a pool table and in the center is a custom-built bar, dark leather couch, and a flat screen television to complete the ensemble in my newly remodeled man cave.

The doorbell chimes and I pull out my phone to the check the app when a familiar face comes into view. I press the microphone button. "Hey Miles. It's open." I lift my head and stare at the man cave. Shit. I race up the stairs two at a time when I come inches away from crashing into Miles on the entry way landing.

"Oh! Where did you come from?" His hand splays against the wall to regain his balance.

"Hey man." I prop myself up with a hand on the wall while collecting my breath.

"Is the remodel done?" He points toward the stairs and shoves past me.

"Uh. No!" I spit out.

He turns to face me. "Oh. Well, can I see the progress, at least?"

"No."

His brows furrow. "Why not?"

Fuck. What do I say? Now, I'm just being a dick. I blow out a breath and motion my hand toward the basement.

He takes my cue and descends the stairs. I'm two steps behind him. When he steps off the last stair, he freezes. He peers left and then right, taking everything in. "This looks more like fully finished instead of a remodel in progress."

"That's because it is." I slide past him and stroll behind the bar. I open the fridge and hold up a bottle. "Beer?"

He waves his hand. "No. I'm good."

I'm not. I twist off the cap and take a long pull.

"It looks pretty awesome down here. You had a lot of work done."

Maybe I'm in the clear. "Thanks. I'm happy with how everything turned out."

"Why did you tell everyone the meeting was going to be at Porter's again?" A stool scrapes across the floor as he pulls it out to sit.

Shit. This is what I was afraid of. I swallow another gulp of the cold amber liquid. "Fuck," I mutter under my breath. How do I say this?

"It can't be for their mini corn dogs. They're good, but not that good." He smirks.

I shake my head as my lips split into a half-smile. "They are good, though. But no, it's not that. Would it be bad if I said it gives me an excuse to see Rylee every week?"

"Rylee?" His eyes widen when recognition hits. "The bartender?"

"I enjoy talking to her." I shrug a shoulder in order to act nonchalant, but Miles sees right through me.

His mouth spreads into a full grin. "You like her."

"I don't like her. That's preposterous. We're just friends." At least that's what she keeps telling me, so it's not a total lie.

"You're totally smitten with her," he teases.

Warmth rushes up to my cheeks. It's an unfamiliar feeling. "I am not. Guys don't get smitten." Casually, I run my palm down my face to see if what I'm feeling is visible. If anything, maybe the short hairs of my two-day stubble will mask my blush. Shit. I am smitten.

"Just so you know, there's nothing wrong with liking her. She seems cool."

If I say the words out loud, I'm confessing my feelings, but I do like her. I enjoy talking to her. I like our verbal sparring and I genuinely want to get to know her more. "Okay. I may like her a little. I'm struggling on what to do. Every time I ask her out to dinner, she keeps turning me down." Once I admit my feelings out loud, it's like a floodgate that's opened, and I can't stop the verbal diarrhea that comes out. "She's the one who put me in the friend zone. I've never been in this position before. It's a little unnerving since I'm at a loss on what to do and that has never happened before. I need to convince her to have another night together." I blow out a breath.

His eyebrows pull together. "Night together?"

"Not to kiss and tell, but we kissed, amongst other things."

"Is that all you want? Another night together."

"Yes. No. Fuck. This is my predicament. I won't be able to stop at just one more night. I'll want another and another." It's the complete opposite of what I've done for the past ten years, which makes it even more complicated.

"And now she's shut you out?"

"She's slammed the door and swallowed the key."

"That's brutal." He glances up to meet my gaze. "But the Trey I know wouldn't give up so easy. Defeat is not an option. If he wants something, he gets it. In fact, it was you who not only helped me with my date but also gave me the confidence to ask for a second one." A cheesy grin takes over his face.

"Holy shit. Congratulations. You took her to The Boat House?"

"I did. They even set us up at the Chef's Table, which I wasn't expecting. I would have been happy for just any table, so the best table in the entire restaurant was a surprise. It really helped me score all the points with Melony."

I square my shoulders and puff out my chest. "The Trey Wilson Special."

He continues to tell me all about his date, from what he wore to what he ate, then what his date ordered, all the way to how the chef flambéed their dessert right in front of them. I fought hard to not tell him he didn't need to give me every minute detail, but he seemed so excited, I didn't have the heart to interrupt him.

"So, thank you for the wonderful dining experience. That's why I came over today."

"Anytime. It's kind of what SBL members do for each

other." One thing that sticks out, is he never mentioned how his date with Melony went, only about the restaurant.

"Even if it's the complete opposite of its namesake?"

"We're... evolving." I shrug a shoulder.

"I like that."

"How did the rest of your date go?"

"Oh. Um. It was good."

"That's... good." He's hiding something. No one should be that excited to talk about food and then say nothing about the date. But I don't want to push him.

"So, Porter's Thursday night? Even though the man cave is finished." He quickly changes the subject.

"Thursday. Porter's." I hold my beer up in salute before taking a swig.

Miles rises to his feet. "Relationships don't have to be scary."

"Until you've found yourself in the most toxic one imaginable," I mumble mostly to myself. One bad relationship can traumatize you, it did exactly that to me.

"I know you've had a string of bad luck in the past, but it's evident there's something different about Rylee since you're pursuing her so hard."

I want to say because she keeps turning me down, but that's kind of an asshole thing to say. This is more than wanting what you can't have. But he's right. There's something that I do like about her.

"You're the poster child for cool, confident, and collected. I'm sure you'll figure something out that will make her swoon at your feet."

It's not for the lack of trying, but so far, she's side stepped all my advances. The only ounce of hope I'm holding on to is she hasn't told me no.

## Chapter 10

## NO HEAD AT PORTER'S

# Rylee

I flip open the box flaps and pull out two bottles of whiskey and slide them onto the shelf. Grabbing two more bottles, I repeat the process until the box is empty. Turning it over, I break apart the glued flaps, flatten it, and toss it onto a stack of other broken down cardboard.

The liquor delivery came yesterday, but being a Friday, we were slammed, and I wasn't able to put it all away. I told Jake I'd come in this morning to finish. So far, all the numbers check out. I'm crossing my fingers the ordering stays consistent from here on out. By late afternoon, I'm almost finished.

As I'm emptying the last box, the storage door opens and Dessa's head peeks through the opening.

"Someone's here to see you." She leans her shoulder against the door frame.

"Who?" I wrap my fingers around the edge of the box, praying it isn't my ex to tell me he's bailing on Abby once again.

"I'll give you one guess. Name starts with tee and ends in ray," she singsongs.

My heart flutters in my chest and I shift my gaze so she can't see the smile that pulls at my lips. I can't explain how he does this to me every time I hear his name or think about him. There's a battle raging between my head and my vagina and it's the latter that's winning the war. "I'll be right there."

Behind me on the wall is a reflective beer advertisement sign. I use it to smooth down my hair even though it's more like a funhouse mirror than anything. What the hell am I doing? I shake my head. Strands flying in every direction. I pull open the door, stroll into the hallway, and peer around the corner to the open bar. Sitting front and center is Trey, looking hotter than any man in this bar should. He's talking to Nora. I feel bad for eavesdropping on their conversation but not that bad.

"Why are you so averse to dating?" Nora asks.

"I have nothing against dating. I just prefer short term. One night. Maybe two if it's good. But that's it. After that, shit gets complicated with feelings and... more feelings."

"You're going to what? Stay single forever?"

"Why not? I can do what I want, when I want. I don't need to ask anyone for permission. I'm wild and free."

"But what happens if you find the woman that sweeps you off your feet?"

"If that happens, she'd better buckle up."

I roll my eyes. Buckle her straight jacket? That's the only thing I could imagine she'd want to buckle. Coming into view from around the corner, our eyes meet and it's as if he knew I was there all along. As I approach, I slow down and come to a stop right in front of him. "I feel like I should be surprised to see you here, but," I shrug, "I'm not."

He rests his elbows on the bar. "I was in the neighborhood."

"You seem to be in the neighborhood often."

"I kind of like it here. Maybe I'll buy a house."

A laugh bursts out of me. "This isn't exactly a white picket fence neighborhood."

"Good thing I don't require a fence."

My gaze roams over his body, eyebrows pinched. "It's Saturday afternoon. Why the suit? Or is that all that's in your closet? Hanger after hanger of suits."

"I've come prepared for our date." He winks.

"You'll be waiting for a while." I shake my head. "What can I get for you?"

"You. On a date with me."

"Unless that comes out of one of these," I point to the row of taps, "it's not going to happen."

"You drive a hard bargain. I guess I'll take an IPA. How about lunch then?"

"I already have a date with leftovers from my favorite Indian restaurant." I grab a frosted pint glass from the cooler and tilt it at an angle as I pull the lever of the tap.

"It's hard to compete with that."

Once it's full, I push it toward Trey. For several seconds, his gaze never leaves mine. It's almost like he can read my thoughts and knows whatever I tell him is the complete opposite of what my body wants.

Slowly, his gaze falls to the beer. Then he lifts the glass so it's eye level. "Wow. That's a perfect pour."

Without saying a word, I point behind me at an

oversized chalkboard with some text flanked by some swirly lines and various beer, hops, and wheat icons. Everything is lightly shaded with yellows, blues, and greens courtesy of Lach.

He lifts his head, following my finger. "No Head at Porter's." He pauses. "Is it odd that I'm both excited and saddened by those words?"

"Words to live by."

He swallows a gulp of his beer. "You know what would be a great word to live by? Yes. As in saying yes to dinner with me."

I pause, trying to piece together his words. My fingers curl around the edge of the bar as I lean in. "That makes no sense."

He shrugs as a half smirk covers his lips.

"Didn't we go over this?" I push off until I'm standing to my full height and hold up one finger. "Dinner sounds like a date." I add a second finger. "Dates lead to relationships."

"It's dinner. It's not like I'm asking for your hand in marriage. Unless that will help my chances. I'll get on one knee right now."

"Guess what I think about that?"

"What?"

With my other two fingers still in the air, I add a third. Then I curl my pointer and ring finger to my palm leaving only my middle finger.

A grin curls around his full lips. "That was good. But I don't speak finger, so you have to give me a good reason why?"

"Because you're... Trey."

"That's not a good reason."

"You're not my type."

"Sexy. Confident. Well-endowed aren't your type?"

I snort a laugh. "More like cocky and full of himself aren't my type. Plus, you wear a suit."

"What's wrong with the suit?" He runs his hands down the lapels of his jacket.

"Nothing per se, but I just don't do suits. They're too... suity. It only adds to the cocky and arrogant thing you got going on." I wave my hand over his body.

"Well, I can fix that." Trey stands and removes his suit jacket and drapes it over the backrest of his stool. His fingers dig into the knot of his tie, loosening it. Next, he pops the button at his collar.

"What are you doing?" I ask.

"Taking off the suit."

"You're going to strip? Right here, in a full bar?"

"Yup." He undoes a couple more buttons.

I want to tear my gaze away, but I can't. Instead, I spit out whatever words I can muster. "Keep your clothes on. No one wants to see you naked."

Nora smacks my arm, and I jerk my head to face her. From the corner of her mouth she says, "Speak for yourself. I kinda want to see what he's packing underneath."

I narrow my gaze at her. She shrugs and slinks away but keeps a close eye on Trey in case he does remove the rest of his clothes. She wouldn't want to miss that. Hell, right now I don't want to miss it either.

Trey clears his throat and I twist around to meet his gaze. "So, what's it going to be? Am I getting naked right here or are we going on a date?

"If she doesn't take it, does the offer extend to others in the room?" Nora asks over my shoulder. I nudge her away and she laughs.

"The entire bar doesn't need to see you naked. Even

though I'm pretty sure over half of the females here already have."

Without missing a beat, Trey locks his gaze on mine. "But there's only one woman I want to see me naked now."

I can't even hide my grin anymore. It's like he controls the strings connected to the corners of my lips and can pull them at his will, forcing a smile. He always has a snappy comeback to one up me. It's infuriating but also weirdly turns me on. Spinning around, I slide down the bar, desperate to distract myself and escape Trey's captivating presence.

"Where are you going? You never answered my question."

I glance over my shoulder. "About dinner? I don't think so."

"You still haven't given me a good reason why."

"I don't do dinner."

"It's one meal. One friendly meal. Since we're friends and all."

"You're relentless, aren't you?" I tap away at the screen until it spits out a receipt.

"You haven't told me no yet." He shrugs his shoulders. "It's one word. Two letters. Say it and I'll never ask you again."

I slap the paper on the bar and push it towards him. "There's your bill. I'm closing out so I can go home. Here's your date. You can walk me out."

"Done." He throws back the glass, swallowing the last gulp of his beer and slams it on the bar when it's empty.

I collect my wallet from the back room. When I'm strolling toward the exit, Trey's already waiting for me like an eager puppy, a beaming smile on his face. He's fully removed his tie and kept the top two buttons undone. It's sexy as hell. I hate myself for not being able to tear my gaze away.

I slide past him inhaling his signature leather and spice scent. It's a unique blend, one not overpowering the other. I push open the door and he follows behind.

"I had a client meeting earlier this afternoon."

I peer over my shoulder. "Huh?"

He catches up and is meeting me stride for stride halfway across the parking lot. "The answer to your question about the suit. I had a client meeting. Today was the only time he had available before leaving town."

I nod. So, he works on the weekends, much like a certain someone else. While I appreciate him sharing something about himself, it's still something I can't do. "You don't want to date me or have dinner with me. There're enough skeletons in my closet to fill a cemetery." This will send him running across the parking lot. It has with every other guy, and they weren't Trey. Self-proclaimed bachelor for life.

"Good thing I have a shovel. Or do we need an excavator? I'm sure I could pull some strings. Call in some favors."

My heart jumps to my throat. That wasn't the answer I was expecting. "Maybe all of the above." I come to a halt at the rear corner of my SUV, and I hike my thumb over my shoulder. "This is me."

"Oh yeah. I remember this car. It was parked next to mine where you rode," he takes a step closer to me, "my dick," another step, "as if it were mediocre and would've preferred to spend the time painting your nails."

I snort out a laugh and slap my hand over my mouth. After I catch my breath, I drop my hand. "Is that more telling of me or you?"

"We can always go a second round to determine the answer."

The corner of my lips tip up into a smile. "Or we don't."

"Okay. Then how about dinner?"

"I thought this was our date." I motion around us.

"But we're missing a key part. Food." He inches closer to me.

"I might have some chewing gum between the seats—"

His fingers brush over my cheeks, holding me in place as his lips press to mine. It's soft and sweet at first until I grip the front of his shirt, pulling him closer. I moan into his mouth, and he deepens the kiss. Twisting us around, the cool metal seeps through the back of my shirt. He breaks away, resting his forehead on mine. I take the few extra seconds to collect my breath. This kiss almost trumps the first kiss, and the first kiss was good. So good.

"Should we finish this somewhere else? Perhaps your place." After a few seconds of silence, he adds, "Or we can have another go at it in my backseat."

"As tempting as that offer is, I can't."

"I guess if you want, we can go to mine."

"No, it's not that." I slide out from under his arm. "It's not just me at my house."

"Wait. Are you dating someone? Is the ex not an actual ex? Because I may do a lot of things, but sharing isn't one of them."

A weak smile floats over my lips. "No. It's not that." I wring my hands together, building up the courage to tell him. It's not that I don't want to tell him, but I'm aware of his stance on kids, and I like to keep my private life private. "I have a six-year-old daughter.

He's silent. Instead, he only stares at me. Is he surprised? Except there's a slight clench to his jaw, so he's angry? His expression is unreadable and a little unnerving. At this point, his silence says more than anything he could say with his words.

"Okay. I'll take your silence as meaning this is over. Thank you. It was fun." I spin on my heels and stomp away. After two steps, a hand wraps around my wrist, spinning me around.

"I'm sorry." His eyes soften, pleading with mine.

"Sorry that this is over or sorry for…"

"Sorry for my silence. You caught me by surprise."

"Either way, it doesn't change anything. I have a kid and you don't like kids. This whole thing we started should have never happened." Immediately, all the walls around me and my heart rise. I was a fool to even get involved with someone like Trey, even if it was just sex.

"It's not that I don't like kids. Some of my best friends have kids and they're the greatest things ever. I just have no plans to have any of my own. You having a daughter doesn't change the fact that I like you. I enjoy what little time we've spend together, and I want to continue spending time with you. Even better if we take it outside the Porter's parking lot."

He grabs my hands and intertwines our fingers. It's comforting and eases some of my reservations about him. He may have made a small hole in the wall I erected.

"So for today, you'll go to your house, and I'll go to mine. Then tomorrow we can do this all over again."

I laugh. "I'm starting to think you like the chase more than you actually like me."

"Don't get me wrong, the chase is fun, but I know what's waiting at the end will be worth it."

A warm blush covers my cheeks. "Do you have a book of lines you memorize so you know exactly what to say and when to say it?"

"No. I actually have a tiny earpiece and Miles feeds me lines." He holds a finger to his ear and pretends to look around.

I slap his chest. "You're so full of it."

"Yeah." He places his hand on mine, holding it to his chest. "No one would buy that. Miles doesn't have any lines."

"As much as I would love to stay and chat with you in the parking lot. I do have to go." I pull away, but Trey stops me.

"Ooor we could always do other things in the parking lot." His eyebrow raises.

"Oh my god. You are relentless."

He flashes me a dimpled smirk. "Okay. Okay. I guess I'll let you go." He releases my hand, and it slides down his chest.

"Have a good rest of your day."

"Once I'm home, thinking about you, it will most definitely be good." He winks.

Warmth spreads over my cheeks. I spin on my heel. Without looking back, I offer a wave over my head. If I see him, I won't be able to resist jumping into his arms and kissing the hell out of him. So, I don't. In fact, I rip open my car door and slam it closed so I don't do just that. I reach over my shoulder and pull my seat belt, locking it in place to also prevent me from jumping out. It's been years since I've felt anything remotely close to this and that scares me the most because I know how it ends.

After pulling out of the parking lot and onto the street, my grip on the steering wheel loosens. The physical distance from Trey is exactly what I need, so there isn't a repeat of the parking lot romp. I glance in my rearview mirror as a late model pick-up truck pulls out behind me. Maybe I should say yes to a date with Trey. Would it be so bad? What am I thinking? Of course it would. Guys like him are a dime a dozen and the last thing I need is another broken heart.

Distracted from all my thoughts on Trey, I notice the truck is still following me several blocks later. With the tinted back window of my SUV, I can't decipher if the truck is black or navy in color. Even from my side mirror the glare from the sun makes it indistinguishable. The hairs on my arms rise as a bead of sweat forms on my brow even though it's a comfortable seventy degrees. I make a right turn and then another, the truck still trailing me, but this time they ride my bumper and then back off almost in a threatening manner. I make note of the missing passenger side mirror and missing license plate. My heart hammers in my chest as I swallow the giant lump in my throat.

There's been a few times where I've encountered suspicious vehicles following me. Sometimes it's been customers from the bar or leaving the parking lot of a store. I keep a bottle of mace in my glove compartment just in case. Thankfully, I've never had to use it, but it's worth being proactive.

Blindly I pat the passenger seat for my phone, preparing myself to call the police over the bizarre driving behavior. When I make another right turn, instead of following me the truck continues straight. Another car passes me, blocking my view of the passing truck before it disappears behind a building. I exhale a deep breath. My paranoia about Trey has led to paranoia about everything else.

# Chapter 11

## UNEXPECTED ADVICE

*Trey*

I stay rooted in place until her taillights blend with the afternoon sunlight. A raging inferno sparked inside me when she mentioned she has a daughter. It's not because she has a daughter, but it's the idea that she's been with someone else to give her a daughter. Not to say I want to be that person. Fuck. I scrub my hands down my face.

She consumes all my thoughts. It's rare for women to reject me, and when they do, I quickly move on. I don't chase women, but I will run to the end of the earth for Rylee. It's been years since I've had to navigate these waters and if I'm not careful, I could easily drown. I need to keep everything at surface level. My thoughts. Feelings. Actions. Nothing deep.

I want to convince myself that it is just sex or friends

with sexy benefits, but it's not. I genuinely enjoy spending time with her. The number of times we've seen each other without having sex outweighs the number of times we've seen each other and have, which is completely unlike me. I don't hang out with single women for fun. We fuck, then I leave, or tell her to leave. No small talk after. She's turned my entire life upside down and I'm clueless on what to do. She's turned me into Miles.

Tomorrow is the SBL meeting. I'll have to recruit the guys for some advice. Even though whatever comes out of their mouths might be questionable, it's all I've got. I climb into my SUV and start the ignition only to go home and be left with thoughts of Rylee instead of worshiping her naked body.

---

The following day, I send a message to the guys to tell them the meeting is back at my house instead of Porter's. Also, I include a list a of pre-approved snacks, so there isn't another cheese incident.

Standing behind my new custom-built mahogany bar, I pour beers out of the tap for Miles, Tim, Darren, and Owen.

"First things first. I never got my gavel back from Jake and the squeaker fell out of the other one, so just pay attention. Anyone have anything they want to discuss?" I wait a second before responding. "Okay. I'll go." I blow out a breath. "I need your help."

The entire room goes silent. So quiet I can hear my hair grow. I quite possibly could have stunned them all to death. But then Owen blinks and I blow out a sigh of relief.

"Can you say that again? I don't think I heard you correctly. You need our help?" The corner of Owen's mouth lifts into a smile.

"There's no way that Trey is asking us for help," Darren says, sarcasm dripping from his tone.

I hold out my hands and curl my fingers into my palm, motioning for them to keep it coming because I deserve all their smart ass comments. But these four are some of my closest friends and I'm glad to have them on my side. "Keep it coming. I deserve it."

Tim leans in and raises an eyebrow. "This all depends on what you need our help with."

My hands fall to my sides. "I need your help with a girl. A woman."

Owen dramatically falls off his chair and onto the floor and everyone busts out laughing, including myself.

He climbs back up onto his chair. "Sorry. I blacked out there for a second because I thought you said you needed our help with a girl."

"That's because I did."

Owen falls off his chair again, except this time he groans as he hits the floor. A few seconds later, he rises to his feet, rubbing his elbow. "Okay. I'm done."

"Do you need some ice?" I nod at his arm.

"Ice would be nice." Owen takes a seat on the stool.

I find a plastic bag and pour some ice inside and pass it to him. "As I was saying, I need your help." I run my hands through my hair. "There's a woman that I kind of like."

Owen gasps and everyone turns their heads his way, waiting for him to black out again. He glances at all of us. "I'm okay." He rests his elbow on the bar top, along with the ice bag.

"I like a woman and I could—"

"It's Rylee. The woman is Rylee," Miles blurts out, and

I shoot daggers at him. He cowers like a child being scolded. "Sorry. I couldn't hold it any longer. I've been told I'm not a good secret keeper."

"Clearly," I deadpan. "It's fine. It was going to come out sooner or later, but yes. It's Rylee."

"The brunette bartender at Porter's?" Tim asks.

"The one and only." I grab a pint glass and pour myself a beer, mostly because I need something to do. I've never been in the position of needing advice when it comes to women. Normally, it's the other way around, so I'm way out of my element. "I don't know what to do. I've asked her to dinner more times than I can count, and she always gives me the I can't excuse, or she'll change the subject."

"So, she's turned you down?" Darren takes a drink of his beer.

"That's the thing, technically she hasn't. I've given her the opportunity to say no and I'll never ask her again but she's never come out and said *no*."

"Sounds like she's holding on to something. Maybe she likes you too," Tim says.

"But why won't she say yes to dinner?" I rest my palms on the cool wood.

Tim sits up in his chair. "I dated a girl a while back."

"Was this after the ex-wife?" Darren asks.

Tim nods. "I needed some companionship. So anyway, she never wanted to go to her house until one day I finally convinced her I wanted to see her space. Big fucking mistake. She told me she was an artist, so her house was littered with art supplies. It was like a kindergarten art class threw up."

"Maybe she's just passionate," Miles says.

"Her paintings were of dogs' heads… with naked human bodies," Tim deadpans. "I'm not an art aficionado, so I wasn't going to do a deep dive analysis for the meaning behind her art."

I nearly choke on my beer while everyone else scrunches their faces.

"That's…" Owen's head tilts toward the ceiling, lips pressed together like he's thinking. "Original."

"I doubt that's the word you're searching for," I say.

"Maybe she likes dogs." Owen shrugs.

"If that's the case, she must like naked people just as much." I raise my pint glass before swallowing a gulp.

"Then mash them together." Owen claps the palms of his hands together.

With his elbows on the bar, Darren leans over to address Tim. "Where do you find these women? Not that I want to find one like her, but where did you find her?"

"Reddit," Tim says.

I swallow a fresh gulp of my beer, needing a few seconds to process all this. I'm trying to put the puzzle pieces together, but it's like I'm working with two different puzzles. I furrow my brows. "How exactly does this tie into my situation?"

"Oh yeah. Moral of the story, if she's saying no or in your case," he waves his hand in my direction, "avoids the question, there must be a reason why. For me, she didn't want to show me her weird ass naked dog head people paintings, and I should have respected that."

"Are you saying I should automatically respect her boundaries and back away?"

"Oh." He rubs his chin. "Not necessarily. Unless she's told you she likes to paint, then I'd be wary."

I shake my head. "Far as I know, she's no Van Gogh, but I've also haven't had time to get to know her more. So, you think she's hiding something from me?"

"What else could it be?" Tim shrugs his shoulders and tilts his head. "I'd be prepared for whatever it may be."

"Expect the worst. Hope for the best," Miles adds.

"You need to give her a date she can't say no to," Owen says.

All I want to do is to get to know her, but it's hard at Porter's while she's working. I'm competing for her attention with fifty other people. Sadly, they always win because it's her job. I'm desperate for some one-on-one time with her. Then I could learn more about her and maybe other things. I won't lie, other things with her would be fan-fucking-tastic. But there's the whole friend zone she put me in. Like what the fuck is that? Is that supposed to deter me? Friends have sex all the time. How many couples end up as friends to lovers? A lot. In fact, this whole friend zone actually sparks a teeny tiny fire of hope. She was hesitant to tell me she has a daughter and an ex-husband, so it can't be that. Unless she's dating someone, but we've slept together. Maybe it started after our tryst. All of this is outside my comfort zone. But this is what she's doing to me.

Owen might be onto something. Give her something she can't say no to. Or let her make the choice. I lift my beer, guzzle down half the glass, and slam it to the bar top. "I got it. I know how I'm going to get my date."

# Chapter 12

## BURLAP LOIN CLOTH

*Rylee*

It's more quiet than usual for a Friday afternoon at Porter's, but I shouldn't complain. It gives me an opportunity to stock the coolers before patrons fill the bar. Jake booked a local band, and band nights always draw a large crowd. As the golden liquid of the IPA rises in the glass, my thoughts drift to Trey. Which they've been doing more and more of lately. It's hard to deny that his persistent pursuit of me is rather flattering. But off in the distance, red flags fly, reminding me of none other than my ex-husband. Even when we're not together, the ex still somehow manages to ruin things for me. Besides that, what else was unsettling is what happened when I left the parking lot the other night.

The cold beer flows over the rim, splashing on my

hand. "Shit." I snap the tap back into place and grab a towel from under the bar. I wipe down the glass and pass it to the customer.

I rest my butt against the edge of the beer cooler and stare at an invisible spot on the far wall. Normally, I'm always levelheaded. I've always had to be, especially in the last six years. But now, suddenly everything is a distraction.

"I'm not staring at your chest. Well technically I am, but just to double check that you're breathing. You've been standing like a statue for the past five minutes. For a second, I thought maybe you were dead, but then your chest rose, and I felt a little better about not staring at a dead person. Is everything okay?" Lach asks, his tone laced with concern.

I crane my neck toward him and furrow my brows. "I don't know how to process everything you just said, but yeah."

He runs his hand through his chestnut locks, moving the strands off his forehead. His normally bright blue eyes darken with concern. "Are you sure?"

"Actually, not really." I sigh. "Have you ever noticed a dark colored, maybe gray or navy, older truck parked in the parking lot? It's missing the passenger side mirror." I tilt my head and roll my lips between my teeth. A part of me wants him to know who the owner is, so I'm not constantly looking over my shoulder every time I leave here.

His eyebrows pinch together. "There are a lot of vehicles in the parking lot."

"Yeah." I pause. Then turn to face him. "It's just when I was leaving yesterday, a truck followed me out and tailed me for several blocks."

He stops, bottles of beer in his hand, and glances up at me. "Did you make three right turns?"

I prop my hand against the beer cooler. "I did, but they never followed me after the second."

"See. It was just a coincidence. Nothing to worry about." He rests his hand on my shoulder and gives it a squeeze.

Something about the whole situation still seems off, but it was one time, and it could very well be a coincidence. "You're probably right." I push all those thoughts aside and finish stocking the cooler.

Several hours later, the traffic inside Porter's picks up. I'm serving customers on one side of the bar while Lach's on the other. Jake is floating and serving customers as needed. Dessa strides in and gives us a head nod. A few steps behind her is Chad. Ignoring our presence, he walks by with his hood pulled tightly over his head. Ever since Jake demoted him, he's been coming into work like a calm bomb. Everyone tiptoes around him because we don't know when he'll detonate.

A sliver of outside light from the door catches my eye and I glance up. Immediately, I'm met with a very familiar face smiling at me. He stalks toward the bar. Since he can't find a seat, he squeezes himself between customers.

He rests an elbow on the bar and leans in. "Go on a date with me?"

"Wow. Right to the point." I finish pouring a beer and passing it to a customer next to him. Then I give Trey my undivided attention. "I don't think so."

Dessa strolls behind me and sing songs, "Just do it."

I swing around and glare at her, but she only smirks.

"See, you're the only one fighting this." He lifts an eyebrow. "Alright, how about this? You can have another ride on the Continental Trey Express. I'll even let you pick your seat, but there are only two options." He points to his mouth then to his lap, an irresistibly sexy smile on his lips.

"Yeah. I got it." I roll my eyes. "I'd rather take the date."

"Perfect!" He slaps his hand on the bar top, startling me and the guy next to him. "I'll pick you up tomorrow at seven."

"Wait. I never said—"

"Oh yes. I do believe you said, and I quote, 'I'd rather take the date.'"

"Of course you'd take that at face value."

"If I've learned anything in life, it's to take any opportunity given to you. I saw it and I took it. But I'll give you an out. Just say the word. Two letters."

Take any opportunity given to you. His words flash through my mind like a marquee. It's only a date. I can spare a date. Plus, I'm a teeny tiny bit curious about what a date with Trey would be like. I peel my gaze off his as I grab a cardboard coaster and flip it over. I scribble my address and phone number on it and slide it across the bar. He flips it over. A sexy smirk pulls at his lips as he scans what I wrote. Then he tucks the cardboard into the inside pocket of his suit jacket.

"But I can't do tomorrow."

"Next Friday?"

"I can't do Friday, either. How about Saturday?" My heart thunders in my chest and I can't explain why. Am I nervous he won't be able to do Saturday?

"Saturday it is. I will text you the details."

A wide smile covers his face. It's not the 'I want to take your clothes off' smile that I've seen so many times, but instead is a boyish grin. Like I've made his entire year. I won't lie, it's a smile that makes me regret not saying yes sooner. "Also, just so we're clear, this is only a friends type date."

"The friendliest." He winks before strolling away.

I can't help but admire how his slacks mold perfectly to his backside. He abruptly stops and I glance up. A woman with honey hair halts his progress with a hand on his arm. Her red stained lips move as she speaks while batting her long, dark lashes.

"I've never actually seen someone crush a glass bottle with their hands. Today could be my day."

I glance at Dessa to my left and she nods at the bottle of rum in my hand.

I loosen my grip and the color floods back into my hand. "Who does that? Take one girl's number and address, then turns around and flirts with another girl."

"If you ask me, Trey isn't doing the flirting."

I roll my eyes, mostly because I know she's right. In fact, Trey has completely ignored every single one of her advances.

A knowing smirk covers her face. "Are you jealous?"

"Yes. No. I don't know. I have no right to be. We're not a couple."

"But you know you could change that."

"You're forgetting one key fact. Trey doesn't do relationships. I don't do relationships with guys like Trey. We're just going on a friendly date."

She faces me, hand on her hip. "And you're forgetting one key fact. He pursued the fuck out of you. Guys who want a friendly date don't do that."

Ugh. She's right. Deep down, I know that, but it's easier if I convince myself that it's nothing more than friends.

"Be a little selfish. Do this for you. And whatever happens," she curls her thumb and pointer finger into an O and stabs her pointer finger on her other hand through the hole, "do it for you." Her mouth falls open as she rolls her eyes, faking an orgasm.

I slap her hands apart, and she laughs. Flashbacks of straddling his lap in his SUV, his cock stretching me while he tongues my nipple flit through my mind and right now, I could use a little finger in the O.

---

All weekend, I've been thinking about my date with Trey. Most importantly, I've been on edge about what he has planned. He did text me what time he'll pick me up but gave me no other clues. It's been months, hell, probably closer to years, since I've gone on an actual date. Dinner and a movie kind of date. And I don't even know if we're doing dinner and a movie. Or what I should wear.

With my laptop pulled out to my online banking and bills scattered across the thoroughly aged dining room table, I let out a heavy sigh. With the measly four figure number sitting in my bank account, it's best I don't go date outfit shopping. Whatever I have in the closet will have to do. But I make a mental note of what I can spend in case he expects me to pay for myself. My foot bounces as I eye my phone next to me. All I want to know is what our date entails so I can dress accordingly. That's not too much to ask, right? I pick up my phone and send a text to Trey.

> **RYLEE**
> What's appropriate attire for our date?

> **TREY**
> Thinking about our date, are we?

> **RYLEE**
> Just thinking of what to wear. I don't want to show up looking like a trash panda.

**TREY**

You could show up wearing a burlap sack and you'd still be beautiful

Heat creeps over my cheeks. It's been a long time since I've been called beautiful. The drunken, slurred compliments at Porter's don't count.

**RYLEE**

My sack's at the dry cleaners. What else do you got?

**TREY**

You're welcome to wear what you'd like. Whatever makes you comfortable.

**RYLEE**

That doesn't help because if that was the case, I would show up in yoga pants and a T-shirt.

**TREY**

That works for me.

**RYLEE**

This isn't helping. What are you wearing?

**TREY**

Burlap loin cloth.

**RYLEE**

HA HA HA

**RYLEE**

What are we doing on our date?

**TREY**

Don't like surprises?

**RYLEE**

In this case, no.

> **TREY**
> I'll give you this, there will be food and activities.

> **RYLEE**
> Still doesn't help me.

> **TREY**
> What we do will depend on you.

> **RYLEE**
> What does that even mean?

> **TREY**
> I'll see you on Saturday. 😉

What the hell kind of date is this? Absolutely zero direction on what to wear, where we're going, or what we're doing. It's time to ask someone who's been on more dates than I have in the recent years.

> **RYLEE**
> What does one wear on a date when you know absolutely nothing about how your date is going to go?

> **DESSA**
> The real question is, how do you want the date to end?

> **RYLEE**
> Trey said I could wear a burlap sack if I wanted to.

> **DESSA**
> This is what I'd do. Dress sexy as hell and be the sex kitten that we all know you can be.

RYLEE

Are you sure you're not confusing me with Nora? Or yourself?

DESSA

Come over to my house. I have a few dresses that will fit you perfectly.

---

After bringing Abby next door to Marcie's apartment, the next hour is spent getting ready. Half the time was figuring out how to get the dress to lay perfectly over one shoulder while not exposing my left breast. Thankfully, Dessa also gave me some double-sided tape which seemed to do the trick. While standing in front of the full-length mirror, I continue to fidget with the dress. There's a reason why I don't wear these on the regular and the spandex tight fabric on my hips is one of them. I shimmy the hem an inch down my thighs, but it's useless, it immediately slides back up. He better appreciate the outfit because come tomorrow my feet with hate me from the three-inch heels. A knock on my front door startles me and I spin around. With one last glance in the mirror, I stroll down the hallway and into the kitchen. My hands rest on the cool wood as I peer through the peephole. My lips split into an enormous grin. I don't even fight to contain it. I grip the doorknob and pull it open.

## Chapter 13

## NO PERSON TO PERSON CONTACT

# Rylee

Trey's eyes darken from steely gray to almost black. His lips part as his gaze starts at the black off the shoulder relaxed upper bodice then drifts down to the fitted skirt and eventually lands on the nude pumps, all courtesy of Dessa.

"You're absolutely, breathtakingly beautiful."

"Thank you." A soft smile covers my lips. His compliment, mixed with the way he can't stop staring, makes me *feel* beautiful. Something Kyle rarely said to me. I shove the thought away. My date with Trey doesn't need to be filled with thoughts of my ex. "Let me grab my wallet and we can go. So, what's our plan?" I ask over my shoulder.

"Well, that's entirely up to you." He reaches inside his charcoal gray suit jacket and pulls out two plain white envelopes, fanning them out in front of him. "You get to pick our date. Pick a card and that's what we're doing."

I peer at him and then at the envelopes, a smile tugging at my lips. Bending down, I examine them, hoping to discover they're semi-transparent, but nothing. I pinch my fingers over the one on the right and pull it from his grasp. I hold it out to him, and he lifts the flap, pulls out a card, reads it, then shoves it back inside.

"What does it say?" I ask eagerly.

A boyish grin covers his face. "That's part of the surprise."

Once at his SUV, Trey moves a manilla folder from his passenger seat. "Can we make a quick detour before our date? I need to drop these papers off with an agent."

"Of course."

"It will be quick. Then we can continue with what's really important. Our date." He reaches across the center console and links his fingers with mine.

"Really, it's okay."

My stomach does somersaults as thoughts of the last time I was in Trey's SUV flash through my mind. In the backseat to be exact, as his cock stretched me, sliding in and out. The way he sucked on my heated skin. My nipples pebble underneath my dress and I rub my legs together to release some of the tension.

From the corner of his eyes, Trey glances over at me. "Are you all right over there? You're squirming in your seat."

"Yeah. Fine," I choke out. *I'm not thinking about you pulling the car over and us hopping in the backseat so I can live out my thoughts.* It's not normal for me to want to ride his cock like a pogo stick every time he's near. In need of a distraction, I force my attention out the window, so I can stop daydreaming about sex with the hot as sin guy next to me.

Trey heads south and pulls into a new housing development. Empty lots and half-built houses pass by us until he pulls onto a dirt driveway. Near the fully erect house, two cars are parked parallel to the building, but one piques my interest.

The SUV comes to a stop kiddy corner to the two vehicles. He pulls the folder off the dash. "I'll be right back."

I nod.

After the door closes behind him, I squint hoping for a better look at the older dark blue truck. It's eerily similar to the one that followed me the other night. I rise in my seat needing a better view, mostly to see if it's missing a passenger side mirror but it's too hard to tell. My hand rests on the door handle ready to step out and check, but Trey emerges from the house.

He climbs in and reverses out of the driveway. "Thanks for waiting."

I chuckle. "Where was I going to go?"

"I don't know." He turns toward me, a grin on his face. "High tail it across the field over there."

"If I wasn't wearing these heels, it might be a different story." I toy with the hem of my dress, contemplating mentioning the truck to Trey. "Do you know whose truck that was?"

"Henry Wilcox. He purchased the property. Do you know him?"

I shake my head. "No. I thought his truck looked familiar though." I brush off any more thoughts of the truck. I'm sure it's nothing.

During the twenty-minute drive from the housing development to downtown Harbor Highlands, we make small talk. Trey tells me about a new housing development that he's involved with, and I tell him about a new movie I watched. Sadly, my life isn't as exciting as his, but he hangs on to my every word and even asks questions as if he's genuinely interested. I could talk about dirt, and it seems he'd still listen with interest.

By the time we reach downtown, the sun dips below the horizon, casting a warm, amber glow on the cityscape. Trey finds an open parking spot along the busy main street. I push open my door and Trey is already waiting for me with his elbow held out on the sidewalk. Unable to mask my smile, I link my arm in the crook of his as we stroll side by side. The air buzzes with a symphony of footsteps, laughter, and snippets of conversations. Illuminated storefronts pass by as we approach the middle of the block.

Up ahead, the awning of Tandoori, a fine dining Indian restaurant, comes into view. I've been there once, and the food was average at best, but it's definitely out of my normal price range. My hand becomes clammy at the mere thought of the hefty price tag attached to dinner. I don't want to be presumptuous about who's paying for dinner, so I made sure to tuck a few twenties into my wallet.

Trey senses my nervousness and glances down. "Is everything okay?"

"Yes. Just a little chill in the air."

"Do you want my jacket?"

"No. I'm okay."

He drops my arm and takes his jacket off and throws it over my shoulders anyway.

His musky leather and spice scent surrounds me. I inhale another deep breath, wanting to savor his scent for as long as possible. "Thank you." I smile up at him. "I thought maybe the long sleeves of the dress would be fine, but apparently not."

As we approach Tandoori, I slow my pace, but Trey's steps never falters.

After we pass the restaurant, I glance up at him. "Where are we going? I thought we were going to dinner?"

"Yes, but not there."

There's only one other restaurant within walking distance. We come to a stop at the crosswalk and wait for traffic to clear before crossing the road. Instead of following the main sidewalk, we veer left toward a side street. I press my lips together, biting back my smile because there is only one place we could be going.

"You mentioned your favorite food was Indian and the only restaurant that made sense was The Curry Kitchen."

Now, I'm fighting my smile for an entirely different reason. "But why did you assume it was The Curry Kitchen? Because the other Indian restaurant is out of my price range?"

"No, because their food is crap and I know you have better taste than that. I'm sorry, curry foam should not be an appetizer. It's foam."

I laugh. Because he's not wrong. Their food is steps below The Curry Kitchen. You definitely don't get what you pay for with them.

When we reach the door, Trey holds it open for me. Immediately the tantalizing aroma of coriander, cumin, and cardamon invades my nostrils, creating an aromatic buffet that causes my stomach to growl.

The Curry Kitchen isn't the usual restaurant. It's more like the dive bar of restaurants, but they have the best Indian food that I've ever put in my mouth. The restaurant only holds roughly thirty customers at a time, with only a hand full of four person tables two person tables. With my hand in his, Trey leads me through the restaurant to a secluded corner to where an empty two person table is situated.

"Did you plan this out beforehand?" I ask as Trey takes his jacket from me and pulls out my chair.

"I had to if we were coming here." He throws the jacket around the backrest of his chair and takes the seat across from me.

"But what if I picked the other card?"

"I guess you'll never know." A sly smirk covers his face.

Before I can ask any more questions, one of the two servers pass us each a single-sided paper menu.

As I scan the two columns, I search for any new dishes, but deep down, I know I'll end up ordering my usual. "I don't even need to look. I already know what I'm getting."

"And what's that?"

"Chicken Tikka Masala."

"I'm ordering the Tandoori Chicken and maybe some Samosas."

"Those are so delicious. You can never go wrong with deep fried pastries filled with potatoes and peas."

"I'll share."

"Wait." I sit back in my chair, eyebrows draw together. "You want to share your food with me?"

"Sure. Why not?" He shrugs. "That way, we get a little of each."

"That's just... not something I'm used to."

"Sharing?"

"Pretty much. Ugh." I lean forward, resting my elbow on the table. "I hate talking about the ex while on a date because it's so cliché, and I definitely don't want him back, but he was and unfortunately still is a part of my life. Anyway, the ex was very much against sharing food. It was just weird. It's not like I was asking him to feed me or anything."

Trey rests his hand on mine before flipping it over and intertwining our fingers. His dark gaze lingers on mine. It's intense. My chest rises and falls with each passing second, waiting for him to say something.

"I'll gladly share my food with you any day."

A soft laugh escapes me. A part of me wonders if this conversation has steered away from food and on to something else entirely.

"I'll even feed you if you'd like."

This time it's a full belly laugh. "Feeding me isn't necessary, but I appreciate the offer."

Hanging out with Trey is just… easy. We can talk about anything and everything and he still makes me laugh, and it's been too long since I've felt this way. Forget doing sit ups, my stomach muscles get a workout just from talking with Trey. But fear firmly plants itself in my gut. What if I fall for this man and he breaks my heart? I don't know if I can survive it a second time.

Luckily, the server arrives with the samosas, and I can concentrate on the amazing food in front of me instead of everything else. Before the server leaves, Trey asks for an extra plate. A couple of minutes later, our entrees arrive, and we dish up as if we're eating family style.

Trey holds out a fork full of chicken and rice toward me. "You have to try this. It's so good."

I eye the fork and then Trey before leaning over and wrapping my mouth around his fork. His heated gaze drops to my lips as they slide off the metal tines.

"Mmm." I finish chewing, then swallow. "That is delicious."

We continue eating while sharing bites of food with

each other. As simple as dinner is for a date, this has been one of the best dates I've been on.

The server drops our bill off at the table and immediately Trey slides it toward him. I reach for my wallet, and he cocks his head to the side. "What are you doing?"

"Oh. Um. I don't want to be presumptuous."

He leans forward, his voice is deep and silky with a hit of seduction. "Know this, when you're out with me, I fully intend to make sure you're treated like a princess."

His words are a direct hit to my lady bits. When I'm with him, he makes me feel exactly that, and while I love the wining and dining, all I need is his companionship. I set my elbow on the table, resting my chin on my hand, and lean forward. "What if I don't always want to be treated like a princess?" I wink.

Trey leans forward, mimicking my pose. "How do you want me to treat you?"

I bite my lower lip before lifting my gaze to meet his. "Like a bad girl."

"But what if I like good girls more?"

"We could get out of here and see which one you get."

He groans. "Fuck. Don't tease me like that." Our server strolls past us and does a double take.

My entire body flames red hot. I drop my gaze to the table and shield my face with my hand.

He chuckles. "You're cute when you blush. On that note, let's get out of here."

I nod.

"Oh, wait." He reaches behind him and digs out two red envelopes from his suit jacket. He fans them out toward me. "You need to pick our next activity."

A wide grin covers my face. My nose scrunches as I

eenie meenie miny moe my choice. I tap the envelope on the right. Trey pulls out the card, reads it, and shoves it back inside. Again, he doesn't tell me what it says, and I know if I ask, he'll only tell me it's a surprise. All he does is rise to his feet and holds out his hand to help me up. Once standing, he wraps his coat around my shoulders before leaving cash and a generous tip on the table for our bill. As he leads me out, I feel the warmth of his hand on the small of my back.

When we reach Trey's SUV, he opens the passenger door for me and I climb in, doing my best to not flash everyone my underwear. A dress this short makes it a challenge. Trey rounds the hood and climbs in.

"So, this requires a location change?"

"It does." As he reverses out of the parking spot, he glances at me. The streetlight causes his eyes to twinkle while his lips tip up into a half smirk. Streaks of light flash past us as we drive down the street. After a left turn and then a right, he's parking his vehicle again.

I peer out the window and a neon sign flashes above us like an old movie theater. "Arcade Palace? Are you going to play Skee Ball to win me a stuffed teddy bear?"

"No. This is even better." He spares a glance my way, a twinkle in his eye.

I'm both nervous and excited for what he has planned. Spontaneity isn't my normal behavior, but with Trey, I'm learning to enjoy it. Before I can ask any more questions, he's slamming his door shut and meeting me at mine. He holds out his hand and helps me out as a breeze from the lake whisps around us. We stroll hand in hand through the wide double doors.

"But seriously, what are we doing here?" I glance up at him with pinched eyebrows.

Trey comes to a stop in front of a long counter, and I stand next to him. "Have you ever played laser tag?"

"Laser tag?"

A boyish grin covers his face as he nods.

I peer down at my dress, landing on the heels. The last time I wore heels was at my wedding and those only lasted an hour. I've already broken my heel wearing record. Now he expects me to run and jump in them. Peering up, I meet Trey's gaze. "I might be at a bit of a disadvantage here."

"The dress? Feel free to take it off." He smirks.

I playfully smack his arm. "The shoes. I can't run around in these."

"Then we need a little wager. If I win, I get to pick the last activity of our date and if you win, you pick."

Unable to turn down a challenge, I hold out my hand. "You're on." His long fingers wrap around mine and we shake. "Also, I failed to mention, I used to be a Duck Hunt champion."

"I guess I'll get to see your moves in action."

The counter attendant greets us and gets us hooked up with all the laser tag equipment. Trey bought out the entire room so it would only be us in a five round elimination battle royale. The teenage attendant gives us the rundown on the rules.

The fluorescent overhead lights dim as yellow, red, blue, and green halogen lights fill the arena. Above us, the countdown flashes on the LCD screen.

Three.

Two.

One.

Go.

The buzzer echoes off the walls. Trey races to the left. My heels clatter on the cement as I scamper to the right and duck behind an obstacle. With my back pressed against the wall, my heart hammers in my chest. It's been years since I've played any type of game like this. It's actually exhilarating. I raise my laser gun into position with my finger on the trigger. Rising to my feet, I peer over the top, thankful that the heels at least give me a couple extra inches. Movement from my left catches my attention and I duck down and inch my way around the corner, careful not to make any noise. I peer over the edge again and I don't see Trey, so I race across the pathway and take cover behind another large block obstacle.

From the other side of the small arena, Trey whistles "Pop! Goes the Weasel".

"I won't lie! That's kind of creepy!" I yell into the air.

Trey's laugh echoes off the walls.

"That's creepy too."

Shit. He probably knows where I am now.

With my back smashed against the wall, I peek around the corner and take off once I see the coast is clear. I hold my breath and keep my gaze trained to my right, hoping to hear any noise Trey might be making.

Suddenly, my vest chimes and flashes red. I glance down and spin around. Trey standing there, the smuggest smile on his lips.

"Pop! Goes the Rylee," he sings.

I rise to my feet.

"I thought you were the Duck Hunt champion." He holds his laser gun out.

"It's only one round. I'll get the next one." I strut past him and shove the plastic gun into his chest.

"*Ooomph*. Feisty. I like it."

I offer a little extra sway in my hips because I know he's watching me from behind.

Once we're at the starting position, I turn to Trey and narrow my eyes. "This round is mine."

"And you'll be mine when I win."

My lips split into a wide grin. "Keep dreaming."

"I do every night."

It didn't take long for laser tag to turn from a fun family game to something more sexual. I wonder what kind of dreams he has? If they're anything like mine, we might be in trouble. Right now, I don't need the distraction of naked Trey and figuring out what this is between us. Instead, I'm going to live in the now. I slam my hand against the button and the countdown starts again, followed by the buzzer.

This time Trey goes right, and I race straight ahead and then hang a left around a big block obstacle. I know I can't let him get me this time. I tiptoe around the corner, holding my laser gun in front of me. If James Bond and Lara Croft had a love child, that would be me right now as I inch my way along the rear wall.

When I was on the right side, I remember there was a little alcove and I can almost guarantee that's where he's hiding. I continue to inch my way along the wall and circle around toward the right before ducking down. With my back flat against a ramp obstacle, I crouch down and peer around the corner. A mop of dark hair peeks out from the alcove. He twists my way and I snap back to hide around the edge. After a few seconds, I dare to take a peek and sure enough, he's moving along the wall away from me. I raise my laser gun, taking aim using the plastic center hold sight. With a steady finger, I pull back the trigger until it clicks. His vest chimes, lighting him up red. Slowly, he turns around, frowning.

I rise to my full height, holding my gun while popping my hip like a sexy Laura Croft. "I saw the duck. I shot the duck. One-One. Game on." I strut past him, but this time, he wraps his hand around my waist, hauling me to him.

"I gave you that one. I didn't want you to feel bad about yourself."

"Oh, you're so full of it."

He bends down and presses a chaste kiss to my lips. "That was for good luck."

"Good luck for me? Or you?"

"For both of us."

I stand in position, gun raised for dramatic effect, ready for round three. Trey hits the button and after the buzzer sounds and we take off in opposite directions. Immediately, I hide behind the first obstacle I come across. Crouching down, my chest heaves as I plan my strategy. Footsteps to my right draw closer and closer. I jump to my heels and shuffle to my left. Within a couple of steps, an arm wraps around my waist.

"Ahhhh!"

Trey's hand covers my mouth, then his warm breath whispers over the shell of my ear. "Shhh. They'll hear you."

He pushes me against one of the block obstacles and spins me around, so we're face to face.

"What was rule six? No person to person contact."

"That's a dumb rule. I'm vetoing."

"You can't just veto the rules."

"Watch me." He slams his lips to mine in a searing hot and demanding kiss.

I forget where we are, that I'm wearing a laser tag vest, and hell, I forget my own name. He does this to me with only a kiss.

He drops his laser gun on a block next to us and then he does the same with mine. I moan into his mouth, and he deepens the kiss. His tongue curls over mine, slow and seductive. Goosebumps prickle my skin as he slides his hand down my rib cage and stops at my waist. Without breaking contact with my mouth, he lifts me up and sets me on top of a block obstacle. He wedges himself between my legs, causing my dress to ride up my thighs. His semihard cock grinds against my lace covered pussy, or I grind against him. At this point, I'm not even sure. Either way, I don't want it to end. His palms cup my cheeks, holding me in place as our tongues slide and caress against each other's. I wrap my legs around his waist and hook my ankles behind him, tugging him even closer to me.

A crackle and hiss fill the air, cutting through the silence. "Excuse me? You can't do that here."

# Chapter 14

## BUCKET LIST

# Rylee

I freeze. My heart jumps to my throat. Is someone else in here with us? Carefully, I refrain from making any noise as I stealthily survey the arena, my eyes scanning every corner without moving my head.

More crackling sounds through the loudspeaker before the young male attendant says, "Rule number six. No person-to-person contact. We have to ask you to leave."

The florescent over head lights flicker to life.

Warmth spreads across my chest and up to my cheeks. Trey pulls away slightly and holds his hands up, palms out. I drop my forehead to his chest and my shoulders shake from laughter. It's like that time as a teenager when I got caught making out with my boyfriend by his parents. I glance up, squinting my eyes as they adjust to the harsh lighting. "See. You can't just veto rules."

He shrugs, then grips my hips to help me down. I run my hands down my thighs to smooth the fabric of my dress, putting it back into place. Trey grabs our laser guns and we quietly exit the arena.

A wide grin covers Trey's face. Not an ounce of embarrassment from being caught. Me, on the other hand, I shield my face, unable to meet anyone's eyes. Trey sets the plastic guns on the counter, then proceeds to help me remove my vest.

Trey rests an elbow on the counter and leans in. "So, you must have cameras in there since you caught us. Any chance you can make me a copy of the tape?"

"I don't think so." I grip his bicep, tearing him away from the counter and drag him toward the exit.

Halfway to the door, Trey turns around. "If either of you had a girl like her alone in the arena, you know you'd do the same thing." He wraps an arm around my shoulder, pulling me into him, and we stroll toward the door.

I playfully backhand his stomach. "Did you really have to say that?"

"Something for them to aspire to."

"To be like you?"

"Nah. To take the most beautiful woman on a date."

Heat spreads across my cheeks for a different reason. He tugs me closer, and I go willingly, wrapping my arm around his waist.

A cool breeze hits us as we step out onto the sidewalk, and I snuggle deeper into his side.

"Here. Take my jacket." He pulls away, rolling his shoulders until the fabric slides down his arms.

"I'm fine snuggled next to you."

"You can have the jacket and a snuggle." Trey wraps

his warm jacket over my shoulders and pulls me into the crook of his arm again.

I sigh, soaking up the warmth. "Well, I have to say that's a first. I've never been kicked out of laser tag before. I guess I can cross that off my bucket list."

"What else do you have on that list? I'd be happy to help you cross off anything else." His hand lazily runs up and down my arm.

A laugh bubbles out. "I've had more excitement than I can handle for one night."

"Since you scored the last point, I'll let you pick our last activity."

I glance around as lamp posts create a warm glow over The Lakewalk. The bright moon shimmers and dances across Lake Superior as waves lap at the rocky shore.

"Let's see what's going on over there." I point down The Lakewalk where a patio is lit up with Edison lights and two firepits.

Upon arriving at the brick patio, the cozy warmth from the nearby firepits immediately greets us, and we spot a couple of unoccupied seats. A server introduces herself, and we order two glasses of wine.

"I'm kinda surprised at how well thought out your date is. I never expected this," I wave my hand over the romantic ambiance of the patio, "would be a date you put together."

"What kind of date did you expect from me?"

"Honestly?" I glance up at the inky sky filled with stars. "A few hours at Sugar Daddy's followed by dinner at The Pink Taco." I tilt my head, a half-smile on my face. "But also, who thought it was a good idea to name a business The Pink Taco?"

A deep laugh escapes him. "Seeing their location is next door to a strip club and they sell tacos, it's kind of brilliant. If they sold soup and sandwiches, it might be a little awkward."

"True. That wouldn't make any sense." I run my fingers along the hem of my dress. "But seriously, this date has been amazing. Is this what all your dates are like?" I'm fishing for information and doing a terrible job at it.

He reaches for my hand, flipping it over, and traces the lines on my palm with his fingertip. The soft touch almost tickles. "No. Dates like this are saved for special occasions."

"What's the special occasion?"

He glances up at me, a smile flirts on his lips. "You finally saying yes to a date with me. It needed to be memorable, so I can persuade you into a second one."

Sitting up, I lean closer, so my lips are poised over his. "If I'm being honest, you've already done it." I bite on the corner of my lower lip, causing his eyes to drift downward. His hand starts at my knee and slides up my thigh a fraction, sending an eruption of goosebumps over my entire body. Then his lips are on mine. It's soft and sensual and everything I'm not used to from Trey. But certainly, it's something I *could* get used to.

He pulls away, making the kiss entirely too short. "What do you say we get out of here?"

First, it's been forever since I've been on a date, but it's been even longer since I've had this much fun on a date, and I don't want it to end. I've fought myself so long because I thought it was the right thing to do, but like Dessa said, I need to be a little selfish. Tonight, I want to do just that.

As I rise, the incessant throbbing from my heel to my toes intensifies and I cringe. Apparently, my feet are done with these shoes. Sitting down for the past hour didn't give them the break they needed. I'll muscle through the three blocks we have back to the car, then they're gone.

Trey reaches down and intertwines his fingers with mine. The gesture is simple, but also the sweetest. At every opportunity, he wants to be near me, touch me. I never expected him to be this sweet. He's the perfect mix of cocky playboy and sweet boy next door. And he's making it hard not to fall for him.

The incessant throbbing much like a steady heartbeat shoots through my feet with every step. Finally, my feet rebel and I stumble forward.

Trey glances down at me, eyes laced with concern. "Are you alright? You only had like half a glass of wine."

"I can't do it anymore." I stop. "These shoes. They have to go." I drop his hand and grip his bicep for support. Kicking up my leg, I reach behind me and flick off one shoe. It clatters to the sidewalk and I repeat the process on the other side. I exhale a sigh of relief as my bare feet are no longer constricted in three-inch heels. "There. Much better."

"You're not walking barefoot to the car."

"I'm not putting these godforsaken things back on." I hold up the pair of heels.

Trey steps in front of me and bends down, wrapping his arms around my thighs and lifts.

A half giggle, half shriek escapes me. "What are you doing?"

"Carrying you."

"Back to the car?"

"Yes."

"That's like three blocks."

"Get comfy then."

"Oh my god. I can't believe you're doing this." I giggle. Other couples stroll past us, and I smile and wave. I'm sure it's not every day they see a grown man carrying a woman down the sidewalk.

"I hope this doesn't kill the romantic mood, but what's the story with Abby's dad?" Trey asks.

My body stiffens. "Mood deflated faster than a popped balloon."

"We don't have to talk about it. Forget I asked."

It's not a giant secret I'm holding on to, but I hate even mentioning Kyle's name. It gives me hives, but Trey deserves to know the truth since he asked. "No. It's fine. But do you want to do this while you're carrying me over your shoulder down the sidewalk?"

"Sure. It gives me a possessive edge. Like I'm whisking you away."

I laugh. Honestly, I wish he could have been the one to whisk me away seven years ago. "Here's the Cliffs Notes version. My junior year I met Kyle. Only a few month into dating I got pregnant. Kyle proposed, and I stupidly said yes. We got married. I took a year off and had Abby. Throughout the following two years, I was constantly wooed and swept off my feet by him, while he shamelessly did the same with countless other women."

His arms wrapped around my legs, tense. "Shit. I'm sorry Rye."

"Thanks."

"Did you leave?"

I huff out a humorless laugh. "Actually, no. He left us."

My body jerks as Trey comes to a halt. "Fuck. Rye." He bends at his knees and releases his grip around my legs. As my body slides down his, my fingertips follow every ridge and valley on his chest until I'm on my feet. One hand threads through the hair on the side of my head and the other grips my waist. "Kyle's a fucking idiot for letting you go. But also, I wouldn't have this moment with you if he didn't." He leans in. I lift my chin and my eyes flutter closed, as I wait in anticipation for his lips to touch mine.

"Trey! Trey!" a woman's voice sounds from several feet away. "Trey. I've been calling you, but you never returned any of my messages."

My eyes pop open as Trey's grip on me loosens. We both turn around. A leggy blonde and her equally leggy friend stand in front of us.

"Uh. Yeah. I've been busy," Trey says as he searches for my hand, linking our fingers.

"You're always so busy. We need to go out for drinks so you can relax," the woman purrs.

"I'm on a date right now."

"Oh, sorry." The woman's gaze wanders over me from head to toe. I'm sure sizing me up. "I thought maybe she was your sister or something since you don't date."

"Nope. This is my date." Trey glances down at me before lifting our connected hands and placing a kiss on the back of mine. "And she's definitely not my sister."

"Oh. Sure. I'll just… call you later."

"Please don't," he murmurs under his breath. Once the woman is out of earshot, Trey faces me. "Sorry about that."

"No. It's okay. You had a life before me. And before whatever this date non-date is." Things were going too good on our date, so it's only natural something would mess it up.

"Don't diminish what this is." He gently squeezes my hand.

My phone buzzes in my wallet. Pulling it out, *Kyle* flashes on the screen and I roll my eyes. He's like Beetlejuice. I said his name too many times tonight. I shove it back inside. Eventually it'll go silent.

"Do you need to take that?"

"No. It's nothing." If it's important, he'll leave a message that I'll ignore until morning. Unfortunately, it buzzes again, and I know I can't continue ignoring it. Dammit for being a responsible adult. "Excuse me."

Trey nods. I step to the side and answer the phone.

"What do you want, Kyle?" I spare a glance over my shoulder and Trey's scrolling on his phone.

"Nice talking to you, too."

"There are no pleasantries when it comes to us. I'll ask one more time, what do you want?"

"I know I have plans this Wednesday with Abby—"

"You are not bailing on her again," I whisper yell in my phone, hoping Trey doesn't hear, but his head lifts my way, so I know my irritation didn't go unnoticed.

"I have this important business meeting."

"Bullshit," I spit out. "You always bail on her. It's like she doesn't even have a father."

"Rylee."

My name coming out of his mouth makes my ears bleed. "Whatever Kyle. I'll be the one to tell Abby you're not coming to see her. Again. I'll be the one who has to bear the disappointment on her face. Again. You need to figure your shit out and act like a father."

I end the call. By now, I'm used to this, but not Abby, and it's always my burden to see the almost tears in her eyes whenever he cancels. I hate him even more because of it.

"Everything alright?"

My heart nearly jumps out of my chest from Trey's voice. For a second, I forgot where I was and who I'm with. "Yeah." I flick my wrist between us. "Just my ex, bailing on Abby… again."

"I'm sorry."

"You have nothing to be sorry about. You're not the one bailing on her."

"I know. I'm sorry that you have to go through that."

"Sadly, I should be used to it by now. He couldn't keep a promise if his life depended on it. At least one to his own daughter." Silence passes between us. "You know what? Let's not talk about him. He's a mood killer. Let's get out of here."

We continue strolling down the sidewalk to where Trey's vehicle is parked. I hate Kyle even more now that he killed the vibe of my date. He always manages to ruin things for me. It's like it's coded into his DNA. Find new and exciting ways to make Rylee miserable. Screw it. I'm taking control. He doesn't get to ruin my date. When we reach Trey's SUV, he unlocks it with the key fob. Before he can open the passenger door, I stop him with my hand on his bicep.

I peer up at him. "Are benefits still on the table?"

He turns toward me. The pad of his thumb caresses the apple of my cheek. His hand continues to glide across my skin until his fingers thread through my hair. His large palm warms my cheek. "No."

My stomach falls. It was inevitable this would have to end, but I was hoping it wasn't tonight.

With his other hand he grips my chin, forcing me to meet his gaze. "I don't want benefits. You're worth more than just benefits. But I'll take whatever you give me."

A slow smile spreads over my lips. "Can we go to your house?"

"Absolutely."

He opens the passenger door and I slide in. While he rounds the hood, I click my seatbelt into place. We've had sex before, but the butterflies are fluttering faster this time. Maybe because it's not a spontaneous, spur of the moment thing. Instead, I have the entire drive to his house to think about it. Trey climbs in and starts his SUV. He glances over at me while reaching his hand over the center console and intertwining his fingers with mine. It's the simplest gesture, but one that calms my erratic heartbeat.

The short ride to his house is silent, but the way his thumb brushes over the back of my hand says everything I need to know right now. I want Trey.

His neighborhood is a far cry from my tiny apartment complex. Enormous houses with even bigger lawns line the streets. A pang of guilt hits me as this is something I'll never be able to give Abby. A neighborhood filled with other kids to run around and play with. Or a backyard to build a fort or play kickball in.

As we approach a navy blue split-level house, he turns left and pulls into the sunken attached garage. I yank myself out of my thoughts. No pity parties tonight. There's only room for one party, and that's between my legs.

The garage door closes, and we both step out, but before we reach the door to the house, my heels that I never put back on slip from my fingers, dropping to the floor with a clatter. Trey twists around and I throw myself into his arms, slamming my lips to his. Without breaking our connection, he twists us around and cages me against the front fender. A shiver runs down my spine as he threads his fingers through my hair, cupping my head as he deepens the kiss. I wrap my arms around his waist and tug him to me, wanting to feel all of him. A low moan escapes his throat.

He pulls away, but his lips linger on mine. "Did I tell you this is the best friendship I've ever had?"

"And if you stop, this friendship is over." I grip his chin and haul his mouth to mine in a bruising kiss. It's frantic and demanding. Mostly, it's everything I've been missing in my life.

I hike my leg over his hip. The hem of my dress tickles my skin as it slides up my thigh. His now rock-hard bulge presses against my pussy and I release a needy moan. Shamelessly, I grind myself against him like a cat in heat. Needing anything and everything that he'll give me. His hand skates up my thigh and between my legs. His fingers rub against the fabric of my panties between my legs.

"You're so fucking wet for me," he whispers, low and growly. "You like grinding against my dick? How bad do you want it?"

His words send an electric current pulsating through my entire body. "Trey," I pant. "I want it. I want it so bad." My hips move in sync with the rhythm created by his skilled fingers, intensifying the pleasure.

He wraps his other hand around the nape of my neck and slams his lips to mine. He slides my panties to the side and runs his fingers down my bare pussy. I whimper into his mouth from the contact. He continues to move his fingers up and down, brushing against my clit with each pass. My hard nipples brush against the fabric of the dress, sending another lightning bolt directly to my core. Trey plunges a finger inside of me and I break our lip lock.

"Oh. Fuuuck." I moan when he adds a second finger, pumping harder and faster.

"Come for me, Rye. Come all over my fingers."

My nails dig into his shoulder while his fingers continue to move inside of me. He adds a third, stretching me even more. A tingle starts in my lower belly. My pleasure cries and pants grow louder with every thrust, echoing off the cement.

His lips move to my ear as his warm breath skates over the shell. "Fuck. Rye. Your pussy is gripping me like a vise. Now be a good girl and come for me."

In that moment, his thumb grazes my clit and that's my undoing. A burst of white-hot heat floods my entire body.

"Oh! Trey! Yes!" I continue to grind against him as I ride out my orgasm until I eventually come to a halt.

Trey pulls his fingers out and slides my panties back into place. My wobbly leg drops, the icy cement does nothing to cool the scorching hot inferno blazing through my entire body. He brings his hand up to his mouth and opens. His lips wrap around his fingers, sucking my orgasm off them.

A deep moan rumbles from his chest. His hooded gaze meets mine. "I've never been the type of man to stop at only one."

---

An hour and two orgasms later, one for each of us, we're standing in Trey's sprawling kitchen. I swear half my apartment could fit in his kitchen. He's sporting nothing but a pair of black boxer briefs while I'm wearing one of his dress shirts.

He passes me a bottle of water from the fridge. "Did I ever tell you that you look fucking amazing wearing my clothes?"

"You like it?" I trail my fingers down the pearl buttons until I reach the hem that kisses the tops of my thighs.

"Fuck yeah I do."

In two long strides he's standing in front of me, caging me between him and the counter. He bends down and runs his nose along the column of my neck. I tilt my head to give him better access.

"The dress you wore tonight is a close second."

"I have a confession. The dress isn't mine. Dessa let me borrow it. I don't own anything remotely close to it. Or the heels."

"The dress was stunning on you. Tell Dessa I'll pay her for the dress because you're keeping it. This isn't the last time I want to see you wearing it."

Heat creeps up my cheeks once again because he knows exactly what to say and when to say it.

"If we're throwing out confessions, I have one of my own. I like you, Rye. I really like you and it's more than this friend's bullshit. It's been a really long time since I've felt like this, so take that for what you will. I'm willing to wait for as long as it takes. Even if that requires me coming into Porter's every day just to see you."

"On the days I'm not working, you'll be so disappointed. I doubt Jake can fill out that dress quite like me."

Trey chuckles. "No, you're absolutely correct. I like it so much. Just thinking about it makes me want to go for round two."

"Should I leave you alone with the dress?"

"Only if you come with it." He presses his lips to my neck, licking my heated skin.

I suck in a sharp breath, something rancid invading my nostrils. It's like passing a farm on a hot summer day. It's nauseating. My stomach does back flips that could rival an Olympic gymnast. Bile creeps up my throat. With both hands, I shove at Trey's chest. He stumbles backward.

"Okay. We don't have to go for round two."

My hand flies up to cover my mouth. I scan the dimly lit kitchen, searching for a garbage can, but I have no idea where it is so I use the only other thing available. Racing to the kitchen sink, my fingers curl over the edge of the counter and I bend over, emptying the contents of my stomach. I dry heave a few times before it settles. A little.

Trey rushes to my side. "Are you alright?"

"Yeah. I don't know what came over me. Maybe it was something I ate? Or I'm getting sick?"

He runs his hand up and down my spine while I'm still leaning over the sink. When I rise to my full height, he passes me a bottle of water. I take a swig and swish it around in my mouth before spitting it out in the sink. Then I turn on the faucet to wash away everything I vomited.

"I'm sorry about that."

Trey passes me a sheet of paper towel to wipe my mouth. "That's the first time someone vomited after having sex with me." He crosses his arms and leans against the counter.

"I'm glad I could cross that off your bucket list." I swallow the last gulp of water from the bottle.

He steps to the side to pull out a drawer with the trash can and recycle bin.

The odor from earlier hits me again, except this time it's like a freight train of stench and I gag.

"Want to go lay down? I'm sure I have some Pepto or Tums you can take for your upset stomach."

"I don't know. If it's the flu, I don't want you to catch it. Maybe it's best if I go home."

Trey moves to stand in front of me. His hands brush up and down my biceps. "Are you sure? I don't mind. I just want to make sure you're okay."

I nod. "Yeah. It's for the best."

Getting sick is not how I wanted the night to end, but Trey was so sweet, wanting to take care of me. Kyle would have tossed me a bottle of water and a blanket and told me to sleep on the couch so he wouldn't catch whatever I had. But not Trey. All he wanted to do was to take care of me, even if it caused him to catch whatever I may have. But I'm not used to sweet. Since my divorce, I never allowed anyone to take care of me, so I wasn't about to start now.

# Chapter 15

## SHODDY CRAFTSMANSHIP

## Rylee

It's been three days since my date with Trey. A date that took me completely by surprise, especially the sex. The first time, even in the backseat of his SUV, was amazing. But the second time was earth shattering. Either it's been too long since I've had sex or Trey has all my buttons on speed dial.

After I got home, I crawled into bed and by morning, I felt completely normal. I have no idea what came over me. Maybe it was food poisoning.

My mind drifts to the sweet way he wanted to take care of me. A jolt of warmth spreads through my entire body from the thought. But I know it's only fleeting, so I shove those thoughts of him wanting to take care of me into a closet and slam the door. Those are feelings I don't need right now.

Instead, I reminisce about how I surprised him at his office yesterday afternoon. Little did I know, I would be his lunch and not the sandwiches I brought. The best part was him bending me over his desk. I can still feel the way his fingers dug into my waist as he thrust into me over and over. That time the sex wasn't sweet. It was raw and primal. Like he needed to be inside of me to survive. I loved every second of it. Instinctively, my thighs clench together as I bite back a smile.

---

I yank open the front door to Porter's and stroll inside. Before I'm two steps in, Dessa and Lach swivel their heads in my direction.

I freeze and my gaze drifts between the two. "Um. Good morning."

"There's something different about you." Dessa taps her finger on her lips.

"I don't know what you're talking about." I scurry past them, but Dessa stops me with a hand on my wrist.

"You're glowing. Wait, you had sex again, didn't you?" Dessa rests a hand on her waist.

Heat creeps up my neck and settles on my cheeks. I can't even hide it anymore. Technically, it's been twice this week, but I keep that information to myself.

"Oh, my god! You did!" Dessa claps her hands.

I roll my eyes. Also, how the hell can she tell? I can't even lie to her because she's some kind of human lie sex detector. "That was over twelve hours ago."

"Damn. And you're still glowing?" Lach croons "Magic Stick" by Lil Kim, while shimmying his shoulders.

I shoot him a death glare and he holds up his hands in defense. He shuffles backward until he's standing behind Dessa, using her as a human shield. He's been on the receiving end of many of my death glares since he likes to push my buttons, and he also knows exactly which ones to push.

"It's a two-time fling. That's it." Shit. Technically three, but they don't need to know every time I have sex.

"You won't be able to stop at two." Her lips spread into an amused smile.

Lach nods along, still behind her.

Of course, I can't, because I'm already at three.

"Yes. I can." My tone is defensive.

"I bet you can't," Dessa counters.

"I'll take that bet." Lach raises his hand.

"Are you two betting on my sex life now?" My gaze flits between them.

A wide grin covers Dessa face. "When you come into work all smiling and giggling, I know you've just had sex." She inches closer to me and sniff my shoulder. "You smell like sex too."

"I do not." I discretely twist my head for a sniff to confirm I don't smell like sex. "And I don't giggle." I cross my arms over my chest.

"Like a schoolgirl, especially when Trey's around," Lach adds.

I shake my head and continue past the bar and down the hallway to the small break room with Dessa and Lach hot on my heels.

"Why are you fighting this so hard?" Dessa asks from behind me.

I yank open my locker and throw my purse inside.

"Because they're all the same. And the last time I was left to be a single mom." While Abby is the best thing to have happened to me, everything after that sucked and I'd rather not live it again.

Dessa leans against the lockers next to me. "Not every guy is going to be like Kyle."

"Or they are. It's best if I keep my guard up. It's just sex. That's all it is." I slam the door shut.

"Guarded is fine, but you've built a fortress equipped with a moat and bloodthirsty alligators around your heart." Lach raises an eyebrow.

I shrug. "Whatever works."

As the saying goes, give someone an inch and they'll take a mile. I know if I give Trey an inch of my heart, he has the ability to take the entire thing. The orgasms are great. Better than great. Mind blowing. Earth shattering. All-consuming. But that's all they can be, just orgasms. I'm not in the market to have my heart broken again and I know if I let my guard down, that's exactly what will happen.

"Also, what's with the double team?" My gaze jumps between them.

"With everything that you've been through, you deserve some happiness. You deserve someone who makes you feel like you've been struck by lightning." Dessa rests her hand on my forearm.

"Who said I wasn't happy? I am perfectly content with my life right now."

"Content isn't necessarily happiness." Dessa purses her lips together, biting back the urge to say more.

She's been my best friend since we both started working at Porter's four years ago. She knows everything about my situation with Kyle, so she's seen me at the lowest of lows, but she hasn't seen me truly happy. Shit. It's been so long since I've seen myself happy. Maybe she's taking whatever this is between Trey and me as happiness.

"You two can continue discussing my happiness, but I'm out." I sidestep the both of them as I strut out to the main bar to take inventory.

Once I'm done restocking the front, I take inventory of the dry storage room and walk-in cooler to give a list to Jake for ordering tomorrow. Ever since Jake passed on the inventory duties to me, I've been able to find ways to make it more efficient while also saving money, which Jake was more than excited about.

By mid-afternoon, I'm finished putting away the liquor delivery with Lach's help. Now, I'm sitting at the bar, waiting for Chad to arrive for his shift. I check the beer bottle shaped clock hanging behind the bar for the tenth time. He's fifteen minutes late and clearly doesn't realize other people count on him to show up to work on time. And it's definitely not the first time.

Finally, Chad strolls through the front door like he's taking a leisurely walk through the park. His hood is pulled over his head while his hands are shoved into his pockets. He's the adult version of a moody teenager.

"Good luck with that. I'm out," I say to Dessa and Lach.

---

I'm climbing the stairs to my apartment when my phone vibrates against my butt. I pull it out and Trey's name flashes with a message.

TREY
I miss you.

**RYLEE**

Barely twenty-four hours have passed.

**TREY**

Twenty-four long, agonizing hours.

**TREY**

If I'm being honest, I missed you the second you left my office, but I didn't want to come off as desperate if I messaged you as soon as you walked out the door.

**RYLEE**

That was a fun afternoon. Now I'm thinking about how you had me bent over your desk. Your long, thick cock stretching me.

**TREY**

Fuck. Now I am too. Are you at home?

**RYLEE**

Yeah. I just got to my apartment.

**TREY**

Alone?

**RYLEE**

Yeah. Abby's at school for another hour and a half.

**TREY**

I'll be there in ten.

Eight minutes later, the alarm on my apartment intercom sounds. After I buzz Trey in, he's knocking on my door thirty-seconds later. When I pull it open, Trey's hands instantly clasp around my cheeks and he slams his lips to mine. It's a dizzying kiss, but every kiss from him sends my head to the clouds. He walks me backward as he kicks the door closed with his heel. He pulls away, but he trails kisses over my cheek and up my jaw.

I moan and tilt my head to give him better access. "We can go to the bedroom."

His warm breath skates over my skin. "No time. I need to be inside you like five minutes ago." He bends at the knees, wraps his arms around my thighs, and lifts. In three long strides, he lowers me until my butt hits the top of my dining table. His lips meet mine in an all-consuming kiss. My tongue presses at the seam and he opens. Our tongues stroke and caress against one another's. His lips massage mine as he swallows my moans. Kisses from him make me forget my own name. Without pulling apart, I slide my hands up his chest until I reach his tie. I pull one end through the loop until it loosens. Then I search for the top button of his dress shirt. With deft fingers, I pop each button until the sides fall open.

Before I can undo the button of his slacks, he pulls away. "I'm craving something sweet," he says with hooded eyes. Then a seductive smile graces his lips.

It's a look that can turn the driest desert into an ocean. Case in point, my panties are no longer dry.

"Scoot back."

I do as he says. With the flick of his wrist, he undoes the button of my jeans. As he yanks on the waistband, I lift my butt so he can peel them down my legs, along with my panties. He runs a hand over my knee and up my thigh. "Look at that. Your pussy is glistening for me. Begging to be licked."

With one hand, he uses his fingers to spread me open. At first, he places a sweet kiss between my legs. Then his mouth is on my clit, licking and sucking. My entire body jolts to life.

"Ah! Yes!" I buck my hips as I thread my fingers through the hair at the back of his head, holding him in place. "That feels so good. Don't stop."

"My girl is greedy."

"Too much talking. Not enough licking."

I grasp whatever hair I can wrap my fingers around and guide him right where I want him between my legs. With the flat of his tongue, he licks up the entire length of me. Then he does it again and again. My entire body buzzes with electricity just from his tongue. Two of his fingers plunge inside, forcing a sharp gasp out of me. He continues to pump in and out as he takes turns between licking my pussy and sucking on my clit. His fingers curl inside and I gasp.

"Oh! Ah! That feels so good. Don't. Stop."

A tingle starts in my lower belly and blasts off like a firework right to my core.

"Fuck Rye. Come for me. Come all over my tongue. I want all your sweetness."

I snap forward, screaming his name as I do just that. I ride out the wave of ecstasy as he licks me dry. My chest heaves as I work to collect my breath, but I know I won't have much time.

He rises to his full height and slides the back of his hand over his mouth. "Fuck. I need in you. Now." He pushes his slacks to the floor. His long, thick cock juts out between us. He yanks me to the edge of the table and in one hard thrust, he's inside me.

My mouth falls open, words failing me as he stretches me wide.

"Fuck. You feel so amazing. You are so amazing." He grunts as he continues to pound into me.

I hook my ankles around his waist as he relentlessly continues to slam into me over and over again. The table creaks below us. Each thrust of his hips causes the table to scrape against the linoleum.

"Oh! Oh! Yes!" I pant. "Harder. Harder." My nails dig

into his shoulder muscles as I desperately hold on. "Right there." Suddenly, a loud snap echoes through the apartment.

"Oh, shit!"

Trey's arm wraps around me as the top of the table plummets to the floor. As I go down, he pulls out of me, and his body falls with mine. He reaches out with his other hand to brace our fall when both of us slam to the ground on top of the table. We freeze, still in a daze over what happened. Then there's another snap and we fall another couple of inches. This time we bust out laughing. After several seconds, we're both still collecting our breaths.

Trey glances up at me. "Are you alright?"

"Yeah. But I don't think my table is." I kick the broken leg with my foot.

"What kind of shoddy craftsmanship is this?"

"To be fair, I doubt it was meant to hold two grown adults."

"That really needs to be the new standard for quality control."

A quiet laugh shivers out of me. I haven't been with a guy that's made me laugh as much as Trey has. It's oddly refreshing. I reach up and cup his cheek. His five o'clock shadow prickles my fingertips. "I'll write a strongly worded letter to the manufacturer."

"I'll get you something of quality." He kisses me. Then he rises to his feet and holds out his hand to help me up.

"You don't have to do that."

"I insist. Since it was kind of my fault that it broke."

"In that case, I have a rickety couch in the living room that you could try breaking."

"Challenge accepted." Without warning, he picks me up and I release a small giggle as he carries me to the couch. "Plus, you've only had one orgasm and I like to work in even numbers." His lips are on mine once again. It's hot and demanding. Broken table instantly forgotten.

Trey sits down and sets me on his lap. His mouth is on my breast, swirling his tongue around my nipple before taking it into his mouth. I arch into him, loving his mouth on me.

I reach between us and wrap my hand around his cock, stroking him while he sucks and licks on my heated skin.

"Put me in you," he mumbles around my nipple. The contrast between his hot breath and the cool air sends a delicious shiver up my spine.

I rise to my knees and guide the tip of his cock to my entrance. Slowly, I sink down on him, relishing in the delicious stretch. "Ooo! Yes!"

Before I'm fully seated, he thrusts up, pushing the rest of the way into me. My mouth falls open as a moan escapes me. With his fingers curled around my waist, he continues to push into me from below. I rock my hips in tandem with his.

"Oh, god! Fuck me. Harder. Don't stop." My fingers clench his shoulders, my nails millimeters away from breaking skin.

"Rye. Fuck. I'm going to come."

"Me too. Keep going."

"Your pussy is gripping me so tight. I can't hold on much longer," he grits out.

He wraps his lips around my nipple and bites down. I throw my head back, the stimulation catapulting me over the edge. My pussy clenches as an orgasm rips through me. I gasp as he thrusts up, his hot cum spilling inside me. He continues to pump into me over and over again until his own orgasm subsides.

My head falls to his chest, both of us collecting our breaths. Leisurely, his hands roam up and down my back.

He presses a warm kiss to my shoulder. The gesture is sweet. Dammit. This isn't supposed to be sweet.

I sit up and fall to the cushion beside him. Tugging the blanket off the back of the couch, I wrap it around me. "That was... wow."

"That's what I do." He collects his boxer briefs and tugs them on, followed by his slacks. He strolls into the kitchen and turns on the faucet.

"You can do that to me anytime you want," I say over my shoulder to his retreating frame.

A few seconds later, he's returning with a damp paper towel. He holds it out for me and I take it. He bends, resting his hand on the couch, caging me in. "And I fully intend to." Then he winks. "But it will have to wait."

"That's okay. I need some recovery time after today, anyway." We share a moment of silence, before I ask, "Is this like our fourth date?"

"Well, if we're counting sex as dates," he rubs his chin, "This would technically be our fifth. I did walk you to your car. Compared to all the other dates, that one is pretty high on the not as memorable meter."

"Only because we didn't have sex."

"You're catching on." His hand tips up my chin as he bends down and presses a gentle kiss to my lips. "From here on out, sex dates only and we should do them more often. Like tomorrow. I'll add you to my calendar."

"You're insatiable," I smile and shake my head, "but also I have to work tomorrow."

He shoves his arms through the armholes of his shirt. Starting at the bottom, he slowly buttons his shirt. "Another time then. I hate to fuck and run, but I do have a meeting at the office in an hour."

"I see how it is. You're only using me for sex." I flash him a playful smile.

He bends down so his lips are inches from mine. "With the way your legs were gripping my head like a vise grip, I'd say you're using me for sex."

"Fair. We can use each other." I grip the front of his shirt and pull him the rest of the way to me, pressing my lips to his in a soft and lingering kiss.

He pulls away slightly. "Just so you know, you're worth more than this. Say the word and I'll show you."

All I can do is press my lips together and nod. How can he give me the world's greatest orgasm and then say the sweetest thing ever? My ovaries can't take it. I rise to my feet and clasp the blanket under my arm. Trey strolls toward the front door and I'm a few steps behind him. He spins around, clasps my cheeks with both hands, and places a kiss on my lips. I fight the urge to deepen the kiss and make him miss his meeting for another round. I guess there will have to be another date. So that's how he does it. Dammit.

We break apart and he points to the now scrap pieces of flimsy laminate pine wood that was once my table. "Is there a dumpster where I can put that?"

"Off to the right when you exit the door there's a dumpster. If you can take the big piece, I can get the rest." I tuck a strand of hair behind my ear.

He lifts the top piece that somehow managed to stay mostly together and tucks it under his arm like it's nothing. I hold the door open for him and he strolls down the hallway. I admire his backside as he saunters away until he's down the stairs and out of sight.

"I was concerned when I heard the loud crash earlier, but the moans that followed soon after told me not to bother you."

I swivel my head to the left to find Marcie with her head poking out of her doorway, an amused grin covering her face. Warmth covers my cheeks, knowing she heard us. "Yeah. It was my dining room table."

"May I recommend you buy yourself some sturdier furniture?" She flashes me a wink before retreating into her apartment.

Then I do the same. When the door clicks behind me, I throw myself against the wood and exhale a deep breath, but I can't fight my own enormous grin.

# Chapter 16

## GENITAL MASSEUSE

# Rylee

**TREY**
Pick one.

**RYLEE**
What's this?

**TREY**
A link to different styles of tables Bennett builds.

**RYLEE**
You're having a table built for me?

**TREY**
Yeah.

**RYLEE**
You don't have to buy me a table, let alone have one custom built.

> **TREY**
> 
> I insist. In fact, the order has already been placed and Bennett would kick my ass if I told him to cancel.

> **RYLEE**
> 
> At the very least, let me help pay for it.

I had no intention of replacing the table since we barely use it. Why waste the money when I can use it for something else? But I can't ask Trey to buy me a new one. Especially a custom built one. That's going to cost a fortune. Anything from the discount store would work just fine.

> **TREY**
> 
> Nope. I broke it, it's the least I can do. Plus, getting one from Bennett, I'll know it's high quality and can withstand our extracurricular activities. Which I plan on doing more often with you. 🍆💦

All it takes is one line from him to completely divert my focus away from my money concerns. I don't know how he does it. But it's been a long time since I've felt like this. Actual happiness. It's a foreign feeling, but one I'm enjoying with Trey.

> **RYLEE**
> 
> And he's tested this. 😏

> **TREY**
> 
> I'll ask.

Oh my god. Bennett must think we're nymphomaniacs.

RYLEE

I was joking. Don't ask.

TREY

Too late. He says, and I quote, "What the fuck is wrong with you? But also, yes." We'll have to test it out when it's ready. For the sake of quality control.

TREY

I'll bend you over the edge and slam my dick inside your tight pussy to test the sturdiness.

TREY

Then I'll lay you out on top to make sure it's suitable for feasting.

A tingle shoots directly to my nipples at the thought of him licking my pussy. Instantly, my thighs clench together, and I shift in my seat.

TREY

Then lastly, we'll test its weight capacity as you ride my dick like a cowgirl. Giddy up.

"You look like you're using Cupid's arrow to pleasure yourself right now."

I slam my phone screen side down on the bar top at Porter's. Heat rushes to my cheeks. Glancing up, I see Dessa staring at me, a sly smirk covering her red lips. My shift technically ended, but I'm waiting for Chad to come in before I leave in case she needs help with anything. "Um. No. Trey's just telling me about the new dining table he's having custom made for me." My phone buzzes again, but I ignore it.

"I wish dining tables turned me on like that."

It's not the table, but what he wants to do to me on top of it. I knit my eyebrows together, feigning innocence. "I don't know what you're talking about." I bite the inside of my cheek, wrestling my smile.

"Oh, come on. Your cheeks are redder than an iron poker sitting in a fire. There's more than just table talk happening."

Lach creeps up behind me. "She has a point. You're looking a little flush."

I jump. Then backhand him in his chest. "Now you're on my case too?"

"Just calling it like I see it." He takes a seat on the stool next to me. "How's it going with Casanova?"

"Really? You want to talk about my... I don't even know what it is."

"Banging and hanging? Insignificant other? Flirtationship? Genital Masseuse? Porn pals?" Dessa supplies.

I glare at her.

"What?" She laughs. "I'm only offering suggestions."

"Genital masseuse is my favorite. I need to find me one of those," Lach says.

"What's wrong with friends who occasionally hook up?" I shrug.

"Nope. It's forever now referred to as a genital masseuse." Lach wiggles his eyebrows.

I sigh. I'm not winning this friends with benefits conversation so I change it. "Where's Chad? He's ten minutes late." I glance at the time on my phone while simultaneously checking if there's a new message from Trey.

"He's been so flaky lately. He's constantly poking at Jake's last nerve. A couple days ago, Jake had to stay late because Chad called in at the last minute," Dessa says.

Lach rolls his eyes. "Someone's just butt hurt because he got demoted. But it's his own fault he sucks at his job."

"That reminds me," I turn to Lach, "there's a small liquor delivery coming later. They forgot a couple of boxes so they're dropping them off at the end of their route. I can trust you to take care of that for me?" I flash him wide, puppy dog eyes.

"For you, anything. Now if it was Dessa… I might need her to be my genital masseuse."

Dessa busts out laughing. "You're such a perv. Be your own genital masseuse." She throws a bar towel at him. He grins and throws it right back.

"Sometimes you need someone else to do it. It's a different grip. A different pressure. A different stroke."

I press my hands to my ears. "I don't need the play by play about your masturbation techniques."

A beam of light floods into Porter's as the door opens. Dessa lifts her head while Lach and I twist in our seats. Chad strolls in. The hood of his black zippered hoodie is pulled over his bowed head and his hands are shoved in the pockets. He strides past without an ounce of acknowledgment. We turn to follow his movements until he disappears down the hallway.

Lach leans in so only we can hear. "Who wears a hoodie when it's almost seventy degrees outside?"

"I'm sweating just looking at him." Dessa fans herself with her hand.

"Well now that Chad's here, I'm out. I'll see you two tomorrow." I rise to my feet. "Don't forget the delivery." I clasp Lach's shoulder.

"Got it," he responds.

I tuck my wallet under my arm, then I'm out the door. The bright sun instantly warms my face as I stroll through the parking lot. As I approach my SUV, my stomach quivers. Glancing down, my front driver's side tire is sitting flat on the pavement. Shit. I unlock my SUV and toss my wallet on the seat. I round to the rear and lift the hatch. After digging around, I pull out the jack, and set it on the ground next to the flat. Then I heave the spare tire out and roll it toward the front of my SUV. The faint sound of my phone buzzing from inside my vehicle catches my attention. I pull open the door and dig it out of my wallet. A message from Trey flashes on the screen.

> **TREY**
> Hey, what are you doing? You left me hanging, so now I have to assume you're lying in your bed touching yourself while you're thinking of me.

> **RYLEE**
> I wish that was the case, but no. I'm in the Porter's parking lot attempting to change a flat tire.

> **TREY**
> Give me five minutes and I'll be right there.

> **RYLEE**
> You don't need to come. I got this.

> **TREY**
> Have you ever changed a flat tire?

> **RYLEE**
> No actually. I've watched others do it a few times, so I understand the concept.

> **TREY**
> I'll be right there.

I tuck my phone into my back pocket. Resting my hands on my hips, I stare down at the flat and blow out a deep breath. I kneel and position the jack on the metal frame. With the vehicle still on the ground, I shove the lug wrench onto the lug nut and twist. It doesn't budge an inch. I wipe the sweat from my brow and try again. Using all my energy, I push down on the wrench and nothing.

Tires rolling on the blacktop draws my attention. Trey's SUV comes into view and parks next to me. He hops out and does a quick inspection of what I've done so far.

"That's pretty good. You got everything in the right position."

"The lug nuts are a little tighter than what I was expecting. I'll have to hit the gym and work on lifting weights. These noodlely arms don't quite cut it." I hold up my arm and flex my bicep.

"You got some muscle there." He squeezes my tiny bicep.

"Probably from lifting boxes of beer."

"It's still sexy." He winks before squatting down to remove the lug nuts.

In a different life, Trey would be everything I'd want in a man. Bold. Confident. Assertive. Cocky, but in a playful non-asshole way once you get to know him. The last one is the one that always gets me in trouble, and that's not what I need right now. That's not what Abby needs. It reminds me of a sign that hung on the wall in my middle school history class. "Those who forget the past are condemned to repeat it." I've made the mistake once. I don't want to do it again.

Trey finishes removing the flat tire and swaps it with the spare. He inspects the old tire, searching the tread for a nail. I'm right beside him, searching as well. Then he freezes.

"I don't think they'll be able to patch this one."

"Why? What's wrong?" My brows furrow.

"It looks like something slashed your side wall." He runs his finger over the gash on the inside of the tire.

"Damn," I mutter to myself as I mentally calculate

how much a new tire will cost. But it's not just one tire. At the very least, I'll need two, so it's even.

"Did you run anything over while you were driving?"

"Not that I can recall."

"We'll buy you a new tire." He rolls the flat tire to the rear of my SUV while I grab the jack and wrench. "I'll follow you to the tire shop. There's a place on Maple that's reasonable."

"Okay." He gives me the address and I type it into my phone's GPS.

Three stop lights and a right turn later, I'm pulling into the parking lot of the tire shop. At the counter, I glance down at the rectangular patch on his dark blue work shirt and read his name. *Clint.* I tell him about the flat tire and needing a new one, but I'll buy two if I have to, but use the least expensive brand. After typing on the computer, he informs me it will be about an hour, and I can wait in the waiting area.

"Shit." I plop down in one of the chairs. "I'll have to ask Marcie if she can wait for Abby for me." I pull out my phone and send her a quick text.

Trey takes the seat next to me. "So, is this considered another date?"

"At the tire shop?"

"Sure. They have food and beverages." He jumps to his feet. "What would you like? Chocolate chip cookie? Blueberry scone?"

"Chocolate chip cookie, please."

"Coffee? Water?"

"Water."

Trey collects two bottles of water in one hand and two cookies in the other. Before sitting down, he passes me one of each.

"A meal and a conversation. This is totally a date."

I shake my head. It's almost impossible to argue with his logic. "If you say so." I sink my teeth into the soft cookie, the chocolate melting on my tongue. At least, one thing has gone right today. This cookie is delicious.

Trey's knee brushes against my crossed leg. "So I was thinking. Um. I would like to meet your daughter."

When he's finished, he spares a glance at me as if he's a little timid in asking me, which is the completely opposite of the Trey I'm used to.

"You would?"

"Yeah." He shrugs a shoulder. "She's your entire world and I want to be a part of it, too."

I'm torn. On one hand, I enjoy my time with Trey. He's so sweet and makes me laugh, but this isn't what I've been looking for. Then there's Abby. I haven't introduced her to anyone I've dated. But we're not dating. "It's a big step. Weird step. She's never met anyone I've been…"

"Friends with?"

A humorless laugh escapes me. "Something like that. Can I think about it?"

The corner of his lips tip up into a small smile. "Of course." He jumps to his feet and holds out his hand for my crumpled napkin.

My phone buzzes and I pull it out of my pocket. Marcie lets me know she'll wait for Abby at the bus stop. When Trey hasn't returned, I glance up, and he's talking to Clint behind the counter. Trey glances my way and flashes me his sexy dimpled smirk. A couple of minutes later, he returns to his seat.

"What was that about?" I ask.

"I wanted to make sure he got the correct tires."

My brows pinch together. Why would he ask the tire guy about the right tires to use? It doesn't make sense. But it's Trey. He does a lot of things that only make sense to

Trey. I brush off the thought. Instead, I mentally plan what I can do to save to pay for the new tires.

When my SUV is done, Clint calls me to the counter. He passes me an envelope of paperwork along with my keys. "You're all set."

"What do I owe you?"

"Nothing."

My gaze twists to Trey, and he flashes me a half-smile. Shock settles in that Trey had something to do with the paid in full receipt.

Clint adds, "It's all paid for. There's also paperwork in there for an extended warranty on all four tires. If you ever drive over a nail or if a tire needs to be replaced for whatever reason, it's covered."

"Wait. All four?"

"Yes. All four have been replaced."

"Thank you," I sputter out. Still in disbelief. I grab my keys and paperwork and spin around. Trey's waiting for me by the front door, hands in his pockets, acting coy. As I approach, he pushes the door open for me.

"You didn't have to do that," I say as I walk past and out to the parking lot.

"It's a date and I always pay for my dates."

I spin around, walking backwards. "This wasn't a date. I can't have you buying me tires. Or anything. You shouldn't even be buying me a table."

Trey grabs my hand, halting my progress. "I did it because I wanted to. And when I asked if this was a date, you told me if I say so and I'm saying so." He shrugs. "Plus, your old tires were shit. I didn't want to find out you were in a car accident because you blew a tire or lost traction." He tugs me closer so we're chest to chest. His thumb brushes over my cheek sending a flutter to erupt in my belly. "Just say thank you. And if you want, you can pay me back in orgasms." He smirks.

I bark out a laugh. "I'm not prostituting myself for tires."

He rests his forehead against mine, dark steely gray eyes with swirling flecks of silver meet mine. "But is it prostituting if I'm giving you the orgasms? Because that's equally enjoyable."

I'm unable to hold back my smile. It's like a permanent fixture whenever he's nearby. "Thank you."

Trey always distracts me from any problem I'm having. He spins it around and lightens the mood. He makes it easy to forget how many obstacles I face on a daily basis. I guess, to me, it's just life. I don't know how to handle anything else. He's thrown my world completely off its axis. I've spent so many years doing everything myself, it's hard to accept help. I lift my gaze, and his eyes are soft and sincere. He's doing this because he wants to. Because he cares. But it's hard to convince myself of that. I tamper down those feelings because I know he won't have it any other way. Brick by brick he's managing to tear down my carefully constructed wall, and it's terrifying because at the end he'll be gone, and I'll be left in the rubble. Alone. Again.

# Chapter 17

## KHAKIS DON'T GET YOU LAID

*Trey*

The gash in her tire didn't look like it was caused by debris on the road—it appeared intentional. Sure, it's a possibility something from the road caused it, but my gut says otherwise. I contemplate if I should say anything to Rylee or not, since I don't have proof. I don't want to cause any extra stress in case I'm wrong. She doesn't have any enemies. None that I know of, anyway.

While changing her tire, I inspected the others and all of them had almost no tread. Since we were going to the tire shop, I was buying her four new tires. The ones she had were beyond unsafe. They were approaching dangerous, and I want to make sure she and Abby are safe. No way was I going to have it on my conscience if something were to happen when I could prevent it. She'd never take my offer, so calling it a date was my excuse. She can be mad at me, but I wasn't taking no for an answer. Not on this. But I knew deep down, she wouldn't be mad at me.

I didn't know what she would say when I asked to meet her daughter. It's a big step, like meeting the parents, but I want to be involved in every facet of her life. I can understand her hesitancy, so maybe I can twist it so it's less like a date and more like two friends hanging out.

I close the fridge, screw off the top from my bottle of water, and swallow a gulp. Staring at me is a birthday invitation to Adventure Land. Sunday at three o'clock. This might be the perfect opportunity to meet Abby. I pull my phone from my pocket, find the correct number, and press call.

"Hey Seth. So, about the birthday party…"

"Oh yeah. Parisa wants me to ask you if you got the birthday present list for Maddox?"

"I did, and don't be surprised if I bought everything on the top half of the list."

"You don't have to do that."

"I know. It's just what I do." I tap my fingers on the counter. "But also, I wanted to ask, is there an option for a plus one. Technically plus two for the party?"

"What do you mean?"

"I want to invite Rylee and her daughter. If that's cool?"

"Yeah man, that's cool. We have plenty of food, probably too much. She'll just need a ticket, though."

"I got it covered. Thanks. I'll see you on Sunday."

I hit end. One problem solved. Now on to the next, though I suspect this one will take a little more convincing. If anything, I'm up for the challenge. I pull up my messages and type on the screen.

> **TREY**
>
> Good morning gorgeous. What are you wearing right now?

It's 7 a.m. and I know Rylee hasn't gotten up yet, so I'm hoping she's wearing some skimpy pajamas that I can picture for the rest of my day.

> **MILES**
>
> Khakis and a navy blue polo. Beautiful.

> **TREY**
>
> Shit. Sorry wrong chat.

> **MILES**
>
> I figured. At least it's better than the unsolicited dick pic you sent me last week. The added caption didn't help either. *shivers*

> **TREY**
>
> Yeah, sorry about that too. I need to be more careful who I send messages to.

> **MILES**
>
> It's just burned in my brain now, so thanks for that.

> **TREY**
>
> It was a good picture.

> **MILES**
>
> Not for me.

> **MILES**
>
> Are we still meeting at that house on Green to shoot some video?

When I found out Miles is a contract drone pilot, I convinced the Blue Stone Group to hire him to give us an edge on the real estate market by offering a first-person walkthrough before arranging an appointment. It's something that's been paying off.

> **TREY**
> Yeah. I'll be there at 2.

> **MILES**
> Perfect, see you then.

> **TREY**
> Also, you should really invest in something besides khakis.

> **MILES**
> What's wrong with khakis?

> **TREY**
> Khakis don't get you laid.

> **MILES**
> Says who?

> **TREY**
> Everyone.

To avoid another wrong message snafu, I find Rylee's number and press call. It rings a few times before she answers.

"Hey gorgeous. What are you doing?"

"Lying in bed, enjoying what little peace and quiet I can before tonight."

"I heard about the big draft party happening at Porter's tonight."

"Too many people fighting over real people to create a fake team sorta. I don't get it. Anyway, did you call for small talk?"

"While I love listening to your voice, my phone call does serve a purpose. Would you and Abby be interested in coming to a five-year-old's birthday party on Sunday? It's for Seth and Parisa's son. It's at the new adventure park in town. I thought maybe Abby would like to go. I remember you telling me that's your day off."

"Oh, wow... Um."

Rustling sounds through the speaker as if she's digging around for something. Her wallet, perhaps.

"I don't know. Abby is already doing this school trip that costs a lot of money."

"The ticket is already paid for, if that's your concern," I spit out. "Another kid had to cancel, so the ticket's going to waste otherwise." I pinch my eyes closed. I hate lying to Rylee, but also, I don't want her to turn it down because she's worried about money. Plus, this is the perfect opportunity to spend time with Rylee and meet her daughter. So, my intentions may be a little selfish, but it's also coming from a good place.

"I'd hate for it to go to waste." Silence fills the phone and I'm worried the call may have gotten disconnected. "Abby would love to go. Thank you. She's going to be so excited."

"Great! I'll pick you two up on Sunday at two thirty."

"H-how about I meet you there?" Hesitancy laces her voice.

A pang of hurt floats through my body. I was hoping to have even a few extra minutes to spend with her.

"Yeah, that's fine. Three o'clock. I'll see you then."

The moment she was hesitant to come, I knew it was a money issue. But I didn't want that to stop them, not only for Abby, because what kid wouldn't want to go to an adventure park, but because Rylee's a strong woman who works hard for everything and it's clear she doesn't want to be seen as needing a handout. But I'd give her everything if she'd let me.

# Chapter 18

## DESPERATE FOR YOU

# Rylee

It was a bad idea telling Trey I would meet him here. If he'd picked us up, I wouldn't have to walk in alone. Instead, I'm sitting in the parking lot in front of an enormous steel building with a colorful Adventure Land sign attached to the side, working up the courage to go inside. While I've had conversations with most of Trey's friends at Porter's, and even offered a few of the guys dating advice, I've never talked to them outside of my work. That's the plus side of not dating. No awkward meet the family or in this case, meet the friends.

Abby's foot presses against the passenger seat. "Mooom. Let's go in," she whines.

I guess we can't stay in the parking lot forever. I twist

around and glance at her. "Do you remember what I told you?"

"Yes. Be nice and listen to the adults."

I smile. Now I wish someone would give me rules, so I know what to do. I push open my door as Abby unbuckles herself from her car seat. When I open the rear passenger door, she jumps out. We walk hand in hand across the parking lot. As I pull open the door, laughter and gleeful screams echo amidst the vibrant colors of the intricate maze of inflatable obstacles, trampolines, and climbing structures. It looks ten times larger on the inside than from the outside. Not even ten seconds after walking in, Trey spots us and immediately rushes over as if he was waiting for us.

"Hi." He flashes me a warm smile that settles my nerves. A little.

"Hi." I glance down. "This is Abby. Abby, this is my—Trey." I'm still not one hundred percent on how I should introduce him to her.

Trey kneels, so he's eye level with my daughter. "Hi Abby. It's nice to meet you. Have you ever been to the adventure park?"

"No." She shakes her head. Her confidence is much higher than mine. At least one of us has our shit together.

"Well, you're going to have a blast. Let me show you and your mom around."

"Okay." An eager grin takes over her face.

Trey plays tour guide as he shows us around the adventure park, pointing out all the cool and fun things to play on. I trail behind as the two of them talk animatedly about the foam ball pit. After the tour, Trey waits for Abby as she removes her shoes and replaces them with the special park socks. After a quick introduction to all the other kids, they all scamper off toward the ball pit.

Butterflies erupt in my belly at Trey's kindness, thoughtfulness, and patience with Abby. And with me. Every day he's proving my preconception about him wrong which makes it so hard to not go all in.

Trey turns around and a slow grin spreads across his face. He stalks toward me, and I hold my breath, waiting for him to catch me. All the surrounding noise dissipates, and the only thing I can hear is the steady thumping of my heart.

When we're toe to toe, he leans down so only I can hear. "I never got to tell you how beautiful you look today."

Heat spreads up my neck and to my cheeks.

"Also, I'm really glad you and Abby could make it."

I love that Trey included Abby. "Me too. It looks like Abby has already made some new friends." Both of us glance at the ball pit where the kids are throwing balls at each other and giggling.

"Let me officially introduce you to everyone." He reaches for my hand and intertwines our fingers.

The gesture is sweet, but I'm sure it will lead to everyone developing the wrong impression of us.

"Ladies," Trey interrupts the table, "you all know Rylee."

"Yes. Come sit." Parisa scoots over and pats the empty bench seat next to her. "Trey, the guys might need your help." She points past us.

We spin around and Seth, Bennett, and Van are being swarmed by all the kids and foam balls.

"I'm needed. These ladies will take care of you." He presses a chaste kiss to my forehead, then takes off toward the ball pit.

I stroll to the opposite side of the rectangular table and take the seat next to Parisa. Hollyn is on the other side of Parisa while Olivia and Charlie are across from us.

My gaze wanders to the ball pit where Trey is fending off balls from Abby and Maddox. Even from across the room, I can see how big her smile is.

Parisa nudges me with her elbow. "So, you and Trey, huh?"

"Oh. Yeah." I glance at her. "We're friends."

"If I'm being honest, with how many years I've known Trey, he's never brought a friend to any birthday parties or parties or get-togethers we've had. You're the first," Parisa adds.

"You popped his plus one cherry," Olivia says, and the table erupts with laughter.

"Trey and cherry don't go together," Charlie adds.

"Oh. I don't know what to say." I nervously roll my lips between my teeth.

"If I had to guess, he might like you as more than just a friend," Parisa says.

"I have to agree with Parisa." Olivia perches her elbows on the table. "Also, before you hear it from anyone else, Trey and I kissed. Once." She holds up a finger. "We wanted to see if there were any feelings there and, rest assured, there's absolutely zero feelings. None. Nada." Her long blonde hair falls over her shoulder as she tilts her head. "Actually, it was like kissing my brother. And I'm engaged to his brother. Funny how things work."

I nod. I wasn't expecting this. Olivia is gorgeous, so I can see why there would be an attraction between them. Trey has a past that I have no control over.

"Anyway, I just want to put that out there. I know Trey. He's never acted like this with anyone. Ever. As much as he may seem like a playboy, he's the most loyal guy you'll ever find." Olivia rests her forearms on the table and leans in. "I'd bet my relationship that he's in love with you."

*In love with you.* My entire body freezes. Love is the last thing on my list, especially with someone like Trey. Thoughts of him as more than a friend pecks at my brain. I don't know what I want. Labeling him as a friend is easier to deal with. There's less hurt that way. I know eventually there will be an end. Needing to change the subject, I turn to Parisa. "By the way, thank you so much for offering the extra ticket to Abby. She's having the best time."

Parisa's eyebrows draw together. "What are you talking about? Extra ticket?"

My heart thunders in my chest. My gaze flits around the table. "Trey said you had an extra ticket because someone canceled..." My words trail off at the end.

Her eyes soften. "I don't want to be rude, but there wasn't an extra ticket."

If there wasn't an extra ticket, but one magically appeared... I glance over at Trey, who is now swimming through the balls like a shark pretending to eat Abby and Maddox. I hate Trey lied to me. That he bought the ticket assuming I didn't have the money to pay for a ticket even though it's true, I don't, but it's still the fact that he lied. Abby's screams and giggles draw my attention to the ball pit. With the sheer happiness on her face, it's hard to be mad at him for giving her that. Ugh. Why does this have to be so complicated?

After I tucked away the information about Trey paying for the ticket, that's a conversation for later, I had the best time hanging out with the girls and laughing at all the stories they had about the guys. I even shared the one about needing a new table. Charlie said it now made sense why Bennett told her they now needed to have sex on their table, claiming quality control.

By the end of the party, all the kids are wiped out, including Abby. She's curled up on the bench, using my leg as a pillow.

"I think it's time for us to leave. Abby seems to be in a pizza and ball pit coma."

"I'll walk you out." Trey jumps up from his seat.

I slide away while struggling to lift Abby's dead weight. A soft groan escapes her, but she never fully awakens.

"I'll help you." Effortlessly, Trey lifts Abby and cradles her against his chest.

"Thanks."

I say my goodbyes to everyone, as Trey does the same. Outside at my SUV, Trey deposits Abby in the backseat, buckles her in, and softly closes the door.

"Thanks for inviting us. Abby had so much fun." A gust of wind blows a strand of hair over my forehead, and I tuck it behind my ear before crossing my arms over my chest.

"I'm glad you two came." He takes a step closer. "Abby's a great kid. And spending time with you is always my favorite part of the day."

I meet his gaze, wanting the truth. "There wasn't an extra ticket, was there? You paid for it." Indignation laces my tone.

Trey rubs the back of his neck.

"Look, I'm not mad. With how much fun Abby had, I can't be mad." I meet his gaze. "But next time, tell me the truth. All I want is honesty."

Trey nods. "I didn't want Abby to miss out. Plus, I wanted to be a little selfish and spend more time with you."

When he says things like that, I can't even be a little mad. He has gone above and beyond what any other guy has done to spend time with me and Abby. Her own father has never shown such dedication in order to spend time with his daughter. Instead, he only calls to cancel, but Trey, whom I've only spent a few months with, is willing to go to great lengths for only a few hours with us.

I close the gap between us, rise on my tippy toes, and press my lips to his. It's short and sweet and if we weren't in public, I'd be tempted to do more. "Thank you."

"So perhaps we can do this again. Maybe replace the adventure park with dinner."

"Perhaps. We'll talk later." I stroll past Trey before I round the hood. His voice stops me.

"Just so you know, I'm going to text you tonight. I'm done waiting the three days to not appear desperate. If you haven't guessed it already, I'm desperate for you."

Warmth radiates through my entire body, settling in my cheeks. I flash him a small smile and he returns it with a sexy smirk of his own. It's a look that will remain with me for the rest of the night. Especially, when I'm lying in bed, needing a visual while I practice some self-love.

# Chapter 19

## EXCLUSIVE FRIENDS WITH BENEFITS

# Rylee

After the adventure park, Trey kept his promise and called me. We spent over an hour talking on the phone until I was practically snoring in his ear. I swear he has some sort of voodoo love doll made of me because it's hard to not spend all my time thinking about him. He turns my insides to goo like a teenager with a crush. Instead of doing work, all I want to do is doodle his name surrounded by hearts in my notebook.

Since I switched my Tuesday shift with Nora, I message Dessa to meet me at my favorite breakfast café. It's the only place in town where you can order a short stack with a side of bacon for under seven dollars. While I wait for Dessa to arrive, I scroll through my social media feed. A post about The Blue Stone Group's latest expansion project flashes by and I pause. Instantly, all my thoughts flood to Trey. He can come over tonight and I'll cook dinner. Afterward, we can watch a movie or play a game with Abby. I pull up our messages.

> **RYLEE**
> Want to come over for dinner tonight? I switched shifts so I'm free.

The three dots start, then stop.

> **TREY**
> I can't tonight. I already have dinner plans.

My heart plummets to the floor. Of course, the one time I initiate the plans, he's busy.

> **RYLEE**
> Okay. No worries. Maybe some other time.

> **TREY**
> Definitely. We'll talk later.

I drop my phone to the laminate wood tabletop. I got my hopes up for nothing.

"Why such the long face?" Dessa sets her purse on the bench and scoots into the booth.

"It's nothing."

"You look like someone ate the last of the pancakes." Both her palms splay out on the table. "Wait? Are they out of pancakes?"

"No. There are pancakes. I've already placed our orders."

"Oh. Good." She dramatically pretends to wipe her forehead. "If it's not the pancakes, what is it?"

I exhale a sigh. "I invited Trey to come over for dinner, but he said he already has plans."

"What is he doing?"

"I don't know. I didn't ask."

"Why don't you ask?" She twirls a dark strand of hair around her finger.

"It's kind of intrusive to pry into his life. If he wanted me to know, he would tell me." I spin the spoon around in my coffee. "He's probably hanging out with the guys or doing a business dinner or something." I glance up at her. "But wouldn't he tell me if that was the case?"

"You put yourself in everyone else's business. Now it's time to do it for your own." She shrugs.

"Not true." I point my spoon at her. "They always come to me for advice, and I tell them how it is."

"Maybe you should take your own advice. You clearly labeled him as just a friend. If he was a boyfriend, then maybe, but as a friend, not really. Unless your feelings run deeper than only a friendship." She quirks an eyebrow at me.

"This is exactly what Kyle would do. Tell me he was having late night meetings when he was actually having himself a late night snack with other women."

"Well, then there's only one thing you can do. See where he's going." She leans against the green vinyl and crosses her arms over her chest.

"Like follow him?"

"Yeah. Why not." She shrugs. "Then you'll know for sure what he's up to. Let me ask you this." She leans forward, resting her chin on her clasped hands. "What would Rylee advise herself to do?"

The server sets plates of buttery pancakes and sizzling bacon in the middle of our table. While Dessa dives in fork first, I toss around the following Trey idea round in my head. It would give me my answer. He'd be none the wiser, as long as I don't get caught. This is dumb. I hate this. I hate that I question something I shouldn't. This is all Kyle's fault.

I slinked down in the seat of my vehicle that's sandwiched between a truck with massive tires and a four-door sedan on the street outside the parking garage of The Blue Stone Group. This isn't the type of advice I'd give to others, so what am I doing? Only going against everything I tell others to do. My excuse... Trey's turning all my rational thinking to mush. I texted Marcie earlier asking if she could pick up Abby at the bus stop and watch her for a few hours. Since she can't let it be what it is, I had to go into a long-winded spiel about my stakeout mission. She said since it's for the good of my vagina, she'll allow it.

When his black SUV comes into view, he turns left, driving away from me. A couple of cars pass before I pull out. I maintain a safe distance but keep him in my sights. Chalk this up as my first low speed pursuit. My sweaty palms slip on the steering wheel as I follow him through a residential area of town. He turns right and my brows knit together. There's only one building down this road.

A large Whispering Pines Assisted Living sign sits on the corner of the road leading to the parking lot. Trey parks near the front entrance while I find a spot farther away. Squinting, I watch him through the glass doors as he enters and talks to the receptionist. Shit. I need to keep a pair of binoculars in my car. I shift to the left for a better angle, but he's gone. Shit. I spin to peer over my other shoulder, and I catch sight of his black jacket headed toward a hallway. Is he visiting someone? What if it's a nurse he's screwing behind my back? Dammit. I jump out of my vehicle and beeline it to the front doors. Behind the desk sits an older woman with salt and pepper hair with a white tag that reads *Loraine*, pinned to her cardigan.

"Hi. How can I help you?" Her voice is soft and smooth like whipped butter.

"I'm here with Trey. Trey Wilson. He just came in here." I point in the direction that I saw him disappear.

"Oh, yes." She tilts her head. "But he didn't mention bringing a helper."

Helper? What the hell does he need help with?

"I just need you to sign in and I'll get you a badge. He's usually in the main dining hall, but sometimes he wanders off."

After she slides a badge across the counter and directs me toward a hallway. I thank her and turn on my heel. My heart pounds in sync with each step. The farther down the hall I get, the more the static in my head increases, drowning out all the other noises around me. I'm on autopilot, preparing for the worst. To see him cuddled up with a nurse. Her head thrown back, giggling at some stupid joke he made. Because that's what he does. Makes stupid jokes. When I reach the opening to the dining room, it's worse than I imagined. I'm an idiot.

Standing in front of the large room behind a table is Trey. He's without the suit jacket and tie but kept the button up and has the sleeves rolled up. His forearm flexes as he spins the bingo carriage until a ball drops out. His deep voice sounds through the microphone. "Bee nine. I have a bee nine." He turns around, his slacks are molded to his perfectly formed ass as he checks off the number on the white board. That explains why the front row is nothing but women.

"Bingo!" an older woman yells from in front of me.

"Doris. You've called bingo for the past two rounds,

and I've only called three numbers. Are you sure you have a bingo?" Trey spins around and immediately our gazes connect. "Rylee?" My name echoes through the dining hall.

Shit. Fuck. I spin around, my hair whirls around me, smacking me in the face as I speed walk down the hallway.

"I'll be right back, folks." There's a muffled bang as the microphone hits the table. "Rylee wait up!" Trey's voice is louder this time, along with his footsteps. "Rylee! Donald! Stop the brunette in the pink shirt coming your way!"

An older man with brown tweed pants jackknifes his wheelchair right in front of me. In that moment, I have two seconds to decide to either hurdle him like a gold medalist or stop. Since I'm not wearing my hurdling pants, I choose the latter.

"Thanks Donald. I didn't want this one getting away." Trey clasps the older man on the shoulder, taking a second to catch his breath. "Next week, I'll give you an extra bingo card."

Donald gives him the thumbs up and continues rolling his way down the hallway.

Trey spins me around to face him. Leather and spice invade my senses and I do everything to not melt into a puddle from embarrassment.

"What are you doing here?"

"Oh. Um. Uh." Words are failing me right now. The puddle may be the better option.

"How did you know I was here?" A smile flirts on his lips. "Did you follow me?"

My shoulders slump, and I blow out a breath. No sense in lying. The running away gave that one away. "Yes."

"Yesss…" His eyebrows raise in question as he waits for me to say more.

"I followed you here."

Two nurses swerve around us, and Trey grabs my hand and leads me to a quiet visiting area by the reception desk. He directs me to take a seat on the blue floral couch. The cushion depresses as he sits next to me.

"Follow up question. Why'd you follow me?"

"Dessa got in my head that maybe your dinner plans were maybe with another woman."

"So, it was Dessa's fault?"

"Ugh. Fine. It was mine. You should really be a cop." I pick at the sparkly nail polish on my fingers. "The first time I asked you to hang out and you shoot me down. I didn't know what else to think."

His lips swoop to one side.

"Dumb." I bury my head in my hands, not wanting him to see my embarrassment. "I know."

He grips my wrists, pulling my hands away. "No. It's not that. You know you could have asked me instead of playing double oh seven."

I huff out a humorless laugh. "Clearly, that would have been much easier."

"Just to ease your mind. There are no other women, except Helen, in the front row. You might have to fight her for my attention."

I move away from him, but he grabs my hand.

"Seriously, there's no one else."

I brush my fingers over his knuckles, staring at the lines on his skin, working up the courage to ask one more question. "Would you call us exclusive friends, then?"

He laughs. "Sure. If that's what you want to label it." He lifts our hands and places a kiss on the inside of my wrist.

"I'm sorry I followed you. It's just... I'm an idiot. Anyway, I should leave. Marcie's watching Abby for me, and I hate to make it longer than needed." I jump to my feet.

He follows my lead. "Why don't you stay? What's an hour? You can help with the board. I suspect the first row likes to check me out each time I put a number up. I think it's causing them to lose their concentration."

"Well, it is a nice view." A smile spreads across my lips as I peer around him for a peek at his delicious backside.

"Hey now." He playfully swats my hand away. "That's only for bingo players. Or for bingo caller helpers."

"Then I better message Marcie."

After I send a quick text to Marcie, letting her know I'll be an hour late, she replies with a slew of Get It Girl GIFs.

I had so much fun calling bingo with Trey. He would call the numbers and I would do my best Vanna White impression while filling in the board. His whole demeanor is infectious. He had the entire room buzzing with energy. Now, I'm sitting on the couch with Abby, curled up with her princess blanket, watching a movie when my phone buzzes. Dessa's name pops up with a message.

DESSA

> What happened with Trey. Did you catch him?

I press my lips together, fighting my smile.

RYLEE

> I did.

DESSA

> Was he with another woman?

RYLEE

> He was.

RYLEE

> In fact, he was with several.

**DESSA**

That piece of shit. I'll get my baseball bat.

**RYLEE**

Men too.

**DESSA**

What the fuck?

**DESSA**

Okay, you lost me there. Was it some sort of sex group orgy?

**RYLEE**

No! 😆 But I'm kind of concerned that's where your mind first went to.

**DESSA**

🙍

**RYLEE**

He went to Whispering Pines Assisted Living to call bingo.

**DESSA**

Awww that's so sweet. So, a bingo orgy.

**RYLEE**

Not really. More bingo, less orgy. But it doesn't change the fact I'm a complete dumbass. I was so embarrassed. But the good news is we're exclusive friends.

**DESSA**

Yay! *hip thrusting GIF*

# Chapter 20

## PAPER RINGS

*Trey*

I unload containers of Chicken Tikka Marsala, Tandoori Chicken, and Samosas on the counter. After Rylee's bingo stunt, I knew her feelings for me run deeper than she wants to admit. I've waited over thirty years to find the perfect woman, I can wait a little longer. That also won't stop me from wooing the hell of her at every opportunity. Tonight that includes me bringing over dinner.

"This smells delicious." Rylee strolls up from behind me and presses a kiss to my cheek.

I wrap my arm around her waist, hauling her to me before she can get away. "You smell even better." I nuzzle my nose right below her ear and press my lips to her neck savoring her sweet vanilla scent.

She tilts her head, giving me better access. "Mmm. As

much as I want you to continue with the kisses, Abby's in the other room."

I give her another quick kiss and break a part.

Abby races down the hallway and into the kitchen. "Trey!"

"Abby!" I bend down on one knee. We slap hands together and then wiggle our fingers.

Rylee's gaze flits from me to Abby, an amused grin on her face. "What was that?"

"Our secret handshake," I say.

"Yeah! Our secret handshake!" Abby repeats.

"Now, I feel left out that I don't get a secret handshake." She teasingly juts out her bottom lip.

Rising to my feet, I lean in next to her ear. I lower my voice to a hushed tone, ensuring that only she can hear. "I'll give you something to shake later." I wink.

She gently pushes me away and softly laughs. "Abby, go wash your hands for dinner."

Abby scampers through the kitchen and the faucet in the bathroom turns on. Rylee's phone buzzes on the counter. Her eyebrows pinch together as she stares at the screen.

"It's work. Let me see what it is."

I nod.

She answers the phone. All I hear is "yeah" and "okay". There's a moment of silence before she ends the call and tucks her phone in her pocket. "That was Dessa. Chad didn't show up to work, and she's swamped. Jake is on his way, but it will be a couple of hours before he can get there. I have to go help her. I hate to ask this, but can you watch Abby?"

"Oh. Um. Yeah. Sure." Sweat dampens my palms. Sure, I've hung out with my friends' kids, but there were always other adults around to supervise me. I've never had to be responsible for keeping one alive by myself. Growing up, I had a younger brother and sister, but by the time they were six, I was sixteen and I never had to watch them.

"Thank you so much. It should just be a couple of hours. You have both my cell and the bar number if there's a problem. Marcie is next door as well." She scrambles to collect her wallet and keys. "Abby! Come here, please!"

Abby races into the kitchen at the only speed she knows, fast.

"I have to go to work for a little bit. So, Trey is going to stay here with you, Okay?"

"Okay," Abby says.

"There's dinner on the counter." Rylee points to the bag of food. "All the emergency phone numbers are on the fridge if anything were to happen. Okay?"

I nod along even though she's speaking to Abby.

"Got it," Abby and I say at the same time.

"I have to go." Rylee leans over, pressing a kiss on Abby's forehead. "I love you."

She straightens to her full height and blurts out, "I love you." before her lips land on mine. We both freeze. Slowly, she pulls away. Her eyes are frantic as they shift over my face, wanting to read my reaction. "I'm sorry," she whispers.

I clear my throat. "Don't worry about it. Everyone drops a casual 'I love you' to me. The other day, the security guard at The Blue Stone Group held the door open for me. I thanked him and he told me he loved me. Another time I was ordering coffee at Roasters, the barista handed me my coffee and told me they loved me. I'm just a loveable guy." I shrug and give her a half-smile. As much as I want to believe that she meant those words, the horror on her face tells me otherwise.

The sharp lines on her face soften. "I'll be back later."

"Mommy?"

Rylee glances down and Abby's holding out her hand in the shape of a half heart. "Right. Sorry." She bends down and completes the heart with her hand. "I love you always."

"I love you forever." Abby beams at her.

A wave of warmth washes over me from their goodbye. It's like the video I watched where a couple took in a stray cat and then, a week later, the cat carried her kittens into the house one by one. That's the kind of shit that would make anyone's eyes leak.

"Now I have to go. See you two later." The front door closes with a click.

"Alright kid, it's just you and me." We silently stare at each other, sizing each other up. She's six and could probably sit like this for hours. I, on the other hand, can't. I shift my gaze, losing the stare off. "Are you hungry?" I pull open a cupboard on the left, then the right, searching for plates.

Abby pulls out a stool next to the fridge and unfolds it until it clicks into place. She places it next to me and climbs up, pulling open a door and revealing a stack of plates.

"I was going to get there. Eventually."

She passes me two plates, and I set them on the counter.

"For your next magic trick, you pull out two forks." I wave my finger in a figure eight as if it's a magician's wand.

Abby throws her head back, cackling with laughter. "No! They're in the drawer." She pulls it open and holds up two forks.

"I'm telling you. It's magic."

I dish up two plates and set them side by side on the

small kitchen counter. Abby climbs up on the stool next to me and plops down.

"You know, I've never known a six-year-old who likes Indian food." I take a bite of the Tandoori Chicken.

"Mommy says I'm a food con dinosaur." She shoves a fork full of Chicken Tikka Masala and rice into her mouth.

My eyebrows knit together, trying to puzzle together what a food dinosaur could be. "Do you mean food connoisseur?"

She nods.

I shrug. "When I was your age, all I wanted to eat was cereal and chicken nuggets. I guess times have changed." I push my plate away and rest my elbows on the counter. Next to me, Abby barks out a giggle. "What's so funny?"

"You look like a squirrel." She giggles again.

"Why a squirrel? I don't sit like this?" I hold my arms in front of me, elbows bent, and let my hands dangle.

"You're doing it now!" She cackles with more laughter.

"Fine. If I'm a squirrel, then your chipmunk."

"I'm not a chipmunk." She bursts out laughing again.

"Yes. You are. Your cheeks are like this." I fill my cheeks with air as if I was a chipmunk hoarding acorns. "Alright, Chipmunk. Are you finished?" Her cheeks puff out and she nods. I chuckle. This kid is my new favorite.

I collect our plates and quickly wash them. Afterward, I close all the takeout containers and place them in the fridge. When I turn around, Abby's gone. Immediately, my gaze jerks to the front door. Still closed. Rustling and banging sounds come from down the hall followed by the patter of footsteps.

"Want to do crafts with me?" She holds out a box filled to the brim with paper, markers, and paints.

"Uh. Sure. What are we doing?"

She sets the box on the counter and climbs up to sit on

the stool. "I got all these different colored papers to make paper rings and necklaces." Within five seconds the entire countertop is littered with paper in every color imaginable.

I now understand how kids can make a mess in such a short period of time. "Okay. You'll have to teach me."

Abby spends the next hour and a half showing me how to fold the paper perfectly to create a ring. Then how to fold a zig zag to create a necklace or bracelet. By the end, we had a pile of different colored paper jewelry.

"You should give my mom one." Her big hazel eyes meet mine.

"Which one do you think she'd like?" I point to the pile of paper jewelry.

Her tongue peeks out from the corner of her mouth as she examines each paper item. "This one." She holds out a purple and green ring.

"A ring. Does your mom like rings?"

She nods. "She has a really pretty one in her jewelry box."

Shit. Does she still have her wedding ring? With how much dislike she has for Kyle, I can't imagine she's keeping it in hopes of reconnecting. What if it's someone else's? Like she has a collection of ex-husbands or ex-fiancés.

"Want to play a game?"

Abby's voice pulls me from my thoughts. "Sure, Chipmunk. What are we playing?"

Her eyes light up with her toothy grin. "Pretty Pretty Princess."

"Great! I've always wanted to be a princess."

# Chapter 21

## PRINCESS TREY

*Rylee*

When I return home, the apartment is dark, except for the soft glow of the television playing an animated princess movie. I drop my wallet on the counter and stroll into the living room. As I round the edge of the couch, Trey's lying down, eyes closed. I tip-toe down the hallway and peek my head inside Abby's room. She's star fished in the middle of her bed. I softly close the door and make my way back to the living room.

*I love you.* I can't believe I said that to him. I'm shocked there wasn't a Trey shaped hole in my front door after I said that. The only reasonable explanation is I was going through the motions after saying it to Abby. I don't love Trey. I can't love Trey. Shit. Do I love Trey? I shove the thought away. Instead, I take this quiet moment to study the man before me. His dark hair is a rumpled mess, with strands poking through the plastic tiara on his head while his long, dark eyelashes fan out against his cheeks. If our friendship started seven years ago, I wouldn't be as broken and maybe things between us would be different.

The cushion dips as I take a seat on the edge and smile. "Wake up, princess." I gently shake his shoulder until his eyes pop open. He stretches his arms over his head before meeting my gaze.

"What time is it?"

"A little after ten. I see you got conned into being a princess for the evening."

His brows furrow. I nod toward the pink plastic jeweled necklace around his neck. His fingers pat his chest until he finds the necklace and lifts it.

"Oh. Yeah."

"The crown is a nice touch, too." I giggle.

"I got hustled playing Pretty Pretty Princess. Your daughter ruthlessly kicked my ass, and she had no issues doing it."

"I always tell her to be proud of her work." I pick at a piece of invisible lint on the couch. "Your babysitting duties are over. Thank you for watching Abby."

Trey sits up and leans on his elbow. He removes the tiara, along with the necklaces, and sets them on the floor. "It was nothing. Abby's a great kid."

"But also…" I pick at my fingernail. Nerves hitting me like a semitruck barreling down the freeway. "With it being so late, if you don't want to drive home…"

He sits all the way up. His mouth inches from mine. "Are you asking me to have a sleepover?"

"Only if you want. So you don't have to drive home. But sleep is the only thing that can happen." I nod toward the hallway. "Abby."

There hasn't been a guy in my bed since Kyle. Sleepovers were off limits. Plus having a toddler who insisted on also sleeping in my bed made things a little more difficult. Dating in general was difficult with a toddler and on those rare occasions I did go out, I lost interest fairly quick, or the sex was mediocre at best, and there was no chance for a second date. With Trey it's different. Any other guy that I've kissed has never felt like this. It's an out of body experience with him, like my nerve endings are all firing at the same time. Even the first time I met Kyle, it never felt like this.

"A chance to spend a few more hours with you… I'll take it." He presses his lips to mine in a chaste kiss.

I grab his hand and lead him to my bedroom. Once inside, I close the door behind us. Trey strips out of his shirt and pants, and I fight every fiber of my being to not stare while he does it. Instead, I change into a long t-shirt that kisses the top of my thighs. When I turn around, Trey has the covers folded back and he's lying on the bed, his mountainous abs on full display.

"Shit," he groans. "You expect me to keep my hands to myself when you're wearing that next to me?"

"Yes. Have some self-control." I bite back a smile. Like I'm one to talk. With Trey next to me, I'm the one who'll need to execute some self-control. I twist the knob on the lamp, and it clicks off, shrouding the room in darkness. In a few short steps, I reach the side of the bed and crawl onto the mattress, pulling the blanket over me.

"I don't know if that's a word in my vocabulary, especially when you're involved." He wraps an arm around me, tugging me close to him, his face nuzzling the nape of my neck. "I'll execute this self-control that you speak. But next time, I can't make any promises."

After a couple of minutes, Trey rolls to his other side.

His hand grabs my wrist and tugs me so my arm is wrapped around his waist.

A ghost of a laugh escapes me. "You want to be little spoon?"

"Uh huh."

"Isn't that demasculinizing?"

"I'm comfortable with my masculinity. Plus, it feels nice."

I cuddle into his warm back, inhaling his signature scent that I love. "This is nice, and for once, I don't have to worry about a dick poking me in the ass."

"Don't worry. The night's still young."

A smile spreads over my lips as I drift off to sleep.

---

"I don't know why he keeps turning down my advances."

"Maybe he's dating someone."

"Trey Wilson doesn't date. Maybe I'll have to double my efforts. I have a meeting set up with him to show me some houses, but maybe I'll be the one doing the showing."

"Oh, you're so bad."

For the past ten minutes I've been eavesdropping on a conversation two women are having at a pub table at Porter's. My molars grind together every single time they mention his name. I hate this, especially after last night. Even though sometime throughout the night we swapped positions, and I did wake up with his dick poking me in the ass, it was sweet. But Kyle was sweet at one time, too. We're just friends with exclusive benefits. But how much does that actually mean? They're just a bunch of random words strung together to make it sound like something it isn't. He could still be poking other women in their ass.

I don't have the mental capacity to listen to women fawn over him, throw themselves at him, and blatantly flirt with him right in front of me. I shouldn't have let him stay over last night. This was all a big mistake, and I should never have gotten involved in the first place. I need to tell him it's over. This is exactly how things started with Kyle. The constant phone calls and late-night meetings, which I assumed were work related but was more like Kyle getting his dick worked.

"I can't do this with Trey anymore," I blurt out.

"Why?" Dessa asks.

"Because every day he has girls throwing themselves at him and flirting with him. There was a girl who did that on our date and she thought I was his sister. Who knows how many times it happens when I'm not around, or how many times he's going to say no until he finally gives in to the temptation."

"Not every guy is like Kyle."

"It's better if I cut my losses now before we're in too deep."

"If that's what you wanna do, but I think you have it completely wrong." Dessa pulls a bottle of beer from the cooler and passes it to a customer.

"He's too perfect. There must be something wrong with him. He's exactly like Kyle." I cross and uncross my arms as anxious energy flows through me.

"They are nothing alike. Kyle is his own special breed of asshole. Plus, that's like breaking up with a boyfriend but telling him you want to be friends. It doesn't work."

"But he was never my boyfriend."

"Or was he and you just labeled it as benefits?" Her hand grips her waist and raises a questioning eyebrow.

I blow out an exasperated breath. "Truth be told, I don't know. The red flags tell me he's just like Kyle."

"What red flags?"

"The constant phone calls. Not to mention the women who flock to him the instant he walks into a room."

Dessa leans against the edge of the bar and crosses her arms over her chest. "Your flags are bullshit. I don't think you're giving him a fair chance."

"I need to do what's right for me and right now I can't deal with all that," I motion my hand over the bar to where the two women are seated, "and sift through whatever feelings I may have. Abby is my number one priority and with that comes dealing with Kyle. I can't do all of it."

She leans in a narrowing her gaze at me. "You have a man who wants to take care of you, who wants to serve the entire world on a silver platter for you, and you keep shoving him away. Do you realize that there will come a time when he doesn't come back."

"He's not the right guy for me. He shouldn't make me feel like this." I blow out a breath.

"Happy? Because that's all I see." Dessa rests a hand on her waist and pops her hip.

"No. I mean, he does." I pause to collect my thoughts. "He makes me feel like I'm a different person. Like I'm doing things completely out of character. For one, I don't stalk guys at assisted living facilities because I have it in my head they're sucking face with a nurse. Second, I don't have sleepovers and introduce them to my daughter."

Dessa pulls out a couple of beers from the cooler, twists the caps off, and passes them to a customer. "He's pushing you outside your comfort zone. You do those things because you care. Genuinely care. That's why you're so upset right now."

I rest my forearms on the edge of the bar and slam my

head down. This isn't supposed to be my life. Simple. Uncomplicated. That's all I want. Not dwelling over my feelings. I lift my head. "I can't. I need to focus on Abby and creating a better life for her. After a few more years of saving, I'll be able to move us out of our crappy apartment. That's where my attention needs to be. Not on… Trey."

Dessa rolls her eyes. "You know you don't have to pick. You can have both. In fact, you deserve both."

Her words dance around in my head. As much as I want to believe them, it's never been like that for me. I never get both. It's always one or the other. When I have a daughter to think about, she'll always take priority. "But what happens when he leaves, and I'm forced to start all over again by myself with nothing?"

"You're the strongest woman I know. Whatever happens, you'll survive because that's what you do. The way I see it, you're not giving him a chance because it's easier to say no than facing your fears."

I hate that she's right. Also, I hate that I feel this way. Mostly, I hate that Kyle did this to me. "It's for the best."

"If that's your excuse." Dessa shrugs.

"It's not an excuse. It's my life." I pull out my phone and send a text message to Trey asking him to meet me at my house later to talk. It's time I put an end to all our benefits. After I hit send, I shove my phone into my pocket, and it immediately vibrates with an incoming message. I know it's from Trey, but I can't work up the courage to read it at the moment.

I busy myself with prepping the garnishes. As soon as I twist off the lid to the pickle jar, my stomach flips. Instantly, I freeze. After a couple of seconds, my stomach settles. I pull out a pickle from the jar, run the knife down its length, and I gag.

"Are these pickles bad or something?" I sniff the

opening of the jar. Bile jumps up my throat and I swallow it down.

Dessa peers over my shoulder and sniffs. "They smell fine to me. What's the expiration date on the jar say?" She spins the jar to find the printed date.

"When my sister was pregnant, she'd get nauseous from olives. Everything from how they smelled, how they looked. If they were anywhere near her, she'd gag. It was the strangest thing," Lach says nonchalantly while continuing to fill the toothpick holders.

My eyes widen to the size of the cardboard coasters as my heart jumps to my throat. When I was pregnant with Abby, the pungent vinegar smell from pickle juice would have me running to the nearest toilet.

"Rylee? Are you okay? You look a little flushed," Dessa asks.

I race past her, practically shoving her out of the way until I find the nearest garbage can. With both hands white knuckling the rim, I bend over and empty the contents of my stomach.

I rise and wipe my mouth with the back of my hand. "I think...I think I might be pregnant."

"With Trey's baby?" Dessa asks.

"Oh, shit's about to get real," Lach says at the same time.

I nod my head. How am I supposed to push him out of my life when we could be having a child together? Let alone having a child with someone who doesn't want kids. Bile creeps up my throat again and I shove my face back into the garbage can.

"Take the rest of the day off. We'll tell Jake you're under the weather. Which technically, with all the vomit, isn't a lie. Go buy yourself a pregnancy test to find out for sure." Dessa rubs small circles over my shoulder blades.

Standing to my full height, I wipe my mouth. "Yeah. I guess I should find out before I jump to conclusions." Even though I know my conclusions are right. If I thought shit was hard now, it's about to get ten times harder.

I lay out the three different pregnancy tests I picked up at the drugstore on my way home. Best two out of three should give me my answer. I twist off the cap to my water bottle and chug half of it. I have an hour before I need to pick up Abby from the bus stop and in less than five minutes, I'll know if my life is changing once again.

Reaching over, I grab the first stick, shove it between my legs, and do my thing. When I'm finished with the first one, I make quick work to pee the other two while my bladder is still full because I don't think I can chug another bottle of water.

Once I'm finished, I flush, wash my hands, and wait. They say a watched pot never boils, well in my case, a watched pregnancy test never changes. In two long strides, I'm on the other side of the cramped bathroom. I spin around and repeat the process to the other side, needing something to do to rid myself of this nervous energy. I stop in front of the sink and lift the hem of my shirt over my stomach. With the pad of my finger, I run it along one of the stretch marks on my belly from my pregnancy with Abby. It makes sense why my pants have been a little more snug than normal, but I thought maybe it was from all the dinners with Trey. I splay my hand over my belly. Am I ready to do everything again? I've always wanted more kids. I just wish it was under different circumstances.

My apartment is only two bedrooms so I guess the

baby will stay in my room for a while first and then he or she will have to share a room with Abby. But what am I going to do about work? Being a single mom and sole provider, I'll need to return to work as soon as possible. I know Jake will do whatever he can to work with whatever schedule I need. Whatever happens, I'll make it work. That's what I do. That's all I can do. But first I should find out If I'm actually pregnant before I conjure up an entire life plan.

With my eyes closed, I grip the edge of the vanity, needing something to keep me grounded in case I pass out. Slowly, I lift my eyelids. Staring back at me are three tests that all say the same thing. I blow out a slow breath before opening a drawer and sliding the tests inside.

I go next door to ask Marcie for a huge favor. Since she can't let it stay a huge favor, and I don't blame her, I give her a brief rundown of my current situation and how I need her to watch Abby for a couple hours while I talk to Trey. Luckily, she agrees.

I've paced my entire apartment about five times and only fifteen minutes have passed. I check my watch for the tenth time. Trey will be here any second now. My heart jumps out of my chest when a knock sounds on my door. I race to it and press my clammy palms against the cool wood and peer through the peephole. Trey's smiling face greets me on the other side.

I twist the knob and pull. When Trey's gaze meets mine, my stomach flip flops, all without the added help of pickle juice. I step to the side to give him enough room to pass through.

"I brought dinner. It's a taco pizza because I know it's your favorite."

At least it's not a bacon cheeseburger pizza like last time. It would be hard to explain the sudden urge to vomit.

Or maybe not. It would really get the point across. As he passes me, he drops a kiss on my forehead. The gesture is sweet, and more than what I deserve for the amount of heartbreak I'm about to deliver.

He sets the pizza on the counter. "Where's Abby?"

"She's with Marcie." I wring my hands together, avoiding eye contact. "I need to talk to you."

"Oh, shit," he mutters. "The expression on your face tells me it's not a let's talk about favorite sexual positions kind of talk."

I huff out a laugh. Even in moments like this he can make me laugh. "No. Not that kind of talk, but something else"

"So, what is it?" In two steps, he's standing in front of me. His hand running up and down my biceps in comfort. "Are you ending this exclusive friends with benefits?"

I shake my head. If he keeps going with all the possible worst-case scenarios, he'll eventually get there.

He lifts my chin, forcing my eyes to meet his. "Then what is it? Are you dying?"

I shake my head again, pressing my lips together. Moisture collects in the corners, blurring my vision.

"There's only one other thing I can think of that warrants the 'we need to talk'. Are you pregnant?"

My gaze drops to the floor.

"Wait. Are you serious? Are you pregnant?"

I lift my head and nod. A giant knot forms in my throat, not allowing me to form words. He drops his arms and I stroll past him to retrieve the pregnancy tests from the bathroom. When I return to the kitchen, I fan them out on the counter.

"Look, I know this is completely unexpected. Hell, I wasn't ever expecting this to happen, but here we are. Just so you know, I don't expect anything from you. I know this isn't something you ever wanted." I swallow. Hard. "I'm happy to do this on my own." A tear wells up in the corner of my eye and I fight to keep it from falling. I don't want him to see me vulnerable.

Slowly, he turns to meet my gaze. His expression is blank. I don't know if he hates me. Resents me. Or never wants to see me again. I wait it out for him to say something, but it never comes. Instead, he storms past me, yanks open the door, and slams it closed behind him.

# Chapter 22

## MARRY ME

### Rylee

Every piece of me wants to cry right now, but I'm too shocked to do anything. I didn't know exactly how he was going to react, but I wasn't expecting him to leave. Or maybe I was and I'm just fooling myself. I message Marcie and ask if she can keep Abby for a couple more hours and to let her know I have pizza if she wants it. I need some time to myself so I can digest everything that just happened and figure out what I'm going to do moving forward.

As I amble into the living room, I pull the blanket off the couch and throw myself down on a cushion. I can do this. I can make this work. It will be trying at times, but I'm resilient. I kind of have to be when others are relying on me. I rest a hand on my belly. A tear rolls down my cheek, until it's absorbed by the blanket. Exhaustion takes over and I close my eyes.

A knock on my door jolts me awake. I blink several times as my eyes adjust to the darkening sky. I peer at the clock on my phone when another knock echoes through my apartment, a little louder this time.

"Rye! Open up!"

"Trey?" I mumble to myself. I leap off the couch and race to the door, pulling it open. His fingers grip the door jamb, turning his knuckles white. The strands of his dark hair are tousled, giving the impression he's been running his fingers through it. Our gazes meet. His normally bright eyes are dull and tired, like he hasn't slept for two days even though it's only been two hours. The deep ridges on his forehead are etched with regret.

He sucks in a deep breath. "I sat in my car for over an hour processing everything. My life. Where I want to go. Where I want to end up."

I exhale the breath I was holding as my hand clutches my heart. "Oh. Trey—"

"Please let me get this out." The lines on his face soften slightly. "I can't let my past dictate my future. I can't let my ex lying about being pregnant affect who I am now. You're nothing like her. I need to move on from the past. You're strong, fearless, independent. Everything that anyone could ever want. You're everything I want. The only thing I need." His hands drop from the door frame. "I don't have a clue what I'm doing, but I want to be there for you and Abby and the baby. I'm going to screw up but know that I will always be there. I've lived my life selfishly because why not? I had no other responsibility besides myself… until now."

He reaches out, his fingers tremble as they wrap around my hand. Slowly, he slides down on one knee. My heart jumps out of my chest. "Trey." My voice quivers. "What are you doing?"

"Rylee. Marry me." He reaches into his pocket and pulls out a white paper ring coated with black ink. Carefully, he slides it down my ring finger on my left hand. "It's a little big. I didn't know exactly what size it needed to be. Abby taught me how to make it, but she never showed me how to size it. Doesn't matter. I'll buy you a real one. The jewelry store isn't open right now."

I don't know if I'm going to burst into tears or pass out. Both are viable options right now. "Trey. Stand up," I grit between my teeth. "Trey." I pull him to his feet. "What are you doing? Why are you doing this?"

His gaze jumps across my face, searching for the perfect words. "Because I want to do the right thing. I want to be there to support you, Abby, and the baby. I want to take care of you." He glances up at the ceiling. "Yeah. That's all I got."

I drag him inside my apartment and close the door. "I'm not marrying you." His face falls as if I told him his puppy just died. "Let me finish. It's not because I don't want to, but we're friends."

He flinches. "I'm starting to hate that word."

"Look, I like you, but I've been down this path before. Get pregnant. Get married." I motion my hand around my meager apartment. "Get left with this. I'm not ready to do it again." I exhale a breath. My hands tremble as I work up the nerve to ask my next question, mostly because of what his answer will be. If yes, I know I won't be able to say it back. If no, then he's doing this for all the wrong reasons. "Let me ask you this. Do you love me?"

Trey's entire body goes still. If he didn't just blink, I would think he was a statue.

"Exactly." Suspicions confirmed. I wrap my fingers around his and press his hand to my chest. "This is far too complicated for either of us to digest right now. Marriage isn't going to fix anything." I snort a laugh. "In fact, it will make things worse. How about this? For the time being, we continue getting to know each other and navigate the pregnancy together."

Trey offers me a sheepish smile.

I pull the paper ring off my finger and hold it in my palm. "You can have this back."

"No." He gently closes my fingers around it. "Keep it. Maybe one day I'll get to put a real one on your hand."

Tears well up in the corners of my eyes. "Dammit Trey." I playfully slap his chest. "You can't say things like that and expect me to not say to hell with it. That my plan is stupid, and we should just go for it."

A salacious grin spreads over his face. "Too bad we're not in Vegas right now because I would carry you over my shoulder to a chapel and make it official." He wraps his arms around my shoulders and pulls me to his chest.

"Again, off track." His body against mine is warm and comforting. But I'm still not at ease. I pull out of his grasp, needing some space between us so I can get out what I need to say. "But there is one thing you need to know. You can't walk away when it gets tough. If you do, you can't come back. See, I don't have that option." I splay a hand over my stomach. "I'm not going to be that girl anymore. You're either in or you're out." Moisture pools in the corners of my eyes, afraid of what his answer will be.

"Fuck, Rye." In one giant step, he's in front of me,

wrapping me in his arms. His hand gently caresses up and down my back. "I'm sorry. I'm in. One hundred percent. I'll be here for you, Abby, and the baby." He continues to slide his hand over my spine, as seconds tick by in silence. He leans back just enough to peer down at me. He brushes a loose strand of hair off my forehead. "I know you don't need me, but I need you. I need you like my next breath."

I snuggle into his chest as a lone tear rolls down my cheek. Those were the words I needed to hear. Maybe things will be different this time. Maybe the universe will give me a happily ever after.

His hands lazily slide over my shoulder blades. "One more question." I peer up at him as a lazy smile spreads across his lips. "We can still have sex, right?"

I drop my forehead to his chest as my shoulders shake with laughter. "Sex is still definitely on the table, but not the actual table because I don't want to get a new one again and I still don't have the one you got me."

"It's being built as we speak." He buries his nose into my hair right above my ear and whispers, "Any thoughts on starting right now?"

I glance up and nibble on my lower lip. "Abby is at Marcie's, so we have the apartment to ourselves."

"I'm all about seizing every opportunity." He bends at the knees and lifts. I wrap my legs around his hips, cup his cheeks, and slam my lips to his. He breaks away long enough to walk us to my bedroom.

I'm lying next to Trey, my cheek resting on his chest as the rhythmic thumping of his heart lulls me to a half sleep. His thumb brushes up and down my bicep as he holds me close to him.

"Can I go with you when you go to the doctor?"

"Of course. I'm going to call and schedule an appointment tomorrow and I'll let you know when." I trail a finger over every rise and dip of his abs.

"When are you going to tell Abby?"

"I'll wait until after the doctor's visit and everything is confirmed."

His thumb stops. "Can I tell her with you? If that's okay. Since I'll be in your lives for the foreseeable future, and I've grown quite fond of my chipmunk."

My heart melts that they've developed a connection and even have nicknames and secret handshakes with each other. "Yeah. We can tell her together."

"Also, there are four bags of baby things in my SUV. I didn't know what to buy, so I started throwing things in my cart."

I sit up, resting my elbows on the mattress. "Baby things? I just told you."

"Well, after I sat in my car for an hour and made your ring. I went to the store. I wandered up and down the six aisles of baby things. How can a baby need so many things? And how do you know where to start? As I was pushing my cart along, I got nervous that people were watching me fumble my way around, so I just threw stuff in the cart and got out of there."

My hand flies up to my mouth as I choke back a half sob, half laugh. "Slow. We'll take this slow. Okay? There is no baby yet to need things."

Bright silvery gray eyes meet mine. They're filled with excitement and nervousness. All the things I'm feeling as well. I press a soft kiss to his lips in hopes of reassuring him we got this.

My phone buzzes from the pocket of my jeans that are haphazardly thrown across the dresser. I roll out of bed and retrieve it. A message from Marcie pops up along with a slew of other messages I ignored while Trey and I were pre-occupied.

**MARCIE**
Why is there so much banging?

**MARCIE**
You do know I share a living room wall with your bedroom, right?

**MARCIE**
Ooooh! The moaning tells me all I need to know.

**MARCIE**
I had to lie to your child. I had to tell her you were moving furniture, that's where all the noise was coming from.

**MARCIE**
When she turns eighteen, I'll tell her the actual story.

**MARCIE**
Are you done? Already? I've had gas last longer than that.

**MARCIE**
Oh! Nope! Just switching positions, I hear.

**MARCIE**
I don't think I've ever heard anyone make that noise.

**MARCIE**
Or that one.

**MARCIE**
Twenty minutes and still going strong.

MARCIE

He's a keeper. You're making me second guess my relationship status. Does he have an older brother? Hot single father?

MARCIE

It's silent. Now you must be done.

MARCIE

Fucking hell. DJ just gave Tonya another rose.

## Chapter 23

## YOU'RE EATING MY CHILD

*Trey*

I motion for Rylee to enter the exam room ahead of me. She takes a seat along the left wall, and I sit down next to her. Rylee kept her word and as soon as she had an appointment scheduled, she called me. It was the most nerve wracking twenty-four hours of my life. I've been in this situation once before, but never made it to the doctor's office. In all fairness, neither did she.

"The doctor will be with you in just a few minutes." The nurse closes the door with a soft click.

My leg bounces on the ball of my foot as I glance around the small room. The pungent smell of cloves wafts around me, reminding me of the dentist's office. Sterile.

I jump to my feet, wandering from one side of the room to the other, examining all the pregnancy anatomy models. I stop in front of a baby anatomy poster. The last time I had to look at this stuff was during sex education in grade school.

"Is everything all right?" Rylee asks.

I tilt my head, trying to figure out how the baby fits out of the vagina. "Yeah. Just nervous energy." I squint.

"That's understandable. I feel it too."

I move on from the poster and continue to wander around the room, poking and prodding at the different displays. In front of me is a poster that shows the growth progression of a fetus but uses food as an example. Now this is something I understand. "What do you think our kid is? A blueberry? Or a kumquat?" I turn and point at the poster.

"I'm pretty sure we're past the blueberry stage."

"I want to go with kumquat."

"You just like saying the word."

"I kind of do. Kumquat." I move on from the food because it's making me hungry and thoughts of eating foods that could be the size of my child doesn't sit well. I stumble upon a model showing two fetuses. Shit. "What if we have twins?" Fuck. If there's two babies, I don't know what I'd do. I'm not prepared for one baby. I don't think I can handle two.

"The chances of two babies are very unlikely, but there's still a chance. I mean you got me pregnant while I'm on birth control. Do twins run in your family?"

I pause to think. "No."

"Me either. So, I don't think we need to jump to that conclusion right this second."

"What if there's three or five or six?"

"Now the statistics are becoming drastically lower."

"I'm a man of chance. Good chance if it were to happen, it would happen to me."

"Trey. Come sit down. You're making yourself nervous and, in turn, making me nervous." She pats the cushion next to her. In two long strides, I'm lowering myself to the chair. Her fingers intertwine with mine. "Let's do this one step at a time. When the doctor comes in, we'll get all the answers."

My leg bounces as Rylee does her best to ease my nerves. The last three months of my life has been a freefall off a cliff. It's been thrilling and frightening at the same time. With Rylee by my side, I feel like I can pull the parachute cord and soar to the ground with ease. Maybe. A couple of restless minutes later, a middle-aged woman with dark hair and a white lab coat comes in and introduces herself as Doctor Lisa Dobb, OB-GYN. They run a blood test and confirm that Rylee is, in fact, pregnant.

"Do you know how far along you might be?" Doctor Dobb asks.

I tap my chin. "Oh man. There's so many. How do I choose?"

"You don't just pick one," Rylee adds.

"It could have been the time after our first date. Or when I bent you over my desk in my office. Or in the backseat..." Rylee slaps her hand over my mouth, but I keep mumbling behind it.

"Honestly, I just found out I was pregnant a couple of days ago, but I'm also on birth control. My period has always been a little irregular and spotty," Rylee says.

Doctor Dobbs nods and makes notes on her clipboard. "As we know, birth control isn't always one-hundred percent effective. We'll also have to take you off your birth control."

"I have some pretty determined swimmers." I sit up straighter and puff out my chest.

"What is the timeframe when you first started having intercourse?" Doctor Dobbs asks.

"The first time was about three months ago," Rylee says.

"Oh. Shit." My eyes nearly pop out of their sockets.

"What's wrong?" Concern is etched all over Rylee's face.

I run my hand over the two-day stubble on my chin. "The condom. That bachelor party was like two years ago."

Her head jerks back. "You didn't think it could have been expired?"

I shrug. "Your boobs were in my face. I wasn't really thinking about the date on the condom. But either way, your birth control should have been the backup. This is your fault."

"My fault? You're the one with the two-year-old condom."

"You said you were on birth control."

"I am. And apparently it failed."

My gaze shoots to the doctor. "So, this is your fault."

Her lips twitch with a smile. "I only insert the birth control. I hold no guarantees on its effectiveness."

"Alright. This is no one's fault. It just happened. So, let's move on," Rylee says, always the voice of reason.

"Will we be using these today?" I swing one side of the stirrup out.

"No. Not today," Doctor Dobbs says.

"With your legs up in these, is this what childbirth looks like?" I glance up to Rylee.

She eyes the stirrup and then me. "It can, but also add in some extra screaming. Didn't you watch the birthing video in seventh grade?"

"Nah. I skipped that day. As soon as I heard what day

it was, I noped right out. They weren't going to ruin sex for me at a young age."

Rylee rolls her eyes. "You were not having sex at that age."

"True. But I also wasn't going to let it traumatize me, either. Like Scott from my class. One day after school, National Geographic was on the television, and they showed a rhino giving birth. I've never actually seen anyone rock in a corner until him. I wonder how he's doing?" I rub his chin. "Is that what I can expect?"

Rylee's eyebrows shoot to her hairline. "A rhino giving birth?"

"Yeah."

She narrows her gaze at me, nostrils flaring. "I want you to think long and hard about that."

My gaze flits to Doctor Dobbs, and she vigorously shakes her head. I turn to Rylee and mimic the doctor.

"How about we get you prepped for a transabdominal ultrasound, then we'll have a better understanding of how far along you are," Doctor Dobbs says.

Rylee lays down on the blue vinyl bed. She lifts the hem over her still relatively flat stomach. The doctor squirts some gel on her stomach and her muscles twitch for a second before relaxing. "Oh, that's cold." Her body shivers and I grab her hand.

The doctor turns the machine on and moves a wand over Rylee's stomach. A grainy image comes into view on the screen. A whooshing sound fills the room. I don't know if it's my hand or Rylee's that's gone clammy. Maybe both.

"Holy shit. We made that." My gaze flits from the screen to Rylee.

A soft smile forms on her lips. "We did."

Fuck. I'm going to be a dad. I can't tear my gaze off the small black and white screen. Not in a million years, or at least the last ten years, did I think this would happen. Especially with Rylee. I can't imagine having a baby with anyone else. With my fingers clasped around hers, I lift her hand, placing a kiss on the back. We both stare intently at the screen. The fetus moves along with a black blob.

"Oh damn! Is that his penis? Are we having a boy?" I drop Rylee's hand and inch closer to the screen.

"Actually, I think that's an arm." Humor laces Doctor Dobb's voice. "It looks like you're about twelve weeks along, so it's a little early to find out the gender. More likely at your next appointment. I'll print you a picture to take home," she says. After the click of a button, she exits the room to collect the picture.

Both of us continue to stare at the black and white screen. "That's our little plum."

"It is."

"I'm a little disappointed it's not a kumquat."

She smiles and shakes her head.

"Do you think if I put the gel on my stomach, we'll be able to see the burrito I ate for lunch?"

Her smile dissipates.

"It's a valid question." I rub my stomach, feeling around for the burrito.

"No. It's not."

"Would it be weird if I asked the doctor if we can try?"

"Yes, I do."

"I'm going to ask her."

She narrows her gaze at me and gives me the motherly scold. "If you ask her, so help me god, we'll no longer play Treyfleupagus Goes Muff Diving."

My smile dissolves. "But that's my favorite game."

Later that evening, I'm sitting at a restaurant with Miles and Bennett. While me and Miles were finishing drone footage for a massive six-bedroom house, Bennett texted me. I told him to meet us for dinner once we were done.

I push the risotto around on my plate. The ultrasound appointment earlier today still hasn't completely hit me. I'm going to be a dad. I'm going to be responsible for the wellbeing of a tiny human.

I glance at Miles' plate. "You're eating my child."

Miles slowly pulls the fork from his mouth and raises a questioning eyebrow.

"You're eating my child," I repeat.

He spits his food out into a napkin. "What are you talking about?"

"Your duck with plum sauce. The plum. It's the size of my unborn kid."

"Wait. Rylee? Rylee's pregnant?"

Bennett's fork falls to his plate with a clatter.

All I can do is nod.

"Congratulations! That's super exciting," Miles' tone would be infectious to any other person, but I'm still trying to process the situation.

I keep my gaze on my still full plate of food.

Bennett chuckles. "Holy shit. Seth is going to get a kick out of this."

"Thanks asshole." I frown. "This is all your fault. You all had to go out and fucking find love and shit. Then you had to be so goddamn happy. And now you're making me question the last ten years of my single life."

Bennett rests his elbows on the table. "Shit is scary. Every day I thank god that Charlie's in my life. That she hasn't left me because she can do better. Every morning, I make sure she knows my world is nothing without her." He lifts one shoulder and lets it drop while his lips tip up into a smile. "That helps reinforce the never leave me part. But you can't let the fear dictate your life. It's more than falling in love. It's finding your soulmate. Someone you can't live without. That's worth more than all the fear in the world."

I scrub my hands down my face.

Miles nods along with everything Bennett says. "That was really beautiful."

I roll my eyes. "Charlie has the rose-colored glasses shoved on his face."

Bennett barks out a laugh. "We waited a long time for cupid to bitch slap his arrow across your face. I guess he used two since you're also having a kid."

I shove my plate away, not even hungry in the slightest. "I don't know how to feel right now." I blow out a breath. "Yes, I'm excited. Yes, I'm scared shitless."

"Well, given your history..." Miles shrugs a shoulder. "She's being honest?"

I pull out the ultrasound picture and slide it across the table. "The doctor handed it to me herself." All three of us stare at the picture. "I also asked her to marry me."

Bennett laughs and shakes his head. Miles coughs and sputters on a bite of food. I prepare myself to give him the Heimlich, which I've done once before. Granted, it was to my neighbor's dog, but tomayto, tomahto.

Once Miles regains his composure, he asks, "You're getting married?"

"Well, I asked. But she killed that idea faster than a knife fight in a phone booth." I motion my hand in a jabbing motion, then flop it onto the table with a smack.

"Do you want to get married?" Miles asks.

I shrug. "Eventually. Rylee has flipped my world upside down. Every day she makes me want to be a better man and no one's ever done that to me. And I absolutely adore Abby." Then she questioned if I loved her. The words were on the tip of my tongue, ready for me to spit them out but I couldn't. Even though I put it in writing, I couldn't get the words out. Not yet anyway, but I will. I've never been one to give up.

Miles takes a drink of his water and sets it down. "Are you prepared to be a stepdad as well? Things like that can be rocky terrain."

Ah. Fuck. The thought never even occurred to me. Not only will I be a dad, but also possibly a stepdad. I'll have to navigate that if and when the time comes. "I've always been one to face a challenge head on. Whatever is thrown at me, I'm ready to face it full force, so yeah, whatever I have to do, I'm ready for it. All of it. Plus, Rylee will be there to keep me in check. She's good like that." All my nerve endings tingle from imagining a future with her.

"Congratulations. I never expected the day our fearless SBL leader would ditch the single life," Miles says.

I run both hands through my hair. "If I'm being honest, I never expected it either, but here we are."

"You'll be a great dad. In your own special Trey way, but I've known you for years and I know you'll give that kid every piece of you," Bennett says.

His words reassure me a little. If someone else can have faith in me, maybe I should have a little faith in myself.

"What will the plans be for SBL? I kind of look forward to hanging out with the guys every week." Miles gives me a weak smile.

I can't imagine giving up the weekly meeting. "We might have to change it up a bit. We'll see. But speaking of dates and ladies, how's everything going with the librarian?"

"She basically dumped me without dumping me. She's never returned any of my calls or text messages."

"I'm sorry. We'll hook you up with someone else. Maybe Rylee has a friend she can set you up with."

"I don't know. Maybe dating isn't for me." A somber expression covers Miles' face.

"You can't spend the rest of your life without dating or companionship. Believe me. I tried it. Now I'm having a kid." Holy shit. I'm having a kid.

After dinner, the three of us go our separate ways. While walking to my SUV, I pass a small bookstore and pause. Might as well acquaint myself with all this baby and parenting stuff. I pull open the door to find some new reading material.

# Chapter 24

## BABY DADDY

*Trey*

It's been a couple of days since the doctor appointment and my nerves have had time to settle. Except being at my parents they're on high alert again. I throw my SUV into park in the driveway, not ready to relive a conversation I had a little over ten years ago, even though this one is different.

As soon as I walk into the foyer, the aroma of stewed tomatoes and garlic leads me to the kitchen. My dad is at the counter chopping vegetables, while my mom's next to him at the stove stirring a pot. I've always envied their relationship. Sure, they've had their fair share of ups and downs, like adjusting to another kid in the house when my half-brother, Ledger, moved in during our teen years. But they made it work and they did it together. And now, they're working side by side in the kitchen, enjoying each other's company. My movement catches their attention, and we silently greet each other with smiles and nods. I plopped down on the stool at the island and continue watching them. The longer I sit here it makes me realize I want this, all the relationship stuff with Rylee.

I've contemplated several ways how to tell my parents. The first one was a King Cake with the little baby inside, but then I figured that would be more fitting if it was closer to Mardi Gras. A temporary tattoo of the ultrasound picture. A singing telegram. Instead, I keep it simple. "You guys are going to be grandparents."

The knife in my dad's hand clatters to the cutting board. Maybe I should've waited until he set it down first. My mom spins around, wooden spoon in hand, dripping tomato sauce on the floor. "Say that again?"

I rub the back of my neck. "You're going to be grandparents." Both of them are stunned silent. I'm sure they're having flashbacks of the last time I told them. I can't blame them. That was a traumatic experience for everyone.

My mom's the first to speak. "Are you sure?"

Her question would shock most people, but I kind of blew the wind out of her "you're going to be grandparents sail" the first time. So, her questioning isn't unreasonable.

"This time it's real."

A thud echoes through the house from the living room as Olivia barrels into the kitchen with Ledger close behind.

"You're absolutely positive?" my mom asks.

"Yes. As soon as Rylee found out, she told me with three pregnancy tests in hand. We went to the doctor together and everything." I pull out the ultrasound picture and slide it across the counter.

"Was this planned?" my dad asks as he picks up the picture for a closer look.

"No. It just happened."

"You're in a much better position with your life now, especially financially. Is she asking for money?" My mom sets the spoon down. Her gaze locks on mine from across the island.

I hate that my mom has to ask these questions, but I understand why she's doing it. She only wants to protect me. "The funny thing is, she offered to do this by herself." My mom glares at me. "Which I said wasn't happening." I pick at an invisible spot on the counter. "Rylee's an amazing woman. She's a single mom to a daughter named Abby. She's the most amazing kid." My heart warms just thinking about them.

"Well, it seems like you have everything in order. Congratulations." My dad claps my shoulder.

"I think so. I really like her, and I want to do everything to be there for her."

"Are you and Rylee dating?" my mom asks as she picks up the ultrasound picture.

I exhale a humorless laugh. "Exclusive friends with benefits. I think that's where we're at now."

"You kids and all your weird dating titles." My mom shakes her head. "Anyway, we would really like to meet her. You'll have to invite her to dinner, along with her daughter, sometime."

"I will. You guys will love her. Abby too."

She rounds the island and wraps her arms around me. "Congratulations." She kisses my temple. "You're going to be an amazing dad. And I can't wait to spoil our grandchild."

It's like a boulder has been lifted off my shoulders. I know my parents only want what's best for me. They often question my behavior but will always stand in my corner. I can't wait until I can offer my kid that kind of love and support.

I spin on my stool, and Olivia and Ledger are standing behind me. Olivia is bouncing back and forth on her toes. I'm sure wanting to ask me all the questions, being one of my best friends and all. I climb off the stool and stroll past them and into the living room. Olivia's hot on my heels as Ledger ambles behind. I flop down on the recliner while Olivia and Ledger sit on the love seat. Several seconds of silence pass while Olivia's stare bores into me, her lips twitching with the urge to talk.

"She really wants to say something, doesn't she?" I ask Ledger, while pointing to Olivia.

"Yep," Ledger replies.

Her face is damn near purple from biting back the urge to speak.

"Do you think this might actually kill her?"

Ledger nods. "Yep."

"I can't do that to you. I know how much you two love each other." Directing my attention to Olivia, I say, "You get five seconds."

She squeals, clapping her hands together. "Oh my God, I am so happy."

"Three."

"I can't believe you actually found a woman."

"Two."

"And an amazing woman."

"One."

Olivia stops talking but still has the cheesiest grin on her face, silently clapping and bouncing back and forth in her seat. "Okay, screw your five seconds. Tell me everything," Olivia squeals.

I bark out a laugh. "I tried."

I go over my entire relationship with Rylee, from friends to benefits to exclusive friends with benefits, and now to baby daddy. But one day I hope to put a ring on her finger and call her mine forever.

I scrub my hands down my face. "As much as I want to push her, I know I can't. She got burned once before and I want to prove to her I'm not her ex. I'm with her one thousand percent and I will do everything to show her that. If that includes waiting until the end of time, I will."

Olivia swoons and falls into the crook of Ledger's arm. "That is so sweet. See, I got none of that from you, that's why it never worked out between us."

I laugh. "And I'm sure Ledger croons all the sweet love messages to you."

"He does in his own Ledger way." She runs a hand down his chest.

"I know what my girl wants and exactly how to give it to her." Ledger pulls her in closer and presses a kiss to her temple.

"Also, don't hate me," Olivia says. "I told Rylee we kissed." She quickly continues, "I told her it was one time. And it was like kissing my brother. No spark."

I cough a laugh. "Did you tell her you then kissed my brother?"

She nods with a beaming smile. "Yep."

"Good." I return her smile with one of my own.

"Never in my wildest dreams did I think you would be having a kid," Olivia says.

"Neither did I, but here we are, doing the things." I lean against the chair and stare at the ceiling. It still hasn't fully hit me. I don't know when it will, but I'll be prepared.

# Chapter 25

## HOW BABIES ARE MADE

# Rylee

Tonight's the night. Tonight, we are doing it. Trey's coming over and we're telling Abby she's going to be a big sister. I'm just as nervous as when I told Trey. It's been Abby and me against the world for the past four years. Six years if I count the years her father and I were still together, but he was basically absent. Unease settles in my stomach. What if she hates the idea and never wants to speak to me again? She's my entire world.

I tap my fingers on the bar top before checking the time on my phone. Chad's late. Again. I'll have to talk to Jake about this because it's getting ridiculous. Plus, every night he's working, the inventory counts are skewed. Sometimes things are misplaced, but other's they just disappear. I hate to point fingers, but it's a little suspicious.

The door to Porter's swings open and Chad strolls in like he isn't twenty minutes late. "You know, when you're late, you screw up everyone else's schedule."

Without sparing me a glance, he struts on by. "Not my problem."

"It will be when you get fired," I mumble to myself. I grab my wallet off the bar and tuck my phone in my back pocket, but before I'm through the door it opens, and I'm greeted by another pain in my ass.

"What do you want, Kyle?" I frown, crossing my arms over my chest.

"What the fuck, Rylee? I have to find out about this shit on the street?" he sneers.

"What are you talking about?" I sigh, dropping my arms. It's always something. It's always me who's done something to ruin his life.

"Do you know who you're spending time with? He's slept with half the city and the other half is male, if you can do the math. I had to hear all about it on the golf course. Do you know how embarrassing that is?"

I roll my eyes so hard I'm surprised they don't pop out of their sockets and roll right past Kyle. I want to ask him if he realizes how embarrassing it is to catch your husband cheating on you not once, but twice. But I'm tired of the same argument, especially when he believes he did nothing wrong. "I know exactly who Trey is. Why do you think you have any say about who I spend my time with. That ship sailed years ago." I fling my arms across my body. "You walked out. You left."

"So, what you're saying is if I stayed, we might still be together." He takes a step closer.

"Hell no." I hold out my palm, preventing him from getting any closer. "After you left, I just finished the job." He flinches for a brief second. A rainbow of emotions float over his face, remorse being the shortest lived one. Honestly, I don't think he has any remorse for his actions. For what he did to me and our daughter. If anything, he only regrets that he got caught.

He shakes his head as if he's disappointed. "Out of all the people in this city, you find the biggest creep of them all."

"No. That's you," I spit.

The half a dozen or so people in the bar turn their heads our way. Our conversation turning more into the headline news of a tabloid magazine.

His lip curls. "You realize while he's spending time with you, he's also spending time with my daughter."

"In the short time we've been spending time together, he's been more of a father figure than you have."

His nostrils flare. Perhaps I hit a nerve. Too bad it's not like the Vulcan nerve pinch, so I can be done with this conversation.

"He's slept with half the town."

My molars clench together so hard I'm surprised I don't crack a tooth. "Are you judging his character right now? Have you looked at yourself in the mirror? You were doing the same exact thing. While. We. Were. Married."

His face reddens but he doesn't say anything because he knows I'm right. He squares his shoulders. "Well, I don't want him anywhere near my daughter."

"She's only your daughter when it's convenient for you. You're not there for school plays, when she falls and scrapes her knee, or when she gets a perfect grade on a school project. None of it."

"I'm not there for any of it because I have a job, Rylee. A real job."

I fling my arms in the air. "I have one of those two. On top of raising Abby, our daughter."

"Well, maybe you should just be more considerate of the company you keep while you're raising our daughter."

I laugh. I don't even think he realizes what he just said.

"You are starting to draw a crowd. Take the conversation outside." Jake's deep voice sounds from over my shoulder.

"No need Jake. This conversation is over." I sidestep Kyle, but he stops me with his arm.

"Wait. You're sleeping with him, aren't you?" When I don't say anything, he throws his hands in the air. "What the hell Rylee? I thought you were better than that."

"What the fuck do you know? But to answer your question, yes. I've slept with him. In fact," I splay my hand over my stomach, "I'm pregnant. With his child. So, what do you have to say about that?"

His mouth opens and closes like a fish out of water, then he shakes his head. "You made your bed. I guess now you gotta lie in it."

"I do. Matter of fact, I'm going to lie in it tonight over and over again."

Kyle spins on his heel but his head turns toward Chad, and he jerks his chin before he storms out the door.

If I wasn't paying attention, I would have missed it. If those two became friends, they can have each other. Two pieces of trash in a pod. When he's out of sight, I unclench my fists. He has no right to dictate any part of my life.

After arriving home from work and in a shit mood because of Kyle, I decided to call the only other person who can make my mood even shittier… my mother.

I remove my phone out of my pocket, pull up her number, and hit call. It rings a half dozen times before she picks up. Water splashing sounds through the earpiece tells me she's lounging at some poolside cabana, sipping mimosas, all on husband number four's dime. At this point, I can't even keep track of their names anymore.

"It's so nice to hear from my daughter."

I pinch my eyes shut. The sound of her voice grates on my every nerve. I fight to keep my tone as neutral as possible. The faster I can get through this, the faster I can be done. "So, I wanted to give you our monthly we're not dead phone call. I'm doing good. Abby is doing good and you're going to be a grandma."

"But I'm already a grandma."

"Congrats. You're going to be a grandma again. Yay." I shake my fist in the air like a cheerleader with a pom pom.

"You're pregnant?" she screeches.

"Yep."

"When's the wedding?"

"No wedding. Just a baby."

"He gets you knocked up and he can't even put a ring on your finger."

Not for the lack of trying on his part. "Nope."

"You need a man who will take care of you."

And be like you on husband number four, while you're sleeping with future husband number five. No thanks. "I'm quite alright, actually."

"Rylee, what are you going to do about money?"

Ten seconds before the money talk. That's a new record. "I'll figure it out."

After I got pregnant with Abby, it was my mother who convinced me I needed to marry Kyle, even though I was hesitant. Her insistent nagging about needing money, someone to take care of me, and not being alone finally wore me down into saying yes. It's something I deeply regret now. She's convinced herself that if she was married to my dad, he would have never left, but I'm pretty sure he had one foot out the door since the day I was born.

"Please tell me he at least has a real job and not working at a bar."

The blows start coming. Number one. "Yes, he has a job and before you ask, yes, he's planning on helping with the baby." I pull open the junk drawer in the kitchen and pull out a nail file to fix a hangnail.

"Well at least there's that. I still can't believe that you're divorced and with another kid on the way. If you stayed with Kyle, you wouldn't be in this predicament."

Blow number two. "No. It was the cheating that kind of made me realize I shouldn't be with him."

"Sometimes you need to brush those things aside and think about your family."

I slam the nail file down. "Being married to someone I don't love isn't thinking about my family."

"You'd at least have some stability. God knows you need that in your life."

And blow number three. "Got it." Sometimes it's easier to nod a smile than trying to argue with her.

"There is only one certainty in life, and it isn't love. So, take your happiness while you still can."

I can't imagine jumping from husband to husband is happiness, but to each their own. "Alright Mother, great chat. Inspiring as always. I'll let you know when I have the baby. Okay bye." I end the call before she can say anything else. It's always a self-esteem boost talking to her.

A knock on my door startles me off the couch. The only two people who knock on my door are Marcie, which is always a knock and barge in if I left the door unlocked, or pancake guy down the hall asking for flour. For whatever reason, he always smells like pancakes and maple syrup which isn't necessarily bad, but it's strong. Trey is still at work, so that eliminates him.

I peer through the peephole and my brows furrow. Trey's friend, Bennett, stands on the other side. His dark hair blends well with the red flannel he's wearing. Twisting the knob, I pull it open. "Hi. What are you doing here?"

"I have a table to deliver." He holds up a piece of dark stained wood.

"Oh! Yes! Come in." I hold the door open for him. "How did you get in? The front is normally locked."

"Your neighbor Marcie. She said something about you needing a sex table so you can stop having sex against her living room wall."

Warmth spreads over my cheeks. Marcie and her big mouth.

Bennett rocks the piece of wood back and forth on the floor. "And she mentioned if I came with the table, I could deliver it to her place."

I bark out a laugh. "She's been binge watching shows about farmers finding love. The red flannel must have given her the vibe, but she's harmless." I point to the empty spot in the dining room. "Anyway. The table can go there."

Bennett leans the piece of wood against the wall.

"It's kind of small." I cock my head to the side. "Do I have to water it and it will grow?"

His gaze jumps to mine, eyebrows drawn together.

"Sorry. Sarcasm. Blame it on Trey." I shrug a shoulder and smirk.

He nods as his head lifts to me. "He tends to do that. Also, congratulations. On the baby. Trey told me."

I rest a hand on my belly. "Thanks."

He rubs the back of his neck. "Trey's a different kind of guy. When he sets his mind to something, he gives it one hundred percent. He's all in, and it's hard to convince him otherwise." He drops his hand and shoves it into the front pocket of his jeans. "But one thing I'll say is that he's loyal to a fault. He always lays his cards on the table, so you know exactly what you're getting. I'll say this, I've never seen him as happy as he is with you."

"Well, we'll be in each other's lives for at least eighteen years."

"I'm sure it will be much longer if Trey gets his way. And very rarely does Trey *not* get his way."

I smile. "That's so true. How does he do that?"

Bennett laughs. "I don't know. Has Trey ever told you about his last serious girlfriend?"

I cross my arms over my chest. "He's mentioned something about her being pregnant and then lying. But I was also shocked by the marriage proposal to ask more about it."

"Oh yeah. I heard about that, too." He smiles. "It's probably not my place to say anything, but also, I don't know if he will. But he was really excited to be a dad. Scared as hell, but excited. Throughout the entire ordeal, she manipulated him with a lot of false hope. It changed him, or at least changed his views on relationships."

"Wow," I mumble, with my hand covering my mouth. To do that to someone… I could never. I can't imagine what Trey went through in dealing with all that.

"That was until you. So, if he's a little over the top, he has his reasons."

A weak smile spreads across my lips and I nod. While I'm glad I can be here for Trey and helping him heal, I just wish we could do it without the added distraction of a pregnancy. "Thanks. These are very unfamiliar waters. Not being pregnant but doing it with Trey."

"He'll be fine. Plus, he needs someone to rein him in every now and then." A moment of silence passes between us. "I'm going to collect the rest of the table and put it together for you."

"Let me help." I pull a pair of shoes from the shoe rack and slip them on.

The six-person rectangular X Trestle table sits perfectly in my dining room. On each end are two custom chairs and bench seating on each side. "The table is beautiful." I run my fingers over the dark, weathered finish.

"It's sturdy too. Trey said that was a requirement." Bennett smirks.

Heat creeps up my neck and to my cheeks and I drop my gaze to the floor in hopes of hiding it.

"I better get going. Enjoy your table and keep Trey on his toes. He needs it." He opens the door and then he's strolling down the hallway.

The door closes behind him and I lean against the wood, exhaling a long sigh. For someone who you'd expect to get what you see, Trey actually has a lot of deep ruts in his seemingly perfect life.

---

I peek through the doorway into Abby's room. Her feet swing in the air as she lies on her stomach on her floor, coloring in a princess coloring book. She's my entire world. Soon there will be one more. I rest a hand on my stomach as warmth fills my chest. I pull my phone out of my back pocket as I stroll into the kitchen, checking to see if I have any missed messages. Nothing. He's thirty minutes late. This better not be a preview of what's to come.

I nearly jump out of my skin when the intercom rings. I buzz Trey up. I'm waiting with the door open as his dark hair comes into view as he climbs the stairs. "Where have you been? You're late."

"Sorry. I stopped at the store and got things to ease the transition from only child to big sister." He holds up two plastic bags in each hand and a helium balloon with big pink letters that says Big Sis.

"This is a bit excessive." I hold the front door open as Trey strolls in past me.

"I would rather be prepared." He sets the bags on the counter and unloads a t-shirt, sweatshirt, books, a teddy bear, a necklace, and a pint of ice cream. "I also found these really awesome baby toys. They light up and play music depending on how fast you move them."

"Seriously, more baby stuff?"

"Yeah. I didn't want to miss out on them being available later." He passes me the bag of baby toys. "Hide this so Abby doesn't find it."

I huff and grab the bag from him. It's been less than a week and this baby already has more stuff than I do. Once in my bedroom, I set the bag down in the corner with the rest of the bags. What are you doing?"

"Getting prepared." He holds out the box of ice cream to me. "Freezer. All news is better with ice cream."

I grab it and smile. It's hard to argue with that logic. I shove the ice cream into the freezer. Spinning around, I face Trey. "Ready?"

"Let's do this." He wraps an arm around my waist and pulls me to his chest, placing a kiss on my lips.

I pull away. A flutter of butterflies fills my stomach. "Abby! Can you come out here?"

The patter of little feet barrel down the hallway. "Squirrel! You're here!" She races to Trey and wraps her arms around his legs.

A flood of warmth washes over my body. I love that these two have developed a connection. I can only hope it will help with what we're about to tell her. "Abby let's sit down in the living room. We have something we need to talk to you about."

"Okay." She sprints into the living room and jumps on the couch.

I follow behind and take a seat next to Abby. The cushion depresses next to me as Trey sits. "What we wanted to talk to you about is... When two people are..." Why is this so hard? I peer over my shoulder at Trey, hoping he has the words I can't seem to find. He just shrugs. I turn toward Abby. "When two people are... together, they do adult things."

Trey chuckles next to me. He leans in, bumping my shoulder, and speaks softly out of the corner of his mouth. "Give her the ice cream."

I'm failing at this parenting thing right now. Just spit it out. "What I'm trying to say is... you're going to be a big sister."

Abby doesn't move a muscle, which is completely out of the ordinary for her. Dammit. She hates me and will spend the rest of her life revolting against me.

Trey jumps off the couch, races into the kitchen, and snatches the balloon and teddy bear off the counter. When he returns to the living room, he deposits them in front of Abby. "We even got you a balloon to celebrate the occasion."

Abby eyes the balloon for a few seconds, then lifts her gaze to me. "Where do babies come from?"

Next to me, Trey stretches his arm over the back of the

couch and leans toward me. "Stork. Go with stork," he mumbles.

I nudge him with my elbow. "Well, when two adults are together. They do things... Sciencey things." The cushion next to me vibrates as Trey's body convulses with silent laughter. Screw it. We're doing this Trey's way. "Two adults get together... and... wait for the stork to deliver the baby."

"Doesn't the baby live in your tummy?" Abby tilts her head.

A bead of sweat forms on my brow. I can give birth to the kid, yet I can't explain to her where they come from. "Yes. The baby's home will be in my belly until the stork comes."

"Okay. Do I have to share my toys?" Her big hazel eyes peer up at me.

"You might have to share, yes."

"Do I have to share my room?"

"It will be a little while until we need to figure that out."

"Give her the ice cream," Trey whispers.

"How about we have some ice cream?"

"Yay! Ice cream!" Abby leaps off the couch and runs into the kitchen.

"I'll be right there," I call over my shoulder.

"Sciencey things?" Trey sits up, resting his elbows on his knees. "I have to admit, science with you is my favorite kind of science."

I drop my head to his shoulder. "I choked."

"If you ask me, it didn't go so bad. No kicking and screaming. Also, the bedroom thing... you two can always move in with me. I have lots of room."

I flash him a small smile. "Let's focus on one thing at a time for now."

"Mommy!" Abby yells from the kitchen.

"But first ice cream." I rise from the couch and stroll into the kitchen, with Trey close behind. The three of us sit at the new table as Trey and I dodge more questions from Abby about how babies are made.

# Chapter 26

## MOODY SIX-YEAR-OLDS

*Trey*

I cut the ignition of my SUV in front of a playground and stare out the windshield as a group of kids run from the swings to the slide several feet away. It's been years since I've been to a playground. Probably since I was a kid. But also, I'm a grown adult, I shouldn't be hanging out around playgrounds without a kid. I scan the area for anyone lurking around who might be kid-less and suspicious. Luckily, I have a kid in the backseat.

Rylee had to go to work, so I told her I would spend the day with Abby to practice the parenting shit. Plus, it'll come in handy if I ever play stepdad. Thanks, Miles, for implanting that into my head. Spending time with my chipmunk is never a chore. We have a good time, except when we play Pretty Pretty Princess. I swear she hides fake necklaces up her sleeves. I vetoed that right away.

The click of a seat belt draws my attention and I glance over my shoulder. Abby pushes herself to the front of her booster seat and pulls the lever of the door handle. A sliver of light fills the backseat before her gaze flits to mine.

"You forgot the safety locks."

"It's usually not something I have to worry about." Note to self: figure out the safety locks. In fact, it's not something I've had to use since college when I gave my dorm neighbor a ride home from the bar and at every stoplight he would yell "red light shuffle", jump out and run around the car before the light turned green. Generally, the prank consists of everyone doing it, but he's the only one who ever played. After the tenth time, the locks were put into place.

Abby jumps out and slams the door behind her. Quickly, I'm following suit. When we reach the edge of the playground where the railroad ties hold in the rubber pellets, Abby veers right to a picnic table instead of toward the jungle gym. She climbs over the bench seat and takes a seat on the top, crosses her legs, and faces the playground. I cautiously sit next to her.

The cheerful chirping of birds blends with the joyful laughter of the other children playing. It's the perfect day to be at the park, yet we're sitting on a picnic table. I peer down at Abby, and her eyes stay fixed on the swings where a guy about my age pushes a little boy. The boy's cheerful laughter grows louder as he yells, "Higher daddy, higher."

While I don't have the slightest idea on what could be going through a six-year old girl's mind, if I had to guess judging by her trying to burn a hole through the swing with her intense staring, it might have something to do with her own dad. And that's a conversation I don't want to touch with a ten-foot pole. Needing to break the silence, I clear my throat and ask, "Didn't you want to come down here to play on the playground?"

She shrugs a shoulder but doesn't offer any more than that.

Good talk. Two of us can be moody six-year-olds.

I mimic her posture and stare off into the distance.

"Are you and my mom going to get married?"

My foot slides off the edge of the bench as I nearly tumble off the picnic table. Shit. Why did she ask that? Did Rylee mention something? Or did she overhear a conversation? Kids are born with supersonic hearing. I found that out when I was having a conversation with Seth about a new beer I tried, and I called it swamp piss. From the other room, Maddox screamed swamp piss. For the next year and a half everything he drank was called swamp piss. Seth wasn't thrilled about that, but it made me chuckle.

I half cough, half choke and I spit out, "Oh. Um. Why do you ask?"

"My mom said she got married to my dad after she got pregnant with me."

"Oh." Shit. What do I say? How do normal people answer this question? I run my palms down my jean covered thighs. "Well, me and your mom… see… we're just taking it one day at a time." Those were her words, not mine.

"Do you love her?"

What the fuck? Life did not prepare me for being interrogated by a six-year-old. Who taught this kid about relationships and love? What do I say? Love… that's a tough one. I've tossed around the words in my head, and they don't make me hurl. I've even written them down and oddly enough, I wrote them with a steady hand. But to say them out loud? I love getting naked with her, but I can't tell her that. Is she doing recon for Rylee? Get the kid to ask questions so I spill everything? Fuck. I scrub my hands over my face and turn to Abby who's staring up at me. She hasn't blinked even once. "I care about your mom. A lot." I hope that'll appease her questioning appetite.

"Okay." She shrugs.

Shit. That was easy. I got this. I sit up and puff out my chest.

"Will you push me on the swings?"

"Absolutely."

She jumps off the picnic table and runs full speed to the swings and I trail a few steps behind.

Once she's on the swing, I stand behind and push as she pumps her legs, going higher and higher with each pass. A smile tugs on my lips as she tells me to push her higher. My phone vibrates in my pocket, and I pull it out. It's a client I've been busting my ass for the past month to find the perfect piece of property for. I wouldn't put much effort into it, but it's a forty-thousand-dollar commission check if I can convince him to sign. That would buy a lot of diapers. I push her with one hand as the phone vibrates again.

Shit. "Abby, I have a really important phone call to take. I'll be right back. Keep pumping those legs."

As I spin around, I press the talk button. "William. I'm so happy for your phone call today. I take it you've made your decision."

"Well Trey, you certainly know how to convince a man to buy something he doesn't need."

I give myself a fist pump. All my hard work on this sale has finally paid off. Normally, I don't deal with the sales, but this is for an old friend. I peer over my shoulder and

Abby is still on the swing, slowly kicking her legs back and forth. Giving William my full attention again, I say, "How about we meet at my office on Monday, and we can sign some paperwork?"

"I'm in meetings all day on Monday. Let's make it Wednesday. Two o'clock."

"Wednesday is perfect. I'll see you then." I press end and shove my phone into my pocket. Holy shit. A wide grin spreads across my face. This is almost as exciting as the time I lost my virginity. Almost. I spin around and my smile plummets to the ground. All the air escapes my lungs. Oh shit. The swing sways back and forth, except Abby isn't there.

# Chapter 27

## PORN STARS NAMED BUNNY

### Trey

I dash toward the swing set as I frantically scan the playground. Where did she go? She was just here a fucking second ago. My heart hammers in my chest as a bead of sweat trickles down my spine. Oh fuck. I lost her. I lost Abby.

"Abby!" I race around the playground, searching under the slide. "Abby!" Then my gaze jumps to the rock-climbing wall. I sprint from one side of the playground to the other but I don't see her anywhere. Rylee is going to kill me. Fuck. I want to kill me. I've lost her daughter. My heart pounds in my ears, drowning out all the other sounds around me. I'm going to be a fucking terrible father.

The distinct sound of a sniffle echoes behind me, and I whirl around. A pair of familiar white sneakers with hearts on them catch my attention from inside a wooden train play set. I sprint toward the caboose and duck inside. Abby's sitting on one side with her face buried in her hands as little sniffles wrack her body.

"Oh shit. There you are!" I shove my large frame through the small opening and sit next to her. I wrap my arms around her shoulders and haul her to me, hugging her tight. "I was so worried. I didn't know what happened to you. That was one conversation I didn't want to have with your mom." I blow out a heavy breath. "Fuck." Adrenaline still courses through my entire body. "What happened back there? You were swinging and then you just left. I thought something happened."

She sniffles and wipes her cheeks with the sleeve of her hoodie. Her voice is soft and shaky as she says, "You left me."

"I had to take a very important phone call. I was coming right back."

"That's what my dad always says, and he never comes right back." She drops her head.

Fuck. I didn't know that's what her dad always does. "Look. Abby. I'm sorry. I won't do that again. Okay?" Her big hazel eyes peer up at me, and she nods. With my back hunched, I rise to my feet, needing to get out of this tiny ass train before claustrophobia takes over, but Abby doesn't move. Instead, she kicks the toe of her shoe against the wood floor. "What's wrong?"

"Why doesn't my dad want to see me? He's always canceling, or on the phone when we're together. Now you're doing it, too. No one wants to play with me." Her bottom lip juts out as her head droops.

Double fuck. Life never prepares you for those types of questions. I plop down on the wooden bench again. "Honestly, I don't know. But what I do know is your mom loves you so much and she loves spending time with you. And I enjoy hanging out with you too."

Her teary-eyed face peers up at me. "You do?

"Hel-heck yeah. We have so much fun together. I'm sorry about earlier. Still want to be my chipmunk?"

She nods and wraps her arms around my waist. I exhale, hugging her tight to me. "We should call the baby acorn."

"Acorn?"

"Yeah. You're squirrel, I'm chipmunk, so the baby is acorn."

"I like it. But does your mom need a name?"

She taps her chin. "Bunny!"

"So, we have bunny, squirrel, chipmunk, and acorn."

"Yeah!"

"I think that's perfect. How about I buy us some ice cream and pizza? Then we can go home and play whatever game you want."

Her eyes light up. "Princess tea party?"

"Uh. Of course. Anything you want."

"Yay!" Abby jumps to her feet. Before she's out the side exit, I stop her with a hand on her shoulder.

"One condition. Don't tell your mom I swore."

She runs her fingers over her lips like she's zipping them closed.

"I knew I liked you." Abby steps outside, and I wiggle my way through the small opening. Once I'm out in the open air, I stretch my arms and neck. Then I follow Abby to my SUV.

After we got home from stuffing our faces with ice cream and pizza, we got through one serving of princess tea party before Abby practically passed out on the floor still wearing her tutu. I tucked her into her bed and turned on her nightlight before softly closing the door behind me. When I'm back in the living room, I throw myself onto the couch. The pink and purple beaded necklaces flop against my chest. Exhausted, I let out a sigh and drop my head heavily against the couch. My scalp tingles as the plastic tiara pulls on my hair. Closing my eyes, I rub my hands firmly down my face. Today could have turned out way differently. I'm glad it didn't, but now I need to tell Rylee. Time ticks by as I stare at the ceiling as dusk turns to night. My eyelids grow heavy until they fully close.

The click of the door startles me awake and I jackknife off the couch. The pink plastic tiara falls to the floor and bounces a couple of times before coming to a rest next to the couch. I jump to my feet and see Rylee standing next to the door toeing off her shoes.

My heart jackhammers in my chest as I blurt out, "I lost your kid."

Her eyes jump out of their sockets as her purse falls to the floor. "What!?"

"I mean, I found her." In five long strides, I'm standing in front of Rylee. "She's sleeping in her bed. But for a brief moment today I lost her."

She clutches her chest and inhales a deep breath. "Back the confusion train up. How about you lead with that instead of 'I lost your kid.' What happened?"

I bend down and pick up her purse off the floor and set it on the counter. "We went to the park, and she was swinging on the swing set. I had to take a phone call, and I turned away for like five seconds and she was gone. I lost your kid. I'm going to be a terrible father. Who loses a kid?" I jab a finger at my chest. "This terrible soon to be father."

"Oh, Trey." Her eyes crinkle in the corners before she bursts out laughing.

"I'm glad you find my traumatic experience so hilarious."

"I'm sorry." She brushes the tears from under her eyes as she regains her composure. "You're not going to be a terrible father. A terrible father wouldn't care." Her warm palms cup my cheeks as she takes a step closer. "Based on your reaction, you care. A lot." She rises on her tippy toes and presses a soft kiss on my lips.

If she wants to show her apology in kisses, I'm all for it. Before I can deepen the kiss, she pulls away.

"Come with me." She grips my hand and leads me past the open kitchen and dining room and into the living room. She takes a seat on one side of the couch and pats the cushion next to her. "You're not going to be a terrible father. You want to know what I did?" She sits up and tucks one leg under her as she faces me. "One time when Abby was an infant, I went to the grocery store. I got her stroller all ready, put her favorite plush toy inside, and I had a bottle in hand. I patted myself on the back for remembering all her things. Halfway through the produce section I realized I left Abby in the car. I had her stroller and all her things, except no Abby."

"Oh shit. Was it hot out?"

"No. It was springtime. But that's not all. Another time I had her carrier with her inside in one hand and two bags of groceries in another. A flight of stairs stood between me and my apartment. Halfway up, one of the bags started to rip. While I was fumbling with not losing all my groceries, I lost my grip when the carrier bumped against the stairs and Abby slid halfway down before coming to a stop on the landing."

"Oh damn. And she was alright?"

"She slept through the entire thing. Not only are they safe enough for a car accident, but they're also safe enough for a half a flight of stairs."

My muscles relax a little as I lean against the back of the couch.

Rylee sits up on her knees and crawls toward me before hoisting a leg over my thighs to straddle me. I run my hands up her thighs, around her hips to her ass, and stop at her waist.

She cups my cheeks and forces me to meet her gaze. "So again, you won't be a terrible father. Keeping another human alive is hard and we all make mistakes, but we just keep doing our best and hope they turn out to be good people." She bends down and kisses me. It's chaste and entirely too quick. "And I'll talk to Abby because she knows better than to run off like that."

I blow out a breath and rest my forehead on her chest. "It was my fault."

She places her finger under my chin and lifts, forcing me to meet her gaze. "What do you mean?"

"When I took that phone call, that's when she bolted. Afterwards, when I talked to her, she said that's what her dad would do. Whenever they would spend time together, he would always take phone calls or busy himself with other things. She thinks that's what will happen with me." I felt like the world's biggest asshole after that. Like it should be stamped on my forehead for everyone to see. My very own scarlet letter, or in this case scarlet word.

Her gaze locks with mine. Soft and sincere. "In the short time I've gotten to know you, you're nothing like her father. And Abby knows that. She's just having a hard time with everything. But we'll get through this. All of it. We'll do it together." She clasps her hand around mine. "I was thinking, maybe we should get out of Harbor Highlands for a few days and spend some time together. Just us two."

"I'd like that. And I know the perfect place. I'll ask Seth and Parisa if they'll watch Abby since she had fun playing with Maddox at Adventure Land." I lift our hands and press a kiss to her knuckles. "Also, I should tell you Abby's name for the baby."

"Oh yeah? What'd she pick?" Her hands roam over my shoulders and chest.

"Acorn."

She softly smiles. "That's cute. It goes with all the other nicknames."

"She picked one for you too." I bit back my grin.

Her hands freeze and she tilts her head in curiosity. "What's that?"

"Bunny," I spit out, unable to hold back my smile any longer.

She drops her head to my shoulder, a laugh bubbling out of her. "Of course, I get the porn star name."

"Now, I fully expect you to live up to your namesake. We can start by doing deep sea fishing."

She quirks an eyebrow at me.

"A little harpooning the salty longshoreman." I thrust my hips up while bear hugging her to my chest. I nuzzle her neck with playful kisses.

She squirms and giggles as she gyrates against me. All thoughts about lost kids and terrible fathers are out the window and we're only left with porn stars named Bunny.

# Chapter 28

## BEG FOR IT

*Rylee*

After weeks of juggling work schedules and meetings, we finally carved out time for a weekend off together. After I picked up Abby from school, I dropped her off at Seth and Parisa's house for the weekend. When I arrived back at my apartment I had approximately thirty minutes before Trey would be here.

Pulling open the small door of the community mailboxes at my apartment, I grab the small stack of letters and slam the door. While climbing the stairs, I thumb through the stack. Bill. Bill. Bill. Junk. Bill. My chest tightens and I come to a halt in the middle of the staircase. Maybe I should pick up an extra shift instead of going away for the weekend. Feed the bank account instead of a mini-vacation. My phone vibrates against my butt, distracting me from my thoughts. I pull it out and read the message.

TREY

> Just left. Be there soon. Also, no need to pack clothes. I plan on keeping you naked and in bed all weekend.

Too late now. I shove the mail into my purse and climb the rest of the stairs.

During the hour drive north along the winding shore of Lake Superior, Trey and I talked about anything and everything. He shared with me the time when he was a kid and saw the northern lights for the first time, and he was convinced that aliens were coming to abduct him and his family. I told him about the time I ran away from home and hid out in my dad's boat behind the house, but as soon as the sun went down, I got scared and hustled back inside. During those three hours, I sat by myself and read books. Later, I found out my dad spotted me and knew where I was the entire time but waited for me to return. Unbeknownst to me, that would be the last time I would see my dad before he left. Perhaps if he never left, my mother wouldn't be so jaded about love and in turn, not have convinced me to marry Kyle for the stability.

Once we hit the scenic small town of Beaver Creek, Trey turns right and meanders down a gravel road through the forest. After a half a mile, it opens up to a giant log cabin with a sign hanging on the gable side that reads Three Moose Lodge.

Trey stops the SUV under the covered entrance. "I'll be right back." He shoves open the door and jumps out.

As he rounds the hood, I roll down the window. "Where are you going?"

"The best thing about this place is they have private

cabins scattered throughout the woods. So, I'm going to check us in and collect our key." His fingers curl around the open window as he leans in and presses his lips to mine. It's a kiss that has me craving more. So much more. Like all night worth of more.

A couple minutes later, Trey strolls out, dangling a key in his hand. Once he's seated, he shifts in to drive, and we snake down a one-way road flanked by luscious cedar, maple, and pine trees until we approach a small A-frame log cabin overlooking Lake Superior.

"This is so beautiful." My face is practically glued to the window as we pull into the single car parking spot. "In all the years I've lived in the area, I never knew something like this existed. It's like having your own lake cabin."

"A friend told me about it." He kills the ignition and turns to face me. "Originally, three brothers owned a single cabin. Over the years, it was passed down through the family and eventually expanded into several smaller cabins." He reaches for my hand and intertwines our fingers. Slowly, he lifts our hands and presses a soft kiss to the back of mine. "What do you say? Should we check it out?"

"Yes!"

He releases my hand as we step out of the SUV. Trey collects our bags as I wait for him under the covered porch. He jogs up the two steps and sets our bags down. With a twist of the key, he unlocks the door. Pushing it open, he motions for me to enter first. The front door closes with a click and Trey's standing next to me in the cramped entryway that leads directly into the only slightly larger kitchen that opens up into a spacious living room and deck.

I push open a door that's nestled between the kitchen and living room and it opens into an enormous bathroom with a gorgeous claw-foot tub nestled in front of a bay window facing the lake. "I am taking advantage of that later."

"You. Naked and wet. Count me in," Trey whispers in my ear.

I twist my head to the side and from the corner of my eye I notice a seductive, dimpled smile spread over his lips. It's the type of smile that sends a jolt of electricity right between my legs. In fact, it's the same smile that got me pregnant in the first place.

"We can do that later." I slide past him before I'm tempted to rip off his clothes and have my way with him. Pregnancy hormones have a mind of their own. In the living room, I spot a set of stairs that lead to a loft. "Is the bedroom up there?"

"Must be. Let's check it out." Trey hoists our bags over his shoulder and leads the way up the narrow staircase.

Once we reach the top, a king size bed rests against the wall in the middle of the room, flanked by two nightstands. A wingback chair and table sit in the corner next to the partial wall. The best part is the view. Straight ahead, a wall of windows sits at eye level as the waves of Lake Superior roll and crash into the rocky shoreline. "This is so beautiful. I never want to leave."

Trey steps in front of me, changing my view of the lake to a gorgeous six-foot two man with the most hypnotizing steely gray eyes. His hands run up and down my arms, sending a shiver through my entire body. "Good thing we have the weekend."

I wrap my arms around his neck and press into him as my fingers play with the short hairs on the back of his head. Rising to my tippy toes, I press my lips to his. His hands slide around my waist and hold me to him as he deepens the kiss. A groan sounds from his chest as he takes a step forward, forcing me backward. Then another. And another. Until my knees hit the edge of the mattress. Slowly, I slide down until my butt hits the comforter. Trey bends at the waist as I inch up the bed, resting on my elbows, all without his lips leaving mine.

Suddenly a rumble sounds from my belly. Trey breaks our kiss and rests his forehead against mine. "It sounds like someone wants lunch."

"There's something else I want more."

He chuckles. "We have all night for that. But first food. I'll grab the cooler from the car, and I'll meet you in the kitchen."

I huff out a breath. "Fine. But it might be a couple of minutes so I can release a little tension."

He growls, deep and gravelly. "Don't you dare touch yourself. All your orgasms will come from me."

Normally, I'm not one to listen when demands are made of me, but when Trey says things like this, it's hot as fuck. I wrap my fingers under the waistband of his jeans and haul him closer to me, so my lips are inches from his. "Then I suggest you do something about it."

"Fuck. You're just saying that to get what you want."

"Is it working?"

"Of course it is." He slams his lips to mine. It's rough and demanding and everything I want.

I moan while I reach out with one hand and flick open the button of his jeans. Breaking away, I hook my thumbs into the waistband of both his jeans and boxers and yank them down. His cock springs free, not fully erect but still impressive at half-mast. I wrap my hand around him, stroking once. Twice. He releases a deep groan from the back of his throat. His cock twitches in my hand, growing harder with each stroke.

His hand brushes a lock of hair off my face, tucking it

behind my ear. "Put me in your mouth. I want to see your pretty pink lips wrapped around me."

My tongue peeks out, wetting my lips before swirling around his head. I flick my tongue over the tip, lapping up the bead of pre-cum.

His hand cups the side of my head while his thumb lazily caresses my cheek. "Fuck. Rye. Let me feel you."

I wrap my lips around his girth and slide down until he hits the back of my throat. A deep moan rumbles from his chest. I pull back, running my tongue along the underside of his shaft.

"Oh yeah. Just like that." His fingers curl into my hair.

As I slide down again, I use my hand to twist around his length. I continue bobbing up and down as he rocks his hips, driving his cock deeper down my throat. Arousal pools between my legs. I moan around him, savoring his salty taste.

"Fuck. Your mouth is fucking perfect. Lips wrapped around me." He continues his shallow thrusts. "I can't. Fuck. You feel too good. I don't want to come in your mouth." He jerks away.

I whimper at the loss.

He bends down and nips at the shell of my ear before he growls, "My turn." The deep baritone of his voice reverberates through my body.

With a firm grip under my arms, he effortlessly lifts me higher on the bed. A half giggle, half yelp escapes me. My back hits the padded headrest. He hooks his thumbs under the elastic waistband of my yoga pants and tugs them down, taking my underwear with them. Once they're off, he throws them over his shoulder, and they land somewhere on the floor.

Desire swirls in his eyes as he takes a moment to admire my body. With his hands under my knees, he lifts, bends, and spreads them in one swift motion. A blast of cold hits me right between my legs, but a second later Trey's hot mouth is on me. A shudder racks my body from the contact.

I thread my fingers through the hair at the back of his head, holding him in place. "Mmm. Oh. Yes."

The pad of his thumb circles my clit as he continues to lap at my pussy. His tongue spears my entrance and I buck my hips while my grip on his hair tightens.

"Oh god. I'm not going to last long. Your mouth on me feels so good."

He replaces his thumb with his lips and sucks.

Tingles shoot through my entire body as my orgasm takes flight and I scream out Trey's name. He continues to lick and suck on my pussy until I'm nearing the brink of a second orgasm. When I'm teetering on the edge, he pulls away and I whimper.

He sits up and wipes his mouth with the back of his hand. "I want your next one to be on my dick. Sit up and turn around."

His demands are sexy as hell. Mostly because I know the pleasure I'll get from them. Rising to my knees, I spin around exactly as he says. With my back to him, he trails his hands up my sides, taking my hoodie and t-shirt with him until he's pulling them over my head. He pulls the elastic band from my hair and my long locks cascade over my shoulders.

The fabric of his shirt brushes against me as he leans forward, his breath against the shell of my ear. "You're so beautiful. I couldn't imagine anyone else carrying my child."

His hand splays over my small baby bump and my breath hitches. I've always underestimated Trey, but the more time I spend with him, he never ceases to amaze me. He's been everything I didn't realize I needed.

Slowly, his hands creep up and settle on my lace covered bra. His fingers dip into the cups and yanks down. Instantly, my nipples pebble from the cool air. "Now grip the headboard. I'm going to fuck you until you're seeing stars."

A pool of desire settles between my legs from his words. I bend over and grip the headboard as I'm told. There's just enough of a gap for my fingers to fit and it's solid enough that it doesn't move. Peering over my shoulder, I watch as Trey reaches behind him and pulls his shirt up. Inch by inch his lickworthy abs are revealed then his sculpted chest. I'll never tire of seeing him strip out of a shirt. A sly smirk covers his face as a blush floods my cheeks from being caught drooling over his bare chest. He tosses his shirt to the floor. I'm instantly drawn to the way his muscles flex with even the slightest movement. My gaze follows the small strip of hair that leads to his long, thick cock.

"If you're going to stare, it's best I give you something worth staring at." He wraps his fingers around his girth and leisurely strokes himself up and down. When he reaches the tip, he squeezes and a bead of pre-cum spills out.

It's hypnotizing. I suck on my bottom lip, my breathing growing heavy as I anticipate him almost splitting me in two with his size. All I want to do is leave my position and twist around to lick the tip of his cock like a lollipop, but I resist. Instead, I wiggle my ass. "Trey, I need you. I need you so much."

He continues to stroke himself. "Are you begging for my dick?"

"Yes. Fuck. I need your cock in me. I need it so much."

"I love when you beg."

With one hand on my hip, he inches closer to me. The head of his cock slides up and down my pussy, teasing my entrance. My fingers clench the edge of the headboard. A second later, he's thrusting inside me.

# Chapter 29

## I KNOW MY ANSWER

*Trey*

Fucking hell. A deep groan rumbles from my chest. Her warm heat surrounding my dick is like home. There is no other place I'd rather be.

She inhales a sharp breath as she adjusts to my size. I pull out an inch and thrust back in. As I continue pumping into her, she pushes into me, needing more and I'm here to please.

"Fuck. Your pussy feels so fucking amazing. Gripping me." My fingers curl around her soft hips as I continue slamming into her. Our skin slaps together, growing louder with each thrust.

"Oh! Yes! Right there. Don't stop." Her breathing grows shallower with each pump of my hips.

I continue to drive into her as her pussy clamps down

hard on me, sucking me in. "Fuck. Rye." My hand runs over the soft flesh of her ass. Softly, I tap her creamy skin. She yelps in surprise, but also her pussy clenches around me. "You like that?"

"Yes. Do it again." She pushes against me with a wiggle and moans.

While I continue thrusting, I slap her ass again, a little harder this time.

"Ah! Yes! Yes!" she chants.

Her pussy pulsates around my dick. My eyes roll to the back of my head as I savor the feeling. I won't be able to hold out much longer. I caress the reddening handprint on her backside.

"Again. Do it again." She slams back into me.

"My girl likes it dirty. But I want you screaming out my name." I reach under her, running a finger up her slit. When I reach her clit, I rub small circles over the tight bud alternating the pressure with my thrusts.

"Oh god! Trey! Ah!" Her pussy spasms around my cock. Her knuckles turning white as she grips the headboard.

"That's a good girl." My hand smacks down on her ass again, and she moans out my name. I continue to drive deeper and harder with each thrust. Her moans mix with my grunts with each slide of my dick in and out of her.

"Fuck Rylee. Give me one more."

"I. Can't." The words come out in breathy pants.

I plunge into her, rolling my hips to hit her g-spot. Doubling my pace, I pound into her over and over.

"Trey. Don't stop. I'm almost. There." Her words are breathy moans.

A second later, her back arches and her pussy clenches around my dick as her orgasm rips through her. Her moans and screams fill the loft. A tingle starts at the base of my spine and shoots directly to my balls.

"Fuck!" A tsunami of ecstasy washes over me as I follow her orgasm with one of my own. My pumps grow shallower and eventually I come to a stop, still inside her. My chest heaves as I work to collect my breath. "That was the best orgasm I've ever had."

The rise and fall of Rylee's back eventually evens out. Then she glances over her shoulder, a pink blush covering her cheeks. "You say that every time."

"That just means you keep setting the bar higher and higher." I lean forward, being careful to not put too much weight on her and place a kiss to the center of her back. "Let me get you cleaned up."

I pull out and race to the small table in the corner where a box of tissues sits. The bed dips as I kneel behind her and do the best I can to clean her up. When I'm done, I collect her clothes that I threw on the floor and place them on the bed next to her. She adjusts her bra as I pull up my boxers and pants.

"Now I'll grab the cooler and make lunch. Unless you're threatening to touch yourself again."

She laughs. It's delicate and sweet. "No. I need a little recovery time after that. Or a lot. I think a nap is in order."

"Good." I press a kiss to her forehead. "Come down when you're ready."

After I get the cooler emptied into the fridge, along with all the other groceries put away in the cupboard, I pull out a bowl and dump a bag of a spring mix lettuce inside. With a knife, I slice chunks of cucumbers and tomatoes and toss them in the bowl.

Rylee strolls down the stairs fully dressed again and with her hair tied up in a messy bun. "Oh yeah. I'm definitely hungry now." She runs a hand over her belly as she moves to stand next to me.

With tongs, I pile the salad into a bowl and pass it to her. "Take a seat and start with this while I make the sandwiches."

"I won't argue with that." She strolls to the circular pub table and pulls out the stool.

A of couple minutes later, I'm joining her with a salad of my own and two turkey caprese sandwiches.

"Mmm. This is so good," she mumbles around a mouth full of bread and turkey.

"I remember you saying that with something else in your mouth." I smirk.

She playfully backhands my arm and swallows down her bite of food. "I've never once said that."

"But you could." I lift my sandwich to my mouth for a bite. My foot bounces on the foot ring of the stool. Curiosity takes over about the sex earlier. I didn't expect her to be so responsive to the spanking in a positive way. She's so strong and independent. I would have thought she'd want to turn the tables and spank me instead. If she'd asked, I would have let her. "How are you feeling?"

"I'm good." She nods.

I set my sandwich on the plate. "Even after the... spanking?"

Pink covers her cheeks. "That was a first for me."

"Did you like it?"

Her lips tip up into a warm smile. "More than I thought I would."

"How's your cheek? I wasn't too rough, was I?" I rub my hand over her thigh and around the back to the top of her ass.

"I think you're using that as an excuse to rub my ass right now."

"I mean... It's a bonus."

She laughs. "It's good. It feels good. Is that something you enjoy doing?"

I move my hand back to the top of her leg, my fingers leisurely stroke her inner thigh. "I've dabbled. Your ass is perfect so I couldn't resist. Is that something we can do more often?"

"You better not stop." She smiles up at me.

After lunch, we take a stroll along the sandy beach. The sheer rock faces rise dramatically from the water's edge surround the bay creating serene waters along the shore. With our hands linked together we soak up the sun and watch as a sailboat floats along the horizon.

I kick at a piece of driftwood. "I told my parents about you and the baby. They'd really like to meet you and Abby."

"Are we at the meeting the parent's stage of this friends with benefits relationship?" She peers up at me, shielding her eyes from the sun.

"Only if you're ready. But they will be grandparents to our acorn."

"True." She rolls her lips between her teeth. "Okay. Let's set something up."

I link my fingers with hers and lift, pressing a soft kiss to the back of her hand. "They're excited. They'll love you and Abby. My happiness means the world to them, and you make me happy."

Her gaze falls to the sand. "Speaking of parents. I told my mother as well. While happiness may not be in her vocabulary, she's aware and may or may not be there when our acorn is born."

My eyebrows pinch together. "Why's that?"

Rylee tells me about her mom and the numerous husbands she's had since her dad left and how it was her mom who convinced her to marry Kyle after she got pregnant. Over the years, her mom hasn't been supportive of her life decisions. While she's maintained a relationship with her, it's been distant.

I halt in my tracks and tug her to me. I wrap my arms around her shoulders and bend down, pressing my lips to hers. "You got me now. And I have no plans on leaving." At one time, a six-year-old asked if I loved her mom, and I think I know my answer.

## CHAPTER 30

## YOU'RE MY FAVORITE

### Rylee

I snuggle deeper into the bed of blankets Trey set up earlier on the deck of our cabin. The moon rises gracefully over the lazy rolling waves of the lake, casting a shimmering reflection on the water's surface. Shades of deep orange, soft pinks, and hues of purple paint the sky as stars fight to push through the darkening horizon.

The sliding door opens and Trey steps out, a mug of hot cocoa in his hand. When he's within arm's reach, he passes me the steaming cup. I wrap both hands around it, inhaling the chocolatey goodness before taking a sip.

"Thank you." I glance up at Trey. "This is perfect. Well, almost perfect." I place the mug on the Adirondack side table next to me. My fingers grip the corner of the blanket and lift. A shiver runs over my body. Trey kneels on the makeshift blanket bed, accepting my invitation. The cool air is replaced by his warmth. He wraps an arm around me, tugging me to his side. His thumb lazily brushes over my shoulder.

Goosebumps spread across my arms for an entirely different reason. I never grew up with dreams of what I wanted my life to be. If I'd told myself I'd be sitting under a blanket on a deck overlooking Lake Superior with a guy who I'm only having a baby with, I would've laughed. Especially when I already have a daughter with another man. Oddly enough, there isn't anywhere else I would want to be.

"Oh." I hold my breath, waiting to see if it happens again.

"What's wrong? Everything alright?"

My lips curl into a smile. I grab his hand and shove it under the blanket.

"Oh!" His eyebrows quirk up as a devilishly sexy smirk crosses his lips. "We're doing this out here?"

"No." I laugh. "Our acorn is moving."

"Oh! Well, that's equally exciting!"

I position his hand on my belly where the baby moved, but after a few seconds of nothing happening, Trey's face falls.

"I'm sorry. This won't be the only time." I drop my hand from his, but he keeps his positioned on my belly.

He pushes the blanket away with his elbow, and it falls to my lap. Scooting down so his head is next to my belly. "Hey acorn. This is your father," he says in his best Darth Vader voice. "So, you might be too young for that, but I promise we'll have a *Star Wars* marathon when you're older. I've been reading a library's worth of how not to screw up your kids' life books. That's not actually the title, but that's the gist of it. Anyway, I'm supposed to talk to you, so you hear my voice. But don't listen while me and your mom are getting it on. Just... earmuffs."

My belly bounces as I'm unable to contain my laughter any longer. I wrap my arm around Trey's shoulders, my fingers playing with the short hairs on the back of his head. My heart swells for this man. Our baby. Everything that's happening at this moment. If I wasn't already pregnant, I would tell him to put one in me. Right now. Instead, I'm basking in the special moment he's having with our baby. This is what it should have been like the first time. Not me in a house—not a home, because living with Kyle didn't give home vibes—waiting for him to walk through the front door. And when he finally did, pretending he didn't smell like some other woman's cheap perfume because I was too scared to be alone.

Trey's cooing at my belly pulls me back to the present.

"After many failed attempts at getting your mommy to go out on a date with me, she finally agreed to let me walk her to her car. Once we were alone, she was unable to resist Daddy's charm. She seduced me into getting into the backseat of Daddy's SUV and had her wicked way with me. And that's the night you were conceived." He glances up at me. "Did I get that right?"

I giggle. "Something like that. But also, we are never telling our child the actual story."

A playful grin covers his face before he whispers to my belly, "Mommy's no fun."

A fluttering sensation takes flight on the right side of my stomach. Trey's shoulders tense.

"Do you feel that?" I whisper.

Trey glances up at me, hand still splayed over my stomach. "I do." Then he stretches, placing a kiss on my lips. "I think our little acorn wants to know more about conception night."

For the next fifteen minutes, Trey continues talking to my belly about each time Daddy convinced Mommy to go on a date with him. "I think our acorn had enough of me talking." He sits up, yanking at the edge of the blanket, covering us again.

Over the lake, the moon rises higher as the last of the daylight disappears into the inky darkness. Crickets break the silence as their chirps sound around us. I fiddle with a loose thread on the blanket, working up the courage to ask Trey about his past, since he has yet to offer anything willingly.

"So, what happened?" My heart thunders in my chest, preparing myself for his answer. "Why don't you do relationships? And why didn't you want kids?"

Trey exhales a deep breath. "Well, it started when a teeny tiny egg started floating down. All the sperm just zipped by while I chill—"

"Really?" I playfully backhand his stomach.

"Okay. Fine." He softly laughs. "I was doing what a sperm does and shot straight into the egg."

I scrunch my nose and glare at him.

"Alright. Alright. Fast forward six years. I'm a strapping young lad minding my business on the schoolyard playground, and Quinn Anderson pulls me under the slide and tells me to kiss her."

"And you did?"

"Of course! It was Quinn Anderson. Plus, she shared her cookie with me." He shrugs.

"Oh God. Please tell me cookie is actually a cookie and not cookie…" I motion my hand over my crotch.

"I was five years old. Who do you think I am? Of course, it was a cookie. They were the best peanut butter M&M cookies I've ever had." Trey stares wistfully off into the distance.

"So that's it?"

Trey shakes his head and narrows his eyes at me. "No. Because what really broke my heart was less than five minutes later, I caught her kissing Travis McNeil next to the merry-go-round."

I raise an eyebrow. "I'm sorry Quinn broke your heart. But that was a long time ago and I think it's best if you move on. I'm going to give you five seconds to grieve your loss, then I'm going to tell you to get over it. Nicely of course. One. Two. Three."

He sits up straighter, resting against the side of the cabin. "I'll have you know, I didn't kiss another girl until I turned ten."

I rest my hand on his and squeeze. "You poor thing. But again, maybe it's time to move on."

Trey stares up past the trees and into the black sky. The breeze rolls through, rustling the leaves. Unsure if the conversation is over or not, I sit patiently, but then Trey breaks the silence.

"During my senior year of college, I started dating a girl. Everything was perfect between us, or that's what it seemed. After graduation, I immediately got hired at The Blue Stone Group, which is pretty impressive right out of college. The money flowed in." He blows out a breath. "Looking back now, that's the moment our relationship flipped from good to red flags. At first, I'd find a few of her things at my place, which wasn't an issue until more and more stuff accumulated. Out of nowhere, she began demanding to know where I was, what I was doing, and who I was with. It got to be too much. When I went to break it off with her, she said she was pregnant."

My heart stops. This must be the woman who lied about being pregnant. I brush my thumb over his hand, encouraging him to continue.

"I was excited. Nervous. Scared. The entire spectrum of emotions ran through me. Between repaying my student loans, I now had a baby to care for. During that time, she told me everything she needed for her and the baby. As each day passed, she continuously asked for more and more. Eventually she asked me to keep the receipts and then told me to only shop at certain stores. She was constantly in my ear, telling me a good dad would do this or buy her that. If I couldn't take care of her, I'd never be able to care for our child. When I didn't buy her something she asked for, she'd tell me how terrible of a parent I'd be."

"That is horrible." My heart shatters for Trey. No one should have to endure that kind of manipulation. I squeeze the top of his hand, offering whatever comfort I can.

"Unfortunately, that's not all." He glances down as he flips his hand so our palms touch. With slow movements, he runs his fingers up and down mine. "A couple of times she'd come home with ultrasound photos. When I asked her why she didn't tell me so I could go, she claimed she forgot, or she had to reschedule last minute, and she didn't want to bother me at work. By the time it got to when you'd expect someone to show, she never did. She said the doctor told her that can happen and it's nothing to worry about. I had no reason not to believe her. Then I hit a wall. I was mentally and physically exhausted from everything. Since I couldn't afford everything myself anymore, I went to my parents about it, and they knocked some sense into me. They demanded that I go to the next doctor appointment because they believed she was lying. When I confronted her about it, she accused me of not believing her and not wanting to take care of her or the baby. That I was selfish. She said a lot of hurtful things. Again, my parents stepped in, threatening legal action if she was not pregnant like she claimed. The threat of a lawsuit must have spooked her because after that she came clean. She lied about everything, then left town."

My jaw falls open. "Oh my god, Trey. That's terrible." I rest my head on his shoulder. "I'm so sorry you had to go through that."

He nods. "It's been years since I've talked about it. Mostly because I've never had to bring it up. I locked it up deep inside and never wanted to let it escape. She ruined the experience for me. After that, it was easier to convince myself that I never wanted kids."

He wraps one arm around my shoulder, tugging me to his chest, and rests his other hand on my belly. "But with you, everything feels different. From the first time we had an actual conversation at Porter's."

"When you tried to save me from the guy hitting on me?"

"I knew you could hold your own. I was there for moral support."

I giggle and snuggle deeper into his chest.

"Since that moment, there was something that made me want to get to know you more. You're strong and feisty. You don't take shit from anyone, including me. That's what I love about you."

Every muscle in my body goes rigid. Holy shit. Did he just say what I think he said? He loves me. Everything in me wants to say those three words back. They're only a breath away, but I can't. He notices my stiffness and squeezes me tighter as if he's afraid I might get up and walk away. But I have no intention of leaving.

"I love you, Rylee and I'm ready to take this next step in our lives. I've loved you since that night at Porter's and then I loved you more every time you turned me down. But I loved you the hardest when you told me we were having a baby. And I will love you every single day from here on out."

Tears prick my eyes. "I can't compete with that speech." I reach up and cup his cheek. The short stubble tickles my fingertips as I haul him down to me, pressing my lips to his. It's soft and gentle and I pray he doesn't hate me for what I'm about to say. "I care about you. A lot. So don't take my lack of saying those three words to mean otherwise, but I just can't. Not right now."

A hint of disappointment flashes over his face, but he quickly recovers, giving me a half-smile. "I understand. Are we still doing the exclusive friends thing?"

"It's better that way."

"Maybe friends who live together?"

"How about one thing at a time? This baby being the first one."

"Okay. Baby steps." A smile flirts on his lips. "Get it. Baby. Steps." He rests his large palm on my belly.

I shake my head but can't help but share in his playfulness with a smile of my own.

"I can wait. You're worth waiting for." He presses his lips to mine. "Honestly, I'm glad you turned me down so many times."

I peer up at him, head tilted. "Why's that?"

"It made me work for it and then it made the reward that much sweeter. Not to say you're a trophy to be won." He rubs the back of his neck. "I'm fucking this up, aren't I?"

I cup his cheek, forcing his gaze to meet mine. "Not at all."

Love and adoration shine behind his steely gray irises. "Not to sound like an asshole, but if you didn't keep your distance, it would have been a one and done situation.

That's what I always did. You gave me a challenge. It made me a better man. You make me a better man."

A tear rolls down my cheek and he wipes it away with his thumb.

"Shit. I didn't want to make you cry."

I laugh through my blurry vision. "Happy tears." It's on the tip of my tongue to tell this amazing man that I love him. The words are right there, but I can't spit them out. Three words. It shouldn't be this hard. All I can do is pray that he'll be patient enough to wait until I'm ready.

I caress his cheek. "You're an amazing man, Trey Alexander Wilson. And you're going to make an even more amazing father. You're my favorite." I rise and press my lips to his in a soft, lingering kiss, hoping he feels everything that I want to tell him but can't.

He pulls away. Lips centimeters away from mine. "Is that your version of the three word phrase?"

I contemplate his words. It is three words and to me the meaning is the same. A smile flirts on my lips. "I guess it is."

"I can live with that." He kisses the tip of my nose. "What do you say, want to go to bed?"

I nod. Trey stands and holds out his hand to help me to my feet. While I push the sliding door open, he collects the blankets. Once inside, he deposits them on the couch. I climb the stairs to the loft and Trey's right behind me. As I change into my pajamas, I notice Trey stripping out of his. I can't help but drool over the way his muscles move and flex as he removes his shirt. After brushing my teeth and splashing some cold water on my face, I fold the corner of the blanket down and crawl under the covers. Shortly after, Trey joins me and turns off the lamp. He rolls away from me and wiggles his butt against my hip. I roll my eyes but can't help but laugh. That's my cue. I throw my arm over his waist and snuggle into his back.

The next morning, I wake up to Trey snuggling me, his semi-hard cock poking me in the ass. This is what always happens. Sometime during the night, we swap positions. He stirs awake and nuzzles my neck with his nose.

"This is my favorite part of the day. Waking up next to you. Especially lazy mornings like this." His hand runs over the swell of my belly. "I figured out why we are meant to be together."

I wiggle my ass against his cock, and he groans. "Do tell."

"My favorite beer is a Rye IPA. Your name is Rylee or Rye. Two of my favorite things."

"That's very serendipitous."

His hand skates down to the apex of my thighs and my breath hitches. "You know what else is serendipitous? How wet I bet you are right now."

"That's not how it works."

"It will be a happy discovery." His fingers slip under the elastic waistband of my sleep shorts. "Bend your knee," he whispers against the shell of my ear. When I do as I'm told, the pad of his finger runs along my slit.

I exhale a breathy moan from the contact. His finger trails down and back up before rubbing a circle around my clit. "Mmm. I definitely love lazy mornings." I rock my hips, needing more contact. His finger teases at my entrance before plunging in. I inhale a sharp breath and exhale a moan.

"So, fucking wet for me. I think I'm going to eat my breakfast, then you can have yours."

I roll over while Trey collects pillows to create a back rest. My phone buzzes on the nightstand. Glancing over, *Parisa* flashes on the screen.

"Ignore it. You can call them back after breakfast."

"I can't. It's Parisa." The phone buzzes again and I reach over to grab it. I press the green talk button. "Hi Parisa." As she talks on the other end, my heart plummets. "Okay. We'll leave right now." I hang up the phone.

Trey's mop of dark hair peeks up from between my legs. "What's wrong?"

"There was an accident. It's Abby."

# Chapter 31

## CLAM JOUSTING

*Trey*

I jump off the bed. "Is she alright? What happened?" I love that kid as much as I love her mom. She's my chipmunk and right now she's hurt. What's even worse is that I'm not there.

"The kids were playing, and she jumped and fell awkwardly on her arm. It might be broken." Rylee casually throws her legs over the side of the bed as if there isn't an emergency right now.

"Shit. Get dressed."

My fingers shake as I tug on a pair of jeans and throw a shirt over my head. "I'll pack the car." In a frenzy, I rush around the room, shoving everything haphazardly into our bags, disregarding whose belongings they are or where they should go. I'll sort everything later. When the upstairs is clear, I toss our bags in the backseat of my SUV along with the cooler. I set a reminder to call the resort and explain that I'll cover the additional cleaning fee since I left all our food in the kitchen.

Once we're on the road, I press the gas pedal to the floorboard. Streaks of brown and green flash by in a blur on the two-lane highway. It's like I have tunnel vision. My only objective is to get to Abby. I hate that we're not there for her.

Rylee's phone buzzes again and she puts it on speakerphone. "Hey Parisa. How's Abby doing?"

"She's asking for you and someone named Squirrel?"

"That's me. Put her on." My chest tightens as if a five-hundred-pound brick is pressing down on it.

"My. Arm. Hurts," Abby chokes out between sniffles.

"Hey, Chipmunk. We're on our way. We'll be there soon." My tone is soft and soothing, hoping to reassure her even though my chest is in a vise grip. "You be strong, okay?"

"Okay." She sniffles again. "I love you."

My heart jumps to my throat. I glance at Rylee, and she smiles softly.

The vise grip loosens a little. "I love you, too. We'll see you soon."

I love that little girl with every fiber of my being. I'm hurting because she's hurting. My knuckles turn white as my grip tightens on the steering wheel.

"Trey. Slow down. It's not going to do us any good if we get in an accident and end up in the hospital ourselves." Rylee grips the grab handle.

"Sorry. I'm just... I want to make sure she's alright." I ease up on the gas pedal.

"She'll be okay." Her warm palm on my thigh eases some of my anxiety. "She's a tough girl."

I exhale a breath. My nerves settling a fraction. "You're right. She's your daughter, after all. I don't know how you can keep your cool."

"Oh. I'm freaking the fuck out but it's not going to do anything to help our situation at the moment."

I curl my hand around Rylee's, intertwining our fingers, offering what little comfort I can give her while she does the same for me.

---

"Wow, this sling is pretty bad a—awesome. It's pretty awesome." I run my fingers over the hot pink sling. "I bet you were a brave girl when they did the x-rays."

Abby nods as she sits next to me on the couch at Rylee's apartment.

Parisa brought Abby to the emergency room and sure enough, she broke her arm. We met them at the hospital right before they took her in for x-rays. Afterward, they set up an appointment for a cast, but in the meantime, they gave Abby a sling to keep her arm still and to wait for the swelling to go down.

"You know, when I was your age, I broke my arm too," I say to Abby.

"You did?" Puffy, red stained eyes meet mine.

"Yeah, I was trying to impress all my friends and show them I could jump from one side of the jungle gym to the other. When I jumped, I didn't quite make it and I hit the ground, breaking my arm."

"Wow. That's what I did." She sniffs, wiping her hand over her face.

"I even have a scar where the bone poked through the skin."

Her face scrunches up. "Eww! That's gross!"

"You want to see?"

"Yeah!"

I twist my arm, so my elbow is facing her and run my finger over the scar that runs down my forearm. Abby leans in to inspect it closer. "Sometimes it pops out of place, and I have to push it back."

She glances up at me, eyes wide. "No, it doesn't."

"It does. Look closely." While she leans in for a closer inspection, I hook my finger in my mouth and pull it out, making a loud pop. She jumps and screams before falling over into a fit of giggles.

"Okay. Maybe it doesn't. But I did get a really cool green cast that all my friends got to sign. What do you say? Should we get some markers so we can have your friends sign your cast?"

"Yeah! Can they be glittery ones?" She kicks her feet.

"We will find you the glitteriest markers. What do you say we put on a movie? We'll just hang out for the rest of the night."

"Yeah! Can we have ice cream too?"

"Go get your pajamas on," Rylee says, "and we'll meet you in the living room with a big bowl of popcorn."

"Okay." Abby scampers off to her room, her little feet patter along the carpeted floor. Rylee struts up to me and I stand to greet her. "You're really amazing with her." She rests her hands on my chest. "I'm sorry we had to cut our weekend short."

"You have absolutely nothing to be sorry about. I'm more than happy to spend the night on the couch watching whatever animated cartoon Abby's obsessed with this week, while snuggling up with my two favorite girls."

Her gaze meets mine as she drags her finger back and forth over my chest. "I promise I'll make it up to you."

"If by promise, you mean we get to play my favorite game, Trey Goes Clam Jousting, then yes. That's the exact promise I want." I wrap my arms around her shoulders, and her hands drop to my waist. Bending down, I press my lips to hers. It's soft and gentle, but fuck, I want more.

"Eww! That's gross!" Abby barrels down the hallway at full speed."

"Slow down," Rylee demands.

She slows her pace, her pink princess blanket dragging behind her. She flops down in the middle of the couch. "Bunny can sit here." She pats the right cushion. "And Squirrel, you can sit here." She twists so she can pat the other side with her good hand.

"Looks like we have a chaperone for this movie." I give Rylee one last kiss since I won't be able to over the next two hours.

"I'll make the popcorn." Rylee spins out of my grasp and saunters into the kitchen.

I can't tear my gaze away from her perfectly round ass sways back and forth with each step. My hand twitches to gently massage the soft skin before giving it a smack. I love seeing my red handprint on her creamy skin. Later. We can do that later. Right now, there are more important matters to take care of first. I lower myself to my designated spot on the couch. "Chipmunk, what are we watching?"

"Princesses!" She shouts. A wide toothy grin covers her face as if she didn't break her arm six hours ago.

Twenty minutes into the movie, Abby's softly snoring as she's cuddled into my side. But there is nowhere else I'd rather be right now.

## Chapter 32

### BABY BOOM

# Trey

"Look at this. You can have custom explosives made." I stare at my phone screen while leaning against the headboard in her bedroom.

After our movie and mini sleepover night, I've made it a habit of staying over at Rylee's apartment. Instead of the occasional once or twice a week, I've upped it to four or five nights. Going to sleep and waking up next to Rylee is my second favorite activity. Granted, my king size bed would give us more room, but her queen gives me an excuse to cuddle next to her. While I would love for her to move into my place, Rylee says it's easier on Abby since all her toys are here. Instead of pushing the matter, I'll take the breadcrumbs she'll give me because I know eventually those breadcrumbs will get bigger and bigger until it's an entire four course meal. It's a lot for Rylee to give up and she's not ready to do that. One thing at a time.

Rylee's in the same position as me, leaning against the headboard, flipping through the pages of a baby magazine. Without sparing a glance my way, she asks, "What are you talking about?"

"For the gender reveal party. You can get custom explosives. When they detonate, a cloud of whatever colored powder shoots into the air." I motion my hands like an explosive blowing up.

"Are you trying to start a wildfire?" She continues flipping through the pages.

"No, but it looks cool as shit. I wonder if they'll make one that spells out baby when it explodes? It would bring a new meaning to baby boom."

Finally, she lifts her head. Her lips trimmed to a harsh line. "We're not blowing anything up, and why are you looking up gender reveal parties?" Her tone is sharp.

"I thought it would be kind of fun to have one." I point to my screen. "How about this? We could hire a sky writer to fly above the house to show everyone if it's a boy or girl."

"That's a little excessive, don't you think?"

"Nothing is ever excessive. Oh. Let's do this." I hold out my phone so she can see the black sports car. "We can rent a car and when you rev the engine, it shoots out colored smoke revealing the gender."

"I don't even know if I want to have a party."

"Nonsense. We have to have a party. How about this? We can wrangle an alligator and have it chomp down on a melon to reveal the gender. Though I don't know where I'll find an alligator in Minnesota." I rub my chin.

"Trey. Stop. You're not listening to me." She slaps my phone out of my hands. "I don't need a party. I don't want a party. I don't need the pregnancy yoga, or the pregnancy walking group you signed us up for." She points to the far side of her small bedroom where bags and boxes of baby things are stacked. "I don't need any baby things. You got it covered for the next five years. Pretty soon, I'm going to be making tunnels out of baby things so I can navigate from one room to the other. Just. Please. Stop. I'm a fucking bartender with a depleting bank account with a baby on the way and you're obsessed with gender reveal parties. I just want you to take this seriously." She throws the blanket off and swings her legs over the side of the bed. She storms out of the room and down the hallway.

"Fuck." I scrub my hands down my face. This isn't what I wanted to happen. In fact, this is the opposite of what I wanted to happen. Quiet sniffles echo down the hallway from the living room. Double fuck.

Rolling out of bed, I follow her. In the living room, she's sitting in the dark on the edge of the couch. Her shoulders shake with silent sobs. With cautious footsteps, I inch my way into the living room and lower myself onto the cushion next to her. She leans into me, and I wrap my arm around her shoulders. She buries her head into my chest as her tears roll down my bare stomach.

"I'm sorry, Rye. I only want what's best for you and our acorn. I'm here. I'll always be here. For anything you need."

She sniffles before wiping away her tears. "I know. I'm sorry I blew up at you. Everything is just... a lot. It's so much, so fast. I've had to do so much by myself, so it's hard to accept the help and support. I never got that with Kyle. Even six years later." She sniffles. "I'm stressing out and I took it out on you. I'm sorry. While I appreciate the enthusiasm, can we slow things down? Starting with no gender reveal party."

I rest a finger under her chin, lifting her gaze to meet mine. "Of course. I'll cool it with all the baby stuff. We have the sealed envelope with the gender, if you want to rip it open. Kind of like a band-aid."

She presses her lips together. "Let's wait."

I nod. "I know it's a boy anyway, so it's cool."

She glances up at me. "And how do you know that? Did you peek?"

"I wished for it. Threw a quarter into a wishing well too. Screw that penny crap. That gets you nothing."

A small smile curls on her lips. "That's not how it works."

"I wished for you and that came true." Her sweet laugh fills the dark room as she playfully shoves at my chest. I wrap my arms around her, holding her to me so she can't move. "It's true." I continue to hold her close. "The offer to move in with me still stands. Then you wouldn't need to build those tunnels."

"Trey…"

"Or I can move in with you."

"What? There's no room. Are you going to sleep amongst all the baby boxes?"

"If I have to, I will. Hear me out. I'm not asking because I want to take care of you. I'm fully aware that you can take care of yourself, but I'm asking because I want you and Abby to have a home. No offense to your apartment, but at my house, Abby can have her own room. She can even have her own playroom. She'll have a yard to play in. Our little acorn will have its own room. Hell, if you get sick of me, you can have your own room too." I brush a finger over her soft cheek, tucking a lock of stray hair behind her ear and she nuzzles into my palm.

"I don't know. This is just a lot at one time."

"Well, I'm here for the long-haul. I'll wait for as long as I have to until you're ready." And I will. I know she's gone through hell and back with her ex. I will continue to fight to prove to her I'm not him.

## Chapter 33

## FIRED. NOT FIRED.

# Rylee

The 8 a.m. message from Jake this morning was a little ominous. He asked everyone to meet at Porter's ASAP. When Jake says ASAP, it doesn't mean as soon as possible. It's more like get your ass here now. My luck, he's telling everyone he sold the bar and we're all fired. Becoming a jobless pregnant single mom is not a good way to start my day.

I park my SUV between Nora and Dessa's vehicles. As I approach the door, something crunches under my shoe. Glancing down, the sidewalk shimmers from the sunlight like tiny pieces of glass. Oh shit! That *is* glass. My gaze shoots up and I'm met with a plywood covered window, glass littered walkway, and a propped open spider web cracked door. My jaw hits the ground. On my tiptoes, I cautiously step through the doorway and into the eerily quiet bar.

My gaze flits around the area, inspecting for any other damage. I find Dessa, Nora, Jake, and a few other employees huddled at the far end of the bar. A somber tone fills the atmosphere. "What happened?"

"Once everyone's here, I'll explain, so I only have to say this once," Jake says.

His normally perfect comb over fade is disheveled as if he's been running his hand through it. Based on the state of his bar, I'm sure that's exactly what he's been doing. I find an empty stool next to Nora and plop down.

"Uh, did you know you have some broken glass out front?" Lach strolls in, hiking his thumb behind him.

"Thanks asshole. I didn't see it there. Take a seat." Jake nods to the stool in front of him.

After Lach sits, we wait around for another ten minutes for Chad to arrive, but it's crickets.

"Fuck it. I'll deal with Chad later." Jake exhales a sigh. "If you can't tell, there was a break in last night or this morning. They stole some bottles of liquor. They tried to break into the safe but weren't successful. Something must have spooked them because they were out before the cops arrived."

We all gasp and sit up straighter on our stools. Over the four years I've worked at Porter's, nothing like this has ever happened. Not to say it can't. This wasn't a place I ever felt unsafe. Plus, Jake has lived here his entire life. Lived in this bar his whole adult life. Everyone knows him or knows of him. He's the last guy you want to mess with.

"Did the cameras catch anything?" Lach asks.

"Nothing that's identifiable." Jake rests both palms on the bar, his gaze cast downward. "Whoever it was seemed to have dodged the cameras. All I have are photos of the back of their head." He pushes off the bar until he's standing straight. "Be on alert, especially for anything suspicious. No one is to be here by themselves. Kind of a rule I've always had, but it's worth repeating. We'll be closed for the next day or two until shit is replaced. That's all." He raps his knuckles on the bar. "Rylee. Can I see you in my office?" He jerks his head and strides around the corner.

Dessa leaps out of her seat. "Jake! Don't fire her! It was me. I ate all the beef sticks. Not pregnant Rylee."

"You're a vegetarian," Jake yells from down the hall.

"Shit." She shrugs. "Sorry. I tried."

"Thanks." I brush my hand on her shoulder as I pass.

My footfalls echo down the hallway in time with the thumping of my heart. Everyone's not getting fired, only me. That's the only logical reason he'd call me to his office. Is he mad about the meat sticks? Son of a bitch. They were so good. Maybe he'll understand that the baby was craving them. Not me. I wipe my sweaty palms on my jeans before peeking my head through the opening. Without saying a word, Jake waves me in.

"I'm sorry. I'll pay you back for the meat sticks. The baby likes meat. I'm blaming Trey."

"This isn't about the meat sticks. Take a seat." He nods to the chair opposite of him. He rests his elbows on the desk and steeples his fingers together. "Have you decided when you'll be taking your maternity leave? Just so I can prepare and figure out everyone's schedule."

So not fired... "In about a month and a half."

He nods. "Okay. Great. Also, I want to say you've been doing a great job. Especially with taking over the inventory and ordering. I would like to offer you a bar manager position."

All the tension evaporates from my body. I huff out a

laugh. "Oh. Wow. I wasn't expecting that. Honestly, I thought you were firing me."

"You're my best employee. I will do whatever it takes to keep you here." Jake drums his fingers on the desk as I strand of sandy brown hair flops over his forehead.

I swallow down the lump in my throat. It's been one hell of an emotional rollercoaster over the past five minutes. Fired. Not Fired. Promoted. "I don't know what to say."

"Just tell me you'll take it. As far as your schedule goes, whatever time you need off or whatever appointments you need to go to, I'll make it work. Since heavy lifting is off limits, either Lach or I will be here for delivery days to move all the boxes."

I nod, soaking in everything he's telling me. With the baby coming, I'll need all the money I can get. "Can you give me a couple of days to think about it?"

"Of course. Take all the time you need. But not too long." He flashes me a half-smile, but in terms of Jake smiles, that's equivalent to a full-blown toothy grin.

"Thanks, Jake." I rise to my feet and stop before I leave. I press my lips together. "About the break in... some time ago, there was a truck that followed me after I left work. It was only a couple of miles, so maybe it was a coincidence, but I wanted to say something, especially now."

"Wait." Jake taps away on the keyboard and twists his monitor to face me. "It's only a partial view, but does that look familiar?"

Leaning in, I study the grainy black and white photo and there's one thing that jumps out at me. "It's missing the side mirror. The truck that followed me was missing one, too."

"Do you know who owns it?"

I shake my head. "No. I don't." I blink. "Oh wait. I was with Trey and I saw a truck that looked familiar." I tap my finger to my lips, racking my brain for the name he told me. "Wilcox. Henry Wilcox. But I'm not one hundred percent if the truck I saw with Trey is the same one that followed me out of here."

"Alright. I'll let the police know. Stay alert and keep everything on the down low."

"Okay. Will do." I stroll through the doorway and down the hallway. The truck and the break in are at the forefront of my thoughts. Are the two related? Or a coincidence? I chew on my thumb nail thinking back to the night leaving the parking lot.

When I step out into the bar, Dessa perks up and jumps off her stool and wraps her arms around my shoulders, catching me by surprise. "Oh my god. Jake fired you. The frown on your face says it all." She squeezes me again before yelling over my shoulder, "Jake! I quit!" She leans closer. "We don't need this place. We'll find something else. Something better."

"Jake didn't fire me."

She frowns. "Then why do you look so sad?"

I keep the talk about the truck to myself. "Because he gave me a promotion."

"So, you're not fired?"

"No."

She leans past me again. "Jake! Just kidding! I love working here!" Her attention focuses back on me. "Congratulations. I'm so happy for you. When do you start?"

"Thanks. I haven't agreed yet though."

"You're taking it, right?"

"Yeah. I just want Jake to sweat it out for a bit." A smirk covers my lips.

"This is why we're best friends." She wraps me in another hug. "Since we have the rest of the day off, want to go get breakfast? My treat."

"Thanks, but Kyle is coming to pick up Abby tonight, so I want to run some errands before Trey comes over." I've been craving a night alone with Trey. I forgot how difficult it is to carve out alone time when you have a kid. Now with another on the way, we want to take every moment available to spend together.

"I get it. You two will be stuffing the turkey. Enjoy it. I'm not jealous one bit." She rests a hand on her hip. "Of the sex. Not Trey."

"Got it." I laugh.

I spent the rest of the morning grocery shopping and in the afternoon, I cleaned the apartment. With only a few minutes to spare, I grabbed a backpack and swiftly packed an overnight bag for Abby, ensuring she had everything she would need for the night.

The intercom for my apartment buzzes. Since Trey texted me he was coming, I knew it was him and let him inside. While I haven't been able to get him a copy of the main door key, I gave him one of my extras for my apartment.

Before he's two steps through the doorway, Abby jumps off the couch and barrels toward him. "Squirrel!"

He bends down and wraps his arms around her. "How's my chipmunk?"

"Good. Come see the picture I drew at school today." She grabs his hand and tugs him toward her room.

As he passes me, he leans over and places a quick kiss

on my lips. "I'll be back for more of those." Abby yanks on his arm and he jerks away. Both of them are absolutely adorable.

While Abby is busy showing him anything and everything, I prepare dinner. When it's finished, I stroll to Abby's room. Trey's on the floor next to Abby looking like they're besties for life. I'm sure the matching tattoos will come next. The floor is a chaotic mess of papers and markers scattered haphazardly. "Dinner's ready. Then you'll need to clean this up before your dad picks you up."

Abby climbs to her feet. She trudges past me, a full blown pout covering her face. I run my hand over the top of her head, brushing away her chestnut brown hair.

At the table, I sit at the end while Abby and Trey sit on either side of me. I scoop a spoon full of peas and dump it on her plate. With her head resting in her hand, she shoves a pea around her plate.

"Abby. Eat your dinner." She stabs at a piece of chicken but doesn't eat it. I drop my fork onto my plate. "What's wrong?"

Her bottom lip juts out. "I want to stay here."

"You don't want to stay with your dad tonight?"

"No," she pouts. Her gaze is fixed on a pea on her plate.

"Abby, look at me." She lifts her head. Her normally bright hazel eyes appear colorless. "Why not? He's renting the new princess movie for you tonight."

"I don't want to watch it."

"Abby. You've been talking about that movie for weeks. Why don't you want to watch it now?" The pea flies off her plate and rolls across the table. I reach over, resting my hand on hers. "Why don't you want to go?"

She drops her fork on her plate. The clatter echoes through the apartment. "I want to stay here with you and

Squirrel. I don't want to go to Dad's. It's not fun. He doesn't play with me. He's always busy."

"He wants to spend time with you," I reassure her.

"I don't want to go." She pushes away from the table and runs across the kitchen to her room.

I turn to Trey. "I'm sorry. She's never done this before. I'll be right back." I walk to Abby's room to find her face down on the bed, her face buried in a pillow. The bed dips as I sit on the edge. "Abby. What's wrong?" I run my hand over her shoulder blades.

She mumbles into her pillow.

"Sit up."

She rolls over. Her cheeks are red and tear stained. "I don't want to go. Dad always works when I'm with him and it's boring. I hate it there. I want to stay here with you and Squirrel. You two always play with me." Her big hazel eyes meet mine. "Do I have to go?"

My heart breaks. If she's this distraught about going, I won't force her. I brush a thumb over her cheek, wiping away the tears. "No. You don't have to go. But can you finish your dinner?"

"I'm not hungry."

"Then can you clean your room?"

She sniffles and nods her head.

I wrap her small body in my arms. "I love you forever."

"I love you always," she mumbles into my shirt.

When I return to the kitchen, Trey's filling the sink with soapy water and scooping leftovers into containers. I lean my butt against the counter next to him. "Sorry. Our alone night for two just turned into three."

He snaps the lid closed on a container. "You have absolutely nothing to be sorry about. I love spending time with both my girls."

My lips pull into a small smile. Even in moments like

this, he knows the perfect thing to say. "I guess she's still upset that Kyle spends his time working when he's supposed to be spending it with her. I can't blame her. That's shitty of him to do. I can't force her to go if she doesn't want to, right?"

"It's the right call on not forcing her." Trey dries his hands on a towel before wrapping me in a hug.

I bury my face into his chest, needing all the comfort I can get. "Parenting is never easy."

"Abby is lucky to have you as her mom." He presses his lips to my forehead.

I huff out an exasperated breath. "I guess I should call Kyle and let him know not to come." Reluctantly, I pull away from Trey's warmth and snatch my phone off the counter. With heavy steps, I make my way into the living room, dreading the phone call I'm about to make. Somehow Kyle will spin it to make it about him because he always does. Blowing out a breath, I pull up his number and press call. After four rings, he finally picks up. "Hey Kyle, just wanted to let you know you don't have to pick up Abby tonight."

"But it's my day with her. I cleared my schedule for this and now she's not coming over?"

Done with his bullshit, I get straight to the point. "She says all you do is work."

"I have shit I have to do, Rylee."

"Apparently, spending time with your daughter isn't one of them."

"I can't ignore important work calls." He grumbles something I can't hear. "I'm doing the best I can. I can't just drop my entire life."

I roll my eyes. If I could reach through the phone and strangle him, I would. "It's called being a parent, Kyle. Sometimes you have to make those sacrifices. I just want to let you know not to bother picking her up." If I was a betting person, I'd placed a million dollars on the only reason he wants to see her tonight is because if he doesn't spend so many days a month with her, he has to pay more in child support. When it involves anyone else, Kyle is the epitome of stinginess.

"You're just going to let a six-year-old do whatever she wants?"

I bite my tongue, wanting to keep my tone as neutral as possible. "I will not force her if she doesn't want to go," I say through gritted teeth.

"None of this was like this until you started dating him."

"Trey?" My fingers clench around my phone. I'm surprised it doesn't snap in half.

"Yeah."

I turn around so I'm facing away from the kitchen and lower my tone. I don't need Abby listening. Who am I kidding? She's six. She hears everything. "This has absolutely nothing to do with Trey, so keep his name out of your mouth," I sneer.

He scoffs. "Brainwashed. Both of you."

"You're so full of it."

The call disconnects. My blood boils. I don't know how I ever dated that guy, let alone married him.

Trey tiptoes into the living room as if he's approaching a wild animal. "Everything all right?"

"Yeah. It's just Kyle being Kyle." I tuck a strand of hair behind my ear. "Why don't you get Abby? I'll finish cleaning up in the kitchen and we'll have our own movie night."

"Or you get Abby and I'll finish cleaning up." He cups my cheek. "Kyle's not the only one who can rent a princess movie."

I lean into his warm palm. The simple gesture gives me the comfort I need. He makes everything better. "Have I told you yet today that you're my favorite?"

"You haven't." The corner of his lips tip up into a smile.

"Because you are."

"Thank you." He winks. "I love you."

From what could have been a disastrous night, Trey turned it around, not only for me, but for Abby. Now, I need to get my shit together to give him everything he's given me. It would be much easier if I wasn't so broken.

# Chapter 34

## MEATCUTERIE

## Rylee

"Wow. This is a lot of food." Dessa places a Crockpot down on the massive white quartz island next to the other twenty Crockpots and platters of food. "Are you expecting a small army?"

"It's a little bigger than what I was expecting." I move the napkins and silverware from the counter next to the fridge to the island. After I vetoed Trey's gender reveal party, I let him take the reins of the baby shower. I told him generally it's just the mother and friends and family, mostly females, but he wasn't having it. He wanted a party for everyone, and he insisted that we have it at his house.

"Look at you compromising already." Dessa rests a hand on her hip.

"Honestly, the sadness in his eyes killed me and made

me cave." I nod to the living room. A giant yellow and gray *A Baby Is Coming* balloon arch display sways as a breeze flows through the open window. "That's your party favor, so don't forget to take that home when you leave."

She tilts her head. "I don't even know where I'd put that."

Trey steps through the sliding screen door from the patio and into the kitchen. He throws an arm over my shoulder and glances down at a tray in front of him. "What's that? With the olives, cheese, and crackers."

"A charcuterie board," Dessa says.

"Oh. That's not going to work." He drops his arm from around my shoulder.

She props a hand on her hip. "What are you talking about?"

"There's no meat. I'm going to the store."

Dessa points to her chest. "Vegetarian."

I throw my hands up in the air. "People will be arriving soon."

Trey's out of the kitchen and in the foyer. "I'll be back in fifteen minutes. Believe me. No one is starting this party without me."

I sigh. I'm too tired to argue with him. He'll just do what he wants. As long as he's not trying to ignite explosives, it's just easier this way.

"Knock knock." Lach wraps his knuckles on the wall as he enters the kitchen. "Trey told me to come in. Where's he going, anyway?"

"Good question." I blow out a laugh. In two slow strides I wrap an arm around Lach's waist in a side hug. "Thanks for coming."

"Of course. I couldn't pass up the opportunity to come to my first baby shower." He holds up a sealed card. "Also,

I have no fucking clue what to buy someone for a baby shower gift, so here's a gift card."

"I'll take that." Dessa plucks the card from his hand and carries it to the gift table.

"Thanks. But perfect timing. Can you help me move some tables? And by me, I mean Dessa, and I'll supervise."

"Sure thing."

We step outside on to an open patio that's surrounded by a meticulously manicured lawn that's filled with even more baby shower decorations that follow our yellow and gray theme. Off to the right on the patio is a seating area of plush furniture circling a stone fireplace.

Dessa blows out a low whistle. "Why haven't you agreed to move in with him yet?" She elbows me in the arm and winks.

"Can I sleep with Trey and move in?" Lach asks.

"You guys are so funny. Ha ha. How about less talking and more table moving?" I clap my hands.

After all the tables are moved to where I want them, movement in the house catches my attention. I pull open the patio door and blink. Not because of needing to adjust to the light, but from who's standing in front of me.

"Hi Mother. I'm glad you could make it." A mixture of surprise and agitation laces my tone.

"You did send me an invitation." She flips her bleach blonde hair over her shoulder.

"It was mostly for politeness." I rest my hand on my hip. Trey insisted that we send her an invite even though I told him there was a ninety-nine percent chance she wasn't going to come. Since I lost that bet, I owe him a game of Conquering the Pink Forest. "I never expected you to actually show up. Especially since you weren't there for the first one."

"Well, better late than never."

"Seems to be your motto."

Her gaze wanders around the expansive open kitchen and living room. "This is certainly a delightful house. All top of the line. No expense spared." Her gaze lands on me. "You did something right by getting knocked up by this guy. What's his name again?"

"Trey. And I didn't get pregnant because of his house."

"At least it has perks." She plucks an olive from the charcuterie board and tosses it in her mouth. "Where's the baby daddy anyway?"

I push the board away from her, even though there's no room for it to go anywhere. "Trey. His name is Trey, and he ran to the store. He'll be back soon."

"Until he puts a ring on your finger, he'll just be a baby daddy. I need a drink."

Me too.

Lach and Dessa stand in the doorway, watching like we're two animals ready to strike. If she's not out of my sight in five seconds, I might do just that. "Lach, can you take my mother out to the patio and get her a drink? There's a cooler with various beverages next to the house."

He waves my mother over and shoots a glare at me and mouths "you owe me."

I give him a silent "thank you." After they exit onto the patio, I rest my hands on the counter.

Dessa steps up next to me. "Well, she's certainly a peach."

"Yeah. That's my mother. I was secretly hoping she wouldn't even show up, but just my luck."

The front door swings open and Trey strolls in with a bag full of groceries.

"What did you buy?"

He pushes a few things on the counter to clear room for his bag. "I'm making my appetizer." He pulls out a knife from the block and cutting board from the drawer. Several times, he shushes me while he works, so I let him be. Ten minutes later he has a plate full of salami, prosciutto, and chorizo that spells out Baby.

"What is that?"

He puffs out his chest. "It's my meatcuterie board."

I roll my eyes, but I can't fight my smile. When it comes to Trey, I have to pick my battles. I won with the not having a gender reveal party. He can have his meatcuterie board and every other overly excessive thing he has planned for this party.

"Also, my mother is here. She's on the patio with Lach. You should go save him."

He grabs his meatcuterie board. "Moms love me. And Lach will appreciate this." He holds up his tray of meat before turning on his heel and going to the patio.

When the door closes behind him, Dessa turns and nudges me with her elbow. "Trey's really into this party planning stuff."

"To say he likes to be involved is an understatement. But it's kind of endearing." The knife in my hand slices through the bottom of the celery stock. "When I was with Kyle, he didn't have an opinion about anything. He always told me 'Whatever you want.' Then he would pay the bill. But with Trey, it's the complete opposite, and I'm learning to adjust my own attitude. But also, I wouldn't want to do this with anyone else but him."

The empty punch bowl falls from Dessa's hands and hits the counter with a clatter. She turns to face me, eyes as big as the bowl, as a knowing grin covers her face. "Oh my god! You love him!"

"Shhh!" I bite my lips together, fighting a smile but unable to contain it any longer. "I do. I love him." I've spent so much time fighting it, not believing it's something in the cards for me, but Trey's flipped the script and has given me a glimmer of hope.

Dessa throws her hands in the air and does a high-knee marching dance before wrapping her arms around me in a hug. "I knew it! You can't keep that shit from me." She squeezes me harder before pulling away, still gripping my shoulders. "I'm so happy for you. You deserve every ounce of happiness. And Abby too. And the baby. You're going to have the most adorable family." She pulls me in for another tight hug before dropping her hands to her sides.

"Now, it's time for you to find love." I raise an eyebrow.

"Ha. That ship sailed away a long time ago to Florida, or California, or Washington." She sneers at the last word. With a large spoon, she scoops out the rainbow sherbet and it plops into the bowl.

"You make it sound like this guy exists."

"Not anymore." She pours a jug of pineapple juice into the punch bowl. "But that's not the point. This isn't about me. It's about you. And the many more adorable babies you're going to make with the man you love," she coos at my belly.

"Let's get through one baby first." I rest my hand on the beach volleyball protruding from under my shirt.

Dessa squeals, "So many adorable babies!" She sighs. "Can I just say I'm giddy that you're in love." She wraps her arms around my shoulders. Sitting on the counter is a bottle of champagne and she lifts it. "I'll have a toast to your pregnancy and your newfound love. You get sparkling grape juice."

I giggle as a wave of warmth rushes over me. "I do. I love Trey." Now that I can finally admit it to myself, the next step will be to say it to him.

# Chapter 35

## EVERYTHING BECOMES REAL

# Trey

The outside is bustling with conversation coming from every corner of the patio. Instead of joining in, I'm a man on a mission. I place the meatcuterie board on the table filled with other appetizers under the tent. On the other side of the patio, I spot Lach as he inches himself farther away from a blonde woman who must be Rylee's mom, but the resemblance is nonexistent. Since this is my first time meeting her, I want to make a few things clear about my family.

I stroll over to relieve Lach of his babysitting duties. When I'm standing next to the woman, I hold out my hand. "You must be Rylee's mom. It's so nice to meet you. I'm Trey."

Lach jumps to his feet. "You can sit here." He leans in

so only I can hear. "Watch her. She gets handsy." I nod and take his vacated seat.

Her perfectly manicured hand grasps mine. "Hi Trey. I'm Darla."

"I'm glad you could make it, Darla." I sit back, taking a laid-back approach, but also ready to fight if I need to.

She crosses one leg over the other. "You have a very nice house."

"Thank you."

"So, do you plan to take care of my daughter?"

"No," I deadpan.

Her hand flies to cover her mouth as an overly dramatic gasp escapes her.

"I don't want you to get the wrong impression." I sit up and rest my elbows on my knees. "But she doesn't need me to take care of her. Rylee is the strongest, most resilient woman I know. But you know that, she's your daughter. If anything, I need her to take care of me. In fact, I will spend every second of every day proving my worthiness to her."

"I can appreciate that." The toe of her red high heel brushes over my knee.

A red-hot inferno rages through me. My fists clench together, fighting the urge to not go Trey-Hulk and flip over the stone fireplace over. I square my shoulders, locking my gaze with her dull and lifeless brown eyes. No. They're loveless. I suspect it's telling about her own life. "With all due respect, Darla," I say, my tone sharp, "that's not happening." I peer down at her foot. She shifts in her seat. "I love your daughter. If you want to stay here at my house for the rest of the party, you'll be respectful. Not only to me but also to Rylee. Any disrespect toward her is disrespect toward me. I have no issues throwing anyone out." I rise to my feet. "Also, I suggest you change your overall attitude toward Rylee because she's already been through a hell of a lot and doesn't need your condescending remarks on top of it. If you can't do that, I'll make sure she never has to deal with you."

Her mouth gapes open. If I had to guess, not too many people put her in her place. But one thing I will not do is tolerate any of her bullshit, especially when it comes to Rylee.

"I hope you'll stay and enjoy the rest of the party." I glide around the firepit and stroll across the patio to where our friends are seated. It's like a boulder has been pushed off my chest. Since Rylee told me about her mom, I wanted to say something to her. I only hope she does change in order to stay in Rylee, Abby, and our acorn's lives.

"Runaway balloon!" Bennett yells, pointing across the yard. Everyone glances up as a yellow balloon dances across the blue sky.

"That wouldn't have happened if Seth tied the balloons," Parisa teases.

"Only if he used bow ties," Van says.

"I'm well versed in tying knots in more than just bow ties. Scarves, ties, rope. I used Christmas tinsel once," Seth adds.

I leap over some hedges and sprint to the front of the house. An array of yellow and gray balloons flutter in the wind. I collect all the strings and re-secure them to the mailbox with a triple knot. I stroll into the house through the front door. Rylee and Dessa are talking in the kitchen.

"I'll have a toast to your pregnancy and your newfound love. You get sparkling grape juice," Dessa says.

The word love halts me in my tracks. I tiptoe down the short hallway, feeling like an asshole for eavesdropping, but this could be important.

"I do. I love Trey." Rylee's voice is beaming with adoration.

My heart pounds in my chest. It's almost hard to hear everything else they're saying.

"Have you told him?"

"I haven't said the words I love you. I feel like once I say those words, everything becomes real."

"Yes! Real! You want real!"

Rylee laughs. "I know. I've kind of created a substitute though. Instead of saying 'I love you,' I tell him 'You're my favorite'. He knows what I mean."

"Ugh! You love him. You need to just tell him."

My heart swells to the size of the fucking universe. My grin is the same size. She loves me. She fucking loves me. As much as I wish she'd tell me, I know she needs time. She does things at her own pace. When the timing is perfect, she'll tell me. In the meantime, I'll have some fun.

I wipe the cheesy grin off my face and stroll into the open kitchen. "What did I hear about love?" I pluck a piece of broccoli off a tray and toss it in my mouth.

All the color drains from Rylee's face. "Oh. Um." Her gaze dances from me to Dessa, back to me, and then to the island of food in front of her. "I would love if you could take these veggies out for our guests." She shoves the wooden board at my chest.

"Done. Next time, give me something more challenging." I press a kiss to her forehead. When I pull away, I wink. Her eyes widen for a split second. If I would have blinked, I would have missed it. In a few short steps, I'm out the patio door to let her stew about if I overheard her or not.

Rylee lowers herself to plush armchair in my living room. "I'm not moving for the next twenty-four hours."

Bending down, I brush a strand of hair off her forehead and press my lips to hers. "How are you doing?"

"Tired. I'm not moving. Ever. I've come to the conclusion Acorn likes to party. He or she has been breakdancing on my bladder all day."

The party was a hit. Everyone had a great time. It felt less like a baby shower and more like a get together with friends and family with the occasional baby shower game. The backyard was filled with laughter from the Guess the Candy Bar game. It's not every day where you watch adults sniff melted chocolate bars in diapers to figure out what the candy bar is. The Snickers had a few people gagging just from the sight. For the rest of the party Rylee's mom was on her best behavior.

"The option to stay here is always on the table. I have a nice pillow top king size bed. The spare bedroom is ready for Abby." I tilt my head, waiting for her answer.

"Is this your way of convincing us to move in?"

"No. But if it helps, I'll take it." I smirk.

"Tell Abby we're having a sleepover." She toes the ottoman as she tries to drag it closer to her. Though she's cute as hell with the tip of her tongue peeking out as she fights the ottoman, I put her out of her misery and push it to her. "Thank you. I'll be right here for the remainder of the evening."

I love having her in my space. Now I need to convince her to make it permanent.

# Chapter 36

## THE THROWDOWN

## Trey

I loved waking up to Rylee's warm body snuggled against mine. We did keep our extracurricular activities PG-13 mostly because we didn't want Abby to get spooked from staying somewhere new and busting in on us in a compromising position. I want to wait a few more years before I start traumatizing the kids.

Earlier in the week, while at the mall to buy a couple of princess pillows and bedding for the spare room, I threw a quarter into the wishing well. I never expected her to say yes but maybe she's slowly rounding the curve to take me up on my offer of her and Abby moving in. I've learned how hard and how often I can push Rylee's buttons, but each time I ask a little more of her hesitancy chips away. Eventually, I know she'll say yes.

I pull into a parking spot at her dimly lit apartment complex. After the baby shower, she kept everything at my house until I could bring things over that she could use right away when our acorn is born. A late meeting kept me from coming over until well after sunset.

I grab one bag from the back seat and slam the door shut. I'll collect the rest after I get her key, then she won't need to buzz me up. My eyes are fixated on the front door when a shadowy figure emerges unexpectedly from behind a parked truck mere feet away.

"This is your fault." The tone is deep and menacing.

I freeze. The hackles rise on the back of my neck. "Excuse me?"

"This is all your fucking fault," the voice seethes. He steps into a ray of light shining down from the streetlamp, revealing his face as he takes a step closer.

Jesus Christ. My shoulders drop with relief. "What are you doing here, Kyle?"

"I'm here to talk to you." His voice is stern as he stumbles forward, nearly toppling over.

"Are you drunk?"

"It's your fault my own daughter doesn't want to spend time with me." He jabs a finger at my chest.

"My fault?" I scoff and brush his hand away. "I think you got that backward. You did that one all on your own. If you didn't bail on her every other weekend, maybe she'd be more excited to spend time with you."

"And what the fuck do you know about raising kids? Oh, that's right. You probably have a shit ton since you fuck anything that walks." His body sways back and forth.

With one hard shove I could topple him over like a tower of building blocks, but the effort isn't worth it. I'm sure he'll fall over all on his own. "Go home Kyle." I shoulder past him and continue toward the front door.

"Trey Wilson, the golden boy," he slurs from behind me. "Gets everything he wants, including my whore of an ex-wife."

At the mention of Rylee, I spin around.

"You think you're some knight in fucking shining armor?" He shoves my shoulder and I stumble back a step. The stench of liquor seeping out of his pores. "You think you can replace me?" he sneers. "All you get are my sloppy seconds. That's all that she's good for."

My fingers clench as I replay his words about Rylee in my head, but I need to be the bigger man. He's not worth it. "Look, I'm not arguing with you. You're drunk. Go home and sleep it off before you do something stupid." Once again, I turn around and continue toward the door.

"You better get to your dirty whore. I'm sure she's waiting with her legs spread wide!"

I jolt to a stop and spin around. In two short strides I'm toe to toe with him. "Here's your only warning. Keep her name, in fact, keep anything about her out of your mouth," I seethe. "Got it?"

"Or what? She'll send her bitch boy to come after me. Imagine that. She's got you fucking pussy whipped. Not surprising, the whore that she is. She'll spread her legs for anyone, including you. The guy who's slept with half of Harbor Highlands. But how does it feel..." he leans closer, his rancid beer and whiskey breath burning my nostrils, "knowing I fucked her first."

Red. All I see is red. Clearly, he's here to push my buttons. Well, he just fucking pushed every single one. I reach out, my fingers grasping the collar of his shirt, and I tug him to me, my face inches from his. "I'm only going to say this once, so listen carefully. Don't you ever fucking talk about her like that again or my fist will be in your face so fucking hard they'll have to surgically remove it. Understand?"

A sinister smirk creeps across his mouth. That look alone sends a rock crashing into the pit of my stomach. I have no idea who this guy is or what he's capable of, and I'm not sticking around to find out. I shove him before turning around to walk away.

"Hey Trey. While you're fucking the whore, just remember she was on my dick first."

I spin around and instantly his fist comes in contact with my left cheek. I stumble back. The bag in my hand tumbles to the ground, all the contents spilling out. Another punch lands in my stomach with an *oomph*. As I lift my head, I'm greeted with a menacing sneer. I lower my shoulder and charge, crashing into his chest, knocking Kyle off balance. His back smacks into the metal dumpster, sending a booming clank echoing between the apartment buildings and cars. He groans and falls forward but quickly regains his posture. It gives me a few seconds to regain my balance.

"You son of a bitch!" He charges toward me, and I pull back. My right fist comes in contact with his jaw. Another howl of pain from him sails through the night air. As he stumbles backward, doubled over, I throw an uppercut into his stomach. Our grunts and groans echo between the cars. He stumbles back a few steps, giving me a moment to shake out my hand. I won't lie, it's been years since I've been in any sort of brawl.

"That's your warning. Stay the fuck away from me." He charges at me once again and I'm able to dodge his attack and spin around, my fingers gripping his throat, not tight enough to choke him, but enough to keep him still. "And you better believe I'm convincing Rylee to talk to a lawyer about this shit." Sirens sound in the distance.

He squirms as he tries to break free from my hold. Suddenly, he stops and there's a sinister glint in his eyes. His arm moves back and lunges forward. Something sharp pierces my side and I immediately release my grip. I touch my side. Something damp coats my fingers. Glancing up through my eyelashes, I find Kyle charging at me again. This time, a metal blade glints under the streetlamp. I dodge to the left, but he slices through the left sleeve of my jacket. In a swift motion, I spin around and launch myself at him with my shoulder, taking him by surprise. As his balance falters, we both collide and crash onto the hard, unforgiving blacktop. I pin his hand gripping the knife with my left hand as my other fist connects with this cheek. Adrenaline and rage race through my veins. I consider myself to be more of a lover than a fighter, but when you fuck with people I care about, you fuck with me, and you don't fuck with me.

Red and blue lights flash off the walls of the building and cars. "Freeze! Put your hands up!"

I roll to the side, landing on the blacktop. I suck in a sharp breath through my teeth and wheeze from the pain. To my right, a white pacifier sits on the ground. The smell of exhaust and burnt rubber fill the parking lot as a truck peels out and onto the road.

I sit up and cringe. With both hands in the air, one cop rushes to my side and clasps a pair of handcuffs to my wrists behind my back. Once they're secure, he helps me up to my feet. I spare a glance at Kyle and he's doing the same but with a little more kicking and screaming. They throw him in the backseat while they place me on a curb several feet away. A few minutes later another squad car pulls in. Fuck. This wasn't how the night was supposed to end.

After I was taken to the hospital to get checked out—

just a superficial scratch on my arm but the wound on my side needed to be stitched up. Luckily, it wasn't too deep and didn't do any damage to any organs but will leave a scar once it heals. Then I got to spend time in a six by eight cement room at the county jail as they ask for my side of the story. The accommodations are shit. Zero stars. Do not recommend. Thankfully, the neighbor that called the cops was able to tell the police everything that happened, which also corroborates my story, so they let me go.

Since I don't have a car, I dig my phone out of my pocket and stare at the now shattered screen and dial the only person I need right now.

# Chapter 37

## SAY YES

# Rylee

Where is he? He was supposed to be here an hour ago. It isn't like him to be this late. I check the clock again. I've sent him a couple of messages, but they've all gone unanswered. What if something happened? I pull out my phone and I'm about to call instead of text, when my phone vibrates and his name flashes at the top of the screen. I blow out a sigh of relief and press the green talk button.

"Where are you? I was getting worried."

"Uh. About that…"

"What? What happened?"

"I'll explain everything, but first I need you to pick me up at the jail."

"What? Oh my god! What happened?"

"I'll explain when you get here."

"Okay. I'm on my way." The call disconnects and I speed wobble to the other side of the room. With my phone in one hand, I dial Marcie while blindly shoving my foot into a shoe.

"Why are you call—"

"I need you to come watch Abby. I'll explain later." I spit the words out in one breath.

"Oh. Okay. I'll be right there."

Luckily, Marcie doesn't ask questions. By my tone, I suspect she understands the urgency. When I hang up, I poke my head in to Abby's room, my heart pounding. She's sitting on her bed coloring in one of her many coloring books. "I need to leave for a little bit. Marcie's coming over to watch you. I'll be right back, okay?"

She lifts her head, taking her eyes off her coloring book. "Um. Okay." Her gaze drops back to the picture.

I close her door but leave it open a crack. By the time I'm back in the kitchen, the front door flies open, and Marcie is wearing a head wrap and bathrobe.

"Sorry to have disturbed your evening. But thank you. I really appreciate this." I throw a light sweater over my shoulders.

"No problem. Now get out of my way. I need to see who gets the last rose. It better not be Tonya." She storms past me and into the living room. Immediately she's flipping on the television to find her show.

"Abby's in her room. I'll be back soon!" I yell through the crack in the door before it clicks closed behind me.

Ten minutes later, I'm parking in front of the jail. I slam my car door and race inside the building. Off to the side, Trey jumps to his feet and meets me in the middle of the reception area. Holy shit. His dark hair is disheveled. A tear in his shirt runs down his bicep.

"Oh my god. What happened to you?" I run my hand over the split fabric before wrapping my arms around his torso and squeezing.

His body stiffens as he sucks in a sharp breath. "Be careful. There are more wounds."

I loosen my grip and peer up at him. "What happened?"

"I met your ex."

"Kyle did this?"

"Yeah. But I think he got the brunt of it. Also, he's booked in a luxurious six by eight room for a little while longer. So, sucks to be him. Let's go. I'll tell you in the car." He throws an arm over my shoulder, and I keep an arm wrapped around his hip.

Once we're in my SUV I start the ignition. "Where am I taking you?"

"Actually, my car is at your place."

"What the hell?"

On the entire car ride to my apartment, he fills me in on the confrontation with Kyle in the parking lot, how a fight broke out and then someone called the cops.

"Also, Kyle stabbed me."

The car jerks to the right as my gaze flies to Trey. "He stabbed you?!"

"Eyes on the road. I was in the hospital once tonight. I don't need to go back." He scrubs a hand down his face. "But yeah. He stabbed me. Twice. Luckily, he's shit aim."

"Oh my god." I press my fingers to my mouth in disbelief. People say their life flashes before their eyes when facing a life-or-death situation. Well, the same is true when you're told someone you care about was in the same position. I reach across the center console to reassure myself that he's really here with me. His fingers wrap around mine and squeezes, easing my fear. "In all the years

I've known him, he never seemed like the type of guy to do something like this. Why'd he do it?"

"Apparently, it's my fault Abby doesn't want to see him."

"What!" The car jerks again. "That narcissistic bastard!"

His hand splays out across the dashboard. "Maybe you should pull over and I'll drive."

"I'm sorry." I blow out a quick breath. "I'm fine. It's just all this has me in a tailspin."

Trey reaches over the center console and grabs my hand, linking his fingers with mine. He's the one who got into a fight and now he's comforting me. Every day, he surprises me more and more.

"I can't believe he's blaming you for Abby not wanting to spend time with him. Maybe if he didn't bail on her every damn time it's his weekend, she'd want to see him. Apparently, nothing is his fault. If he's done this, who knows what else he's capable of."

His thumb brushes over the back of my hand. "He was pretty drunk. I don't think he would do this under normal circumstances."

"Drunk or not, it's not an excuse. Every time I go to my car, I'll be looking over my shoulder. Normally, I'd be able to hold my own, but it's not just me."

Trey releases my hand and spreads his fingers over my growing belly. "I'll make sure nothing happens to my girls and Acorn."

If there's anything that can distract me from all the chaos happening in my life, it's Trey being sweet. So sweet that I want to veer the car to the shoulder and do what started this pregnancy in the first place.

Once we're at my apartment, we fill in Marcie about what happened before she leaves. I poke my head in

Abby's room and she's curled up on her bed. In the corner of her room, I grab a blanket and spread it over her.

Back in the living room, Trey's sitting down on the couch, his head tilted toward the ceiling. His suit jacket drapes over the edge next to him. Bags droop under his normally full of life eyes.

I stop in front of him, straddling his knee, and cup his cheek. "I'm sorry this happened."

"What do you have to be sorry for? You didn't stab me." The corner of his mouth tips up.

I rest my hands on his shoulders. "I know. But Kyle is my ex and this would have never happened if we weren't involved."

His head rolls to the side and he places a kiss to my wrist. "None of this is your fault. It's all on him. Got it? Either way, I would fight until the end of the world for you." He nudges me with his nose, softly running the tip up and down my arm.

Tears well up in the corners of my eyes. I've never had someone care this much for me. To fight for me. For once, I might not have to do this on my own. Not wanting to be vulnerable in front of Trey, I step away. "I think I have one of your shirts in my room. I may have borrowed it after our first date."

While strolling to my bedroom, I brush away the tears that have now fallen. He's been there every step of the way, never demanding more than what I can give him. It's only fair I meet him halfway. I'm ready. After regaining my composure, I pull the thread bare Onyx Stone concert tee from a hanger in the closet. When I'm back in the living room, Trey stands, holding out his hand and I place the shirt in his open palm.

Starting at the neck, I pop the button through the hole. I've thought long and hard about this, but after tonight it's a no brainer. I need to be willing to accept help, not just for me, but for Abby and our acorn. Deep down, I know Trey will do whatever it takes to ensure our safety.

"My answer is yes." I work the next button through the hole and push.

Trey presses his hand against mine, halting my progress. "I've asked you a few questions recently. Which one are you saying yes to?"

I peer up at him. His steely gray eyes meeting mine. "Yes. We'll move in with you. I can't fathom the idea of Kyle possibly doing that again. He knows where I live. I'm sure if he tried, he could find out where you live too—"

"But I also have security cameras. It'll be harder for him to hide."

"Exactly, and you're right. Abby needs somewhere to run around and play. Acorn can have their own room. This will be more than good." I press my lips together, once again fighting back tears. "It will be the start of our new life together."

"And the answer to my other question?"

"One thing at a time." A smile plays on my lips. "But it's still on the table."

"That's all I need to hear."

# Chapter 38

## HE'LL KNOW WHAT IT IS

## Rylee

As soon as I agreed to move in with Trey, he didn't hesitate on arranging a moving company. He wanted us moved in and settled with plenty of time before the baby came. His strict instructions were to pack everything I wanted to keep, set aside the donate or throw away items, and the moving company would take care of the rest.

After Acorn finishes using my bladder as a punching bag, I use the bathroom and wash my hands. In my bedroom, I set a packing box on the floor. I pull open a drawer in my jewelry box and the paper ring Trey made for me sticks out like my belly. I pluck it out and run my finger over the folded edge. Slowly, I slide it down my ring finger. My lips tip up into a smile. It fits a little better now. A drop of water from my hand soaks into the paper. The black ink bleeds around the center, but something about it is off. I delicately drag it off my finger and carefully open a fold. Then I do another and another until it's a strip of paper. Written in smudged ink are the words: One day this will be a real ring. One you can wear forever. You are my forever. I love you.

Tears spring to my eyes. He wrote this when I told him I was pregnant. These were his feelings all those months ago. I shove the piece of paper into my pocket. Scanning the room, I find my phone and wallet laying on the bed. I scoop them up and waddle down the hallway as fast as I can. Unfortunately, I'm pretty sure a turtle left me in a cloud of dust. "Oh my god! Why do I have to be growing a baby elephant?"

I shuffle past the movers. "You guys are doing great! Keep packing things. Label the boxes." The front door slams behind me. I waddle down the flight of stairs one at a time. I'll miss these stairs as much as the acid reflux I got from this pregnancy.

I race across town, almost running three stoplights until I'm parking in front of The Blue Stone Group. I throw on my flashers, praying they don't tow my car and instead take pity on the woman growing an adult linebacker inside her. I push through the double doors. The sun shines through the atrium. I stop at the reception desk and ask if Trey's in his office.

The young woman with black swooping bangs types away on the keyboard, but I don't wait. This can't wait. By the time she answers me, I'm a quarter of the way to the elevator.

"Do you want me to buzz him down?" she yells to my back.

I throw a hand up, waving her off. "No worries. I know which office is his."

I waddle to the elevators and press the button for the third floor. Exhaling a breath, I'm thankful I don't have to deal with stairs. When I reach his door, I half ass knock before I'm pushing through.

Trey jumps to his feet and steps out from behind his desk, concern etched on his forehead. "Rye, what are you doing here? Is everything okay? Is it our acorn?"

I pull out the piece of paper and slam it on his desk. "What is this?"

He glances down and his fingers run along the worn paper. Slowly, he lifts his head, his gaze meeting mine. "That's the paper ring I gave you."

"No. The words. Did you mean them? Even all those months ago?"

He rubs the back of his neck. "I'm pretty sure I've known that's how I felt since I watched you man handle the guy at Porter's."

I step close and grip his tie and yank him to me, crashing my lips to his in a searing kiss. He clasps my cheeks, holding me to him as our lips press and move against each other's. I pull away but keep my lips centimeters from his. "I want to be your forever. You're my forever. You're Abby's forever. Acorn's forever." I kiss him. "You're my absolute favorite." Another kiss. "I want to be struck by lightning. Metaphorically, not literally, and you do that. With you it's like I'm stranded in the middle of a lightning storm."

He pulls me to his chest and places a chaste kiss on my lips. "You're my absolute favorite. That's four words." He winks.

A laugh bursts out of me. "Fine. How about this? I love you."

His eyes crinkle at the corners as a grin splits his face. "I love you. And Abby. And our little Acorn." He kisses me again. "I can take the afternoon off and show you exactly how much I love you." His lips brush over my cheek and down my jaw line.

I can't help the moan that escapes me. "As much as I want to do that. I can't. I left the movers alone at my apartment and my car might get towed."

"Where did you park?"

"On the street. But I put my flashers on. The parking lot is way too far away for me to waddle across. They really should have pregnant parking."

A laugh drifts from his throat. "I'll be sure to mention that at our next board meeting." His thumb brushes over my cheek. "But tonight. In our home. In our bed. You're all mine."

When he says things like that, I have the urge to say to hell with it. The movers can manage. I can collect my car from the impound lot. But I digress. "Promise?"

"Only if you don't fall asleep mid lick." His eyebrows lift.

Laughter erupts from me. "That was one time, and I was exhausted."

"You're always good at keeping my ego in check." He spins me around and playfully smacks my ass. "Go finish bossing around the movers so you can officially be moved in."

I flash him a flirty smile over my shoulder as I leave his office.

The next day, I wake up to a buzzing from my phone with another ominous message from Jake requesting to meet him at Porter's a little early, if possible. Today is my last day at work until I start my maternity leave and two weeks until the baby is due. And I am ready. After a six-year break, I forgot how different life is when you're the size of a hot-air balloon.

When I pull in, the parking lot is empty except for Jake's truck. I park next to it and weeble-wobble my way inside. The outside light from the door draws Jake's attention from behind the bar. He sets the glass bottle down in the empty row behind the others.

"Hey Rylee. Take a seat." He points to a smaller table against the wall. He steps out from behind the bar and takes a seat across from me. "First off, you're not working today."

My eyebrows knit together. "Why?"

"I'm giving you the day off. You can start your maternity leave early. But I called you in to let you know they caught the person who broke in."

"Who was it?"

"Chad."

I'm stunned silent. Chad turned into an asshole in the past six months, but I never expected him to steal from Jake. "Wow. I wasn't expecting that. But at the same time, I can see it."

He folds his hands on the table. "That's not all. They caught him because of the fight Kyle had with Trey."

My jaw drops. "At my apartment?"

"Yeah. Your neighbors who called the police about the fight caught the license plate of the truck that sped away. They concluded that the truck was the same truck I caught on camera the night of the break in. The owner is Henry Wilcox."

All the puzzle pieces magically fit into place, except one. "That's the same name Trey told me." I purse my lips. "But how does he fit into the picture? I don't know him."

"Apparently, it's Chad's step-uncle."

My head draws back. "I never would have guessed that. I wonder how those two connected."

"I have no idea. I just wanted to call you down here and let you know. I'll be telling everyone about Chad later."

"Thanks." All the news about Chad, Kyle, and uncles ping pong through my mind. It must have been the truck that followed me. Shit. It could have been Chad who gave me a flat. Jake's voice pulls me from my thoughts.

"Now, you go do whatever you need to do." He rises to his feet, and I do the same, only slower. "But before you go, I have something for Trey." He strolls across the bar and down the hallway. A minute later he emerges, a hammer in his hand. "Give this to your boyfriend."

"He's not—" *My boyfriend* sits on the tip of my tongue. I swallow it down. Boyfriend doesn't sound so bad. I kind of like it, actually. It beats baby daddy.

He holds his hand out and drops a wooden gavel in mine. "He'll know what it is."

## Chapter 39

## POP GOES RYLEE

*Trey*

"Why won't Acorn come out of me," Rylee groans from the plush chair and peering down to her belly. "You're supposed to fall off the tree when you're ready." With her back arched, she pushes off the backrest and stands. "So fall." She blows out an exasperated sigh, then glances to me. "If you give me any of that 'because you've made such a good home, it's so nice and cozy' bullshit, I'll punch you in the jugular."

I heed her warning and take a step back, making sure I'm out of arm's reach. Acorn is a week overdue, and everyone can tell. I take a big breath and then let it go. My patience will be tested once our acorn arrives, so this is great practice. "I love you, Rye." Her glare slingshots to me, and I retreat another step.

"Have sex with me right now. Like fuck the baby out of me," she demands.

"As much of an amazing offer as that is, the hostile tone doesn't draw the appeal."

"Appeal is the least of my concerns. I want this baby out. I've tried walks, spicy foods, and this baby is holding firm. Picket sign in hand. The only thing we haven't tried is sex."

I glance down at my crotch. "I think he's out of commission, like on vacation. Yep. There's the out of order sign."

With a hand on the small of her back, she waddles across the living room and into the kitchen, grumbling about being done with being pregnant. "We're never doing this again," she sneers.

I slink toward her as if approaching a wild animal. "You're absolutely beautiful and amazing and you're so strong. You'll get through this."

"If I'm so beautiful, why won't you fuck meee," she whines. Her lip juts out as her wide, chocolate doe eyes stare back at me. "Just stick it in. It only needs to be a little. I'll do the rest."

I laugh to myself. She doubles her efforts in giving a little extra pout. It kills me inside that she's bearing all the responsibility for carrying our acorn. If I could take it away from her, I would, so this is the least I can do for her. In two long strides, we're toe to toe. I cup her cheeks. "The doe eyes are my kryptonite." I brush my thumb over her cheekbone.

"Does that mean you'll have sex with me?"

"That means I will fuck our little acorn out of you." I slam my lips to hers. She moans into my mouth as I deepen the kiss.

She jerks away. "Oh! Ah!"

"Oh yeah. Rye." I press my lips to her cheek and across her jaw.

"No. No. My water broke." She rests a hand on her belly.

"Oh shit. That was fast." I mentally run through the Pop Goes Rylee checklist. "Grab your shoes. I have the slip-ons next to the door. I'll grab the bag." Racing through the house, adrenaline pumps through my veins as I reach the bedroom and hastily grab the bag. When I return, Rylee has made it halfway to the door. "You gotta move faster than that."

"Fuck off. I only have one speed and it's not fast," she says over her shoulder.

I race into the garage, throw the duffel in the back seat, and pull out and park as close to the door as possible. I push open the front door and Rylee has both her shoes on. Linking my arm with hers like I'm helping an elderly lady across the street, I escort her to the SUV. Once she's inside, with two fingers, I guide her face to meet mine and kiss her. "I love you." I don't wait for her to say it back, instead I shut the door, round the hood, and jump in.

I shove it into drive and peel out of the driveway. Trees zip by in a blur like streaks of paint. It's happening. I'm going to be a dad. My hand white knuckles the steering wheel as I glance over at Rylee. She's calmly sitting there with her hand on her belly. I wish I could be that calm.

I pass her my phone. "Want to message everyone. Let them know we're on our way to the hospital." My phone connects to the LCD screen and Bennett's name pops up. "No, use the group chat."

"I'm not using the group chat."

"Use the group chat. That's why I set it up."

She huffs, then types out a message and hits send. It pops up on the LCD dash screen.

Pop goes Rylee

**TREY**

This is Rylee. Trey's driving. Baby is coming.

**DESSA**

Oh my God! Yay!

**BENNETT**

Congrats you two!

**PARISA**

Where's Abby? Do we need to pick her up from school?

**TREY**

Yes, that would be fantastic. Thank you!

**SETH**

I never thought the day would come where someone would call Trey, Daddy.

**BENNETT**

I thought that was an every weekend occurrence.

I press reply on the dashboard.

**TREY**

That was then. From now on there's only one person who's calling me Daddy.

**SETH**

Is that Rylee?

**TREY**

Rylee here. I never once called him Daddy. We'll see you all at the hospital.

I peer at Rylee from the corner of my eye. "Don't worry, you can start now."

"Trust me, I'm not worrying."

"Just say it. Daddy. It rolls off the tongue." I smirk.

She sucks in a short breath as her eyes pinch closed.

"You doing all right?

"Yeah. Contractions."

I press the gas pedal to the floor.

Seven hours and a possibly broken hand later, I'm sitting on the bed next to Rylee as she's holding our little acorn. "We made that." I stare at the chubby cheeks and button nose swaddled in a blanket.

"We did. What do you think is a good name?"

"We weren't sticking with Acorn?"

"As much as Abby would love that, no." She runs the tip of her finger over the bridge of our daughter's nose and peers up at me. "What about Kaelyn?"

"Let's ask her." I lean down to our acorn. "What do you think? Do you like Kaelyn?" Her little mouth wiggles open and she squeaks out a noise. "I think that's a yes."

"I think so too." Rylee beams up at me.

I wrap my arm around Rylee as we both lovingly glance down at our daughter. "Welcome to the world Kaelyn Marcie Wilson."

# Chapter Epilogue

## ONE MONTH LATER

# Rylee

My eyelids crack open, and I stretch my legs, the couch is not as comfortable as my bed. Noise echoing from the basement draws my attention. I roll off the couch, almost tripping over the stack of college enrollment papers. Trey encouraged me to finish my degree since I was only twelve credits shy from graduating. I told him I don't have plans of leaving Porter's to pursue a different career, and he told me to do it for myself. Finish what I started. Then he showed me exactly what finishing what you start means… from between my legs. When he does things like that, I can't argue with his logic.

I tiptoe across the room and slink down the stairs, eavesdropping on the conversation.

"I'll have another apple ale," Abby says.

"Coming right up," Trey says, followed by the clanking of glasses. "Wait a second. Do I need to check your ID?"

"I'm seven."

"So, you're not driving?"

She bellows out an infectious laugh. "I can't drive."

"Okay. Just checking."

After Kyle attacked Trey, the court charged him with aggravated assault, resulting in the revocation of his parental rights of Abby. With the way Trey has stepped up as a father figure, she's hardly even noticed. He thinks of Abby as if she is his biological daughter. Last week, he started the adoption paperwork so it can be official. Every day I fall harder and harder for him, if that's even possible.

At the bottom of the stairs, I come to a stop and rest my shoulder against the wall. Trey's standing behind the bar, Kaelyn's strapped to his chest in a tactical baby harness, as Abby sits on a stool across from him. A golden liquid pours into a glass from the tap, filling it to the rim. He slides it across the bar in front of Abby. She lifts it and takes a big gulp.

"Ah! That's a good ale." Abby sets down the glass.

I drop from the last step and stroll to the bar. "So, this is what you do while I nap?" I quirk an eyebrow.

"Day drink apple ale? Absolutely." Trey grabs a glass and pulls down the tap, filling my glass halfway before passing it to me.

I take a sip and smile. "Apple juice."

Abby busts out laughing, nearly falling off her stool. "We fooled you, Bunny!"

Sadly, the name stuck with Abby. Trey likes to use it in the bedroom. "You sure did." I tickle her sides as she squirms and squeals on her stool.

Trey shrugs. "She wanted to hang out with the guys, so

I had to make it as authentic as possible. And who doesn't want apple juice on tap?"

I smile and shake my head but take another drink of my apple juice. Even though Trey's not single anymore, he continues the weekly SBL tradition, except now it's turned into an evening with everyone. All the guys, their significant others, and even the kids come over to hang out for a few hours.

"Alright. Day drinking is over. Abby, I need your help upstairs." I climb off my stool.

"But I'm not done with my ale," Abby whines.

"Bring it with you."

"But Squirrel says no glasses can leave the bar."

"I'll make an exception this time. Just be careful," Trey says.

"Okay." She hops off her stool and reaches for her glass of apple juice.

When we're upstairs, I pull Abby into her room. "I need your help. Can you show me how to fold a paper ring?"

Trey sits in the plush chair, Kaelyn nestled in the crook of his arm, as he feeds her a bottle. If there's anything that can make me want to have another baby, it's watching Trey with a baby. Swoon. Plus, Kaelyn is so tiny compared to his large frame, especially when he holds her in his palms. Instant baby making material.

"Abby, it's time for bed," I say.

She rolls over on the living room floor. "But I'm not tired."

"You're never tired, but that doesn't change the fact it's bedtime."

She groans but climbs to her feet. She runs over to Kaelyn and kisses her forehead. "Good night, Acorn. Good night, Squirrel."

"Good night, Chipmunk."

"I'll come tuck you in." I run my hand over her head as she runs past me.

"I think this one is ready for bed too. But first it's time to deactivate the bomb she just dropped." His face scrunches up.

I take the bottle from him. "You do that. I'll say good night to Abby. We'll reconvene in the bedroom in, say, ten minutes."

"I love when you talk dirty to me." He winks.

After Abby and Kaelyn are in bed. Trey strolls into our bedroom and closes the door with a click. I sit up in bed then with one hand in front of the other, I crawl on my hands and knees to the end. Trey's hooded eyes watch my every move.

"Is this the type of night we're having?"

At the foot of the bed, I rise to my knees. With my fingers curled around the waistband of his jeans, I pull him to me. With deft fingers, I push the button through the hole. "Well, there is something I want to ask you."

He rests a finger under my chin. "If the question is if I'll go yodeling in the gully? Absolutely." He winks. Then he reaches behind his head and pulls his shirt. The fabric slowly slides up, revealing every dip and valley of his abs. All thoughts and questions disappear from my head.

With a glint in his eyes, he prowls over my body. I fall backward hitting the mattress, forcing a giggle out of me. His hand glides from my knee and up my thigh. Goosebumps spring up over every inch of my body. A single touch from him sets my body ablaze. I cup his cheek. His scruff tickles my fingers as I haul his mouth to mine.

The kiss is both scorching and desperate. Two words that describe exactly how Trey makes me feel.

Breaking away, he starts at my jaw and kisses his way down the column of my neck. His hand slides up my stomach, taking my shirt with him. I arch my back as he moves to below my breastbone. He trails kisses down my stomach, making sure to kiss each and every one of my stretch marks.

"I love you so much."

My fingers thread through his hair, gripping the strands." I love you even more."

When he reaches my hip, his thumbs dig under the fabric of my yoga pants and slowly drags them down my legs. "Let's put my yodeling skills to the test." He kisses my inner thigh on one side, then the other. The tip of his tongue slides up my slit.

"Ahhh! Yes!" My fingers grip tighter around his strands.

He alternates his licks between the flat of his tongue and the tip. My hips buck each time he hits my clit.

"Fuck. Rye. You taste fucking sweet as honey." With his fingers, he spreads me open. His lips wrap around my clit and he sucks.

"Oooh! Mmm!"

"Shhh. You'll wake the kids." His finger teases at my opening before he pushes into me.

I blindly reach for a pillow and slam it over my face. "Oh god. More. I need more." My muffled words spur Trey on. He flicks his tongue over my clit as he continues to plunge his finger in and out. A tingle starts at my toes and shoots off through my entire body like a rocket. I cry out his name as my fingers clench his hair, keeping him right where I want him. My orgasm subsides and so does my grip on his hair.

I move the pillow to the other side of the bed and sit halfway up on my elbows.

He lifts his head from between my legs and licks his lips. "I think my yodeling skills are on par."

"You're a professional yodeler."

He pushes his jeans off, and they hit the floor with a thud. He crawls up my body and nuzzles his nose in my neck. "What did you want to ask me?"

"Oh. Yes," I say with a playful nudge, causing him to shift to the side. With a gentle tug, I pull open the nightstand drawer and retrieve the delicate paper ring I made earlier. "I wasn't planning on doing this while we were half naked, but it doesn't matter." I sit sideways, knees bent on the bed. Gently, I grasp his left hand and carefully slip the paper ring onto his finger. Peering up, I meet his gaze. "Seven months ago, you put a paper ring on my finger and asked me to marry you so it's only fitting that I return the gesture. Will you marry me?"

He glances down at the ring, then at me. "There's only one flaw with your gesture."

I tilt my head. "What's that?"

"I'm not going to tell you no." He cups my cheek and pulls me to him with a kiss. It's soft and sweet. He pulls away, resting his forehead on mine. "Just so you know, I expect nothing less than two carats, princess cut, and white gold."

I wide grin covers my face. "I'll work on that."

He wraps his arms around my waist and twists us around so my back is on the bed. "Also, in case you missed that, my answer is yes."

## Dessa

I peek my head over the ledge of the side window into the Porter's parking lot.

"She's here! Get ready!"

I scamper to the main bar area where everyone is gathered. A corner of the banner we got that says *Welcome Back Rylee* dangles from the ceiling. I climb up on a stool and re-secure it. As I step down, a sliver of light pours in through the front door as Rylee strolls in. A roar of claps and cheers rolls through the bar as everyone rises to their feet.

The widest grin takes over her face as pink tinges her cheeks. "What is all this?" She glances around the packed Porter's. She strolls toward the end of the bar where Lach, Nora, Jake and I are standing. As she passes, everyone offers their congratulations. "You'd think I won a Nobel Peace Prize, not have a baby."

When she's within arm's reach, I squeal and pull her to my chest. "I'm excited you're back.

She giggles under her breath. "You've come over every week since I've been gone."

"I know, but working with those two," I hike my thumb between Lach and Jake, "has been boooring."

"Hey, I heard that," Lach says.

I glance behind me. "I wasn't trying to be quiet."

From behind, he rests his chin on my shoulder. "If I was gone for a month, you'd miss me."

She rolls her eyes. "Hardly." I playfully jab my elbow into his chest.

He chokes out a laugh. "Son of a bitch. I need to find

some less violent friends." He rubs at his chest before wrapping an arm around Rylee. "Glad you're back."

"Me too." She smiles up at him. "Now everyone, get back to work."

"Listen to the boss." Jake clasps a hand on her shoulder. "Glad to have you back."

Rylee and Lach are on the ends while I'm in the middle behind the bar. I grab a frosty pint glass from the cooler and hold it under a tap, pulling the lever down. Once it's full, I pass it to a customer and pour another. A sliver of sunlight shines in as the front door opens and my gaze drifts up.

A tall, rugged man with dark jeans, a fitted white shirt that accentuates his toned arms, with a tattoo peeking out from beneath the sleeve stands just inside the doorway. A baseball cap is perched on his head, the dark hair spilling out from the sides. His scruff covered jawline rivals any stone statue. He turns my way and pulls the aviators off his face. A half smirk tugs at his lips. Time stops. My breathing stops. Noise stops. Everything stops. All the people in Porter's disappear. Standing before me is a ghost of a man. One I knew years ago and hoped I would never have to see in person again. My eyes roll back, and my entire world goes black.

Thank you for reading Love Is Ale You Need! Want more Trey and Rylee? Claim your copy of their fun and steamy bonus scene when you join my newsletter!

Dessa's in for a surprise of a lifetime when her ex-best friend comes back to town after not speaking to her for ten years. And he has some unfinished business to settle. Make My Heart Malt. The second standalone book in the Brews and Flings series.

***A sizzling enemies to lovers, unrequited crush standalone novel by romantic comedy author Gia Stevens...***

**Dessa should have been mine... until my brother kissed her first.**

Ten years is a long time to be infatuated with your former best friend, especially when she's dating your brother. So, when I receive a wedding invitation with his name embossed on the front, it feels like a fastball to the heart. But it turns out, my unrequited crush isn't the blushing bride after all.

Now's my only chance to make amends for my past mistakes and give her the kiss I've desperately been holding onto. Unfortunately, she thwarts my efforts with every drink she throws at me.

When we find ourselves locked in a storage closet, we're forced to hash out the real reason I left town—and it wasn't for baseball. Turns out, there's a fine line between anger and passion and it doesn't take long for her to scream my name.

Even after hitting third base, she still hates me. However, I'm determined to prove I'm not the man who ghosted her all those years ago. This time I'm not walking away.

My last game ended in a devastating miss—costing us the postseason, but this is one game I refuse to lose.

**Because when it comes to Dessa... I'm playing for keeps.**

Get Make My Heart Malt Today

Love Is Ale You Need Cocktail

Backseat Smash

**Ingredients:**
- 1 ounce White Peach & Rosemary Vodka*
- 1 ounce Peach Schnapps
- 1/2 ounce Triple Sec
- 3 ounces Orange Juice
- 1/2 ounce Grenadine*

**Directions:**
Fill a glass with ice. Pour in vodka, peach schnapps, and triple sec. Next add the orange juice and then top with grenadine. Stir and Enjoy!
**Optional Garnish:** Orange Wedge, Maraschino Cherry

*Substitute grenadine for Cherry Smash Monin Cocktail Mixer*
*Substitute white peach and rosemary vodka for regular vodka*

Drink Created By: Cindy C. -Cocktail Concoctionist

# Acknowledgments

First and foremost, I want to thank everyone who picked up this book. I think I will forever be in awe that you want to read my stories.

I have to thank my husband. I don't know if I would have ever started writing without his words of encouragement.

A big shout out to Brandi Zelenka. You were there for me every step of the way and I don't think I could have done this without you.

To my creative team, you pushed me to put out the best book possible and I am so thankful to have you on my side. Thank you to my editor, Brandi at My Notes in the Margin. I tend to give you a hot mess and you make it brilliant.

Thank you to Katy Cuthbertson for all your work and support, especially your eye for commas. You've been a huge help.

Thank you to my beta readers Rachel Story, and Randi Gauthreaux. You gave me invaluable feedback to help make my manuscript sparkle. Thank you to my proofreaders Jessie Bailey and Tonya Fender. You've helped me out so much.

Thank you Indie Pen PR for your amazing PR work. You made everything run smoothly.

Most of all thank you to all the bloggers, bookstagrammers, and booktokers for reading and sharing your excitement for this book. It means the world to me and I can't thank you enough. And of course, thank you to all the readers for reading my words. I hope I've been able to give you a fun escape for a few hours.

See you at the next book! Stay sassy!

# About The Author

Gia Stevens resides in Northern Minnesota with her husband and cat, Smokey. She lives for the warm, sunny days of summer and dreads the bitter cold of winter. A romantic comedy junkie at heart, she knew she wanted her own stories to encompass those same warm and fuzzy feelings.

When she's not busy writing your next book boyfriend, Gia can be found binge watching TV shows that aired five years ago, taking pictures of her cat, or curled up with a steamy romance book.

Visit my website for more information.
https://authorgiastevens.com

# Also by Gia Stevens

Want to read more sassy heroines, swoony heroes, and fun and flirty romance books?

Visit Gia's website to find a complete list of all her books.

Made in the USA
Monee, IL
12 April 2024